Montana Hearts:
Sweet Talkin' Cowboy

By Darlene Panzera

The Montana Hearts series
Montana Hearts: Her Weekend Wrangler
Montana Hearts: Sweet Talkin' Cowboy

The Cupcake Diaries series
The Cupcake Diaries: Sweet On You
The Cupcake Diaries: Recipe for Love
The Cupcake Diaries: Taste of Romance
The Cupcake Diaries: Spoonful of Christmas
The Cupcake Diaries: Sprinkled with Kisses

Other Novels
Bet You'll Marry Me
(Originally appeared in shorter form as "The Bet" in the
back of Debbie Macomber's *Family Affair*)

Montana Hearts: Sweet Talkin' Cowboy

DARLENE PANZERA

AVONIMPULSE
An Imprint of HarperCollinsPublishers

Excerpt from *Montana Hearts: Her Weekend Wrangler* copyright © 2015 by Darlene Panzera.

Excerpt from *Guarding Sophie* copyright © 2015 by Julie Revell Benjamin.

Excerpt from *The Idea of You* copyright © 2015 by Darcy Burke.

Excerpt from *One Tempting Proposal* copyright © 2015 by Christy Carlyle.

Excerpt from *No Groom at the Inn* copyright © 2015 by Megan Frampton.

EPub Edition DECEMBER 2015 ISBN: 9780062394705

Print Edition ISBN: 9780062394712

Avon, Avon Impulse, and the Avon Impulse logo are trademarks of HarperCollins Publishers.

10 9 8 7 6 5 4 3 2 1

For Joe, Samantha, Robert, and Jason.
And for Tom and Donna Altmann for the
many years of adventures together.

Acknowledgments

I'D LIKE TO thank my editors at Avon Impulse: May, Chelsey, and Elle; and my critique partners, friends, and family for all your help and support. I thank God for His ever present guidance. And I'd like to give a big shout out to my Start To Finish class team; Jeri, Beverly, Carol, Karen, Robin, Julie, and Debby for your prayers and support, which truly made the completion of this book possible.

Chapter One

A LOUD SCUFFLE sounded from within the cabin, followed by a thud, as if something had bumped against the interior wall. Luke Collins stopped his trek down the dirt path in front to listen, and wondered who or what was inside. The two unfinished cabins at the end of the row on his family's guest ranch were *supposed* to be empty.

He glanced down at his two-and-a-half-year-old niece and tightened his hold on her small hand.

"Onkle Uke, what's that?"

"What's *what*?" Luke asked, keeping his tone light to hide his alarm.

Another thud creaked the woodwork beside them.

"*That*," Meghan said, her blue eyes wide.

Luke's gut tightened as he noticed the front door had been left ajar. "Could be a squirrel," he told her. Then he remembered the other creature they'd found in a cabin the month before and forced a smile. "Or a skunk."

"Pee-yew!" Meghan said, scrunching up her nose.

Luke nodded. "Yes, skunks smell pee-yew. Stand back while I check and see."

The first of the two unfinished cabins had been framed, roofed, and sheeted with plywood—nearly complete. He stepped onto the wooden porch and, adjusting his weight to his good foot, pushed the door in with the tip of his cane. Although he'd never dreamed he'd be using an old-man stick while still in his twenties, the cane *did* come in handy from time to time and provided him with a ready weapon—if ever he should need one.

The hinges on the door were new and didn't screech like some of the older cabins when opened. Luke waited a second to see if anything would run out. Nothing did, but another bump sounded on the inside wall, letting him know something was in there.

Something a whole lot larger than the creatures he'd mentioned to his niece.

A shot of adrenaline coursed through his veins, and, glancing over his shoulder, he told Meghan, "Go over to the garden and stay with your great-grandma for a moment."

He watched until the toddler had joined the eighty-year-old white-haired woman a safe distance away. The day before, a few of the guests at Collins Country Cabins had reported seeing two men in black ski masks looking through their windows while they were undressing. What if the Peeping Toms were holing up in *this* unfinished cabin?

Luke pressed himself against the outside wall and

strained his ears to listen, but all was silent. Then, despite the limp from his left leg, he used the stealth he'd maintained from his past military training to move inside.

His first glance around the rough interior revealed a man's jacket lying on the floor. The savory scent of pepperoni pizza permeated the air. He heard a soft murmur of voices and spun toward his right, his cane raised high, ready to strike. And standing not ten feet away from him there was indeed a man . . . with his arms around Luke's older sister.

Bree jumped away from her fiancé, Ryan Tanner, with a start. "Luke! What are you doing here?"

"My job," he said, shooting them each a grin as he lowered the cane. "Which is more than I can say for the two of you, unless you've added kissing to your list of ranch duties."

Ryan chuckled and wrapped an arm around Bree's shoulders. "Absolutely. No cowboy can work at peak performance without a few stolen kisses."

"If you say so," Luke said, unconvinced.

"I worked all morning on the finances and future bookings," Bree informed him. "And Ryan doesn't have to lead the mini-roundup until tonight."

Meghan peeked her blond, double-ponytailed head through the doorway. "No pee-yew?"

"No skunk," Luke assured her. "Just Aunt Bree and Cowboy Ryan."

"Looks like Delaney has *you* working hard," Bree teased, referring to their younger sister. "She's got you babysitting?"

Luke picked Meghan up with one arm and lifted her onto his shoulders. "Del's getting ready to take a few guests on a trail ride, and Ma, Dad, and Grandma plan to take a trip into town, so Meghan's gonna watch me work. I need to finish siding this cabin and continue framing the next."

Bree gave him an earnest look. "We need the cabins finished before the Hamilton wedding in August."

"Don't I know it." His family was depending on his carpentry skills to get the job done and reminded him at every turn.

Luke couldn't blame them. As co-owners of Collins Country Cabins, they each needed the large amount of money the wedding with its one-hundred-person guest list would bring in. Especially after their previous ranch managers fled at the beginning of the summer season with most of their cash. Their father had trusted Susan and Wade Randall, but when a fall from his horse landed him in the hospital, the couple used the opportunity to embezzle as much as they could.

"When are you going to start planning your own wedding?" Luke asked, trying to take the focus off himself.

Bree glanced at Ryan and smiled. "Sammy Jo agreed to help me plan an engagement party, set for the end of next month, but the actual wedding won't be for another year."

Ryan nodded. "I tried to convince her to marry me *now*, but she says she needs time to plan out all the details."

"I just want it to be perfect," Bree said, her cheeks

coloring. "And I'm hoping the Hamilton wedding will give me some good ideas. You know, I thought we could decorate all the guest cabins with white garlands and . . ." Bree's voice trailed off and Luke watched her gaze drift toward his cane. "Of course I'll do all the decorating. I don't expect *you* to have to get up on a ladder, Luke. In fact, why don't you let Ryan and I help you right now?"

Luke stiffened. "Nope. I've got this. No offense, Bree, but you don't know the first thing about construction."

"Well, then, why don't you let *me* watch Meghan," she persisted, "so she doesn't get in your way and—"

"Trip me?" Luke frowned. "No, I promised little Meggie that she and I would spend the afternoon together."

Bree pursed her lips and her gaze drifted toward his cane again. "But it would be easier if—"

He shook his head. "The days are longer now that it's the tail end of June. I'll get it done," he promised.

Without anyone taking pity on me.

He knew his sister didn't mean to look at him like that, but he and his siblings hadn't seen each other for close to a year before they returned to Fox Creek to help out on their family's Montana guest ranch six weeks before. And up till then, he'd kept his injury to himself.

They still weren't used to the idea he needed a cane to get around, but then again, neither was he. The sooner he got the money for the knee surgery, the better, except . . . he cringed every time he thought of being knocked out for the procedure.

Greg Quinn, one of his friends in the army, survived

a horrendous helicopter crash only to die twenty-four hours later due to complications from the meds used to put him to sleep prior to surgery to remove a damaged kidney.

Luke swung Meghan off his shoulders and, in one swift move, set her back on her feet. "Like I said, I've got it handled."

"Okay, then," Bree said, her voice still hesitant. A second later she smiled. "If you *do* need help, you know where you can find us."

"Yes, I do." Luke glanced down at his niece. "We'll leave them be and work on the other cabin," he told the blond-haired cutie. "The other one's more fun anyway."

Back outside, Meghan giggled as she ran toward the open-slatted two-by-fours framing up the walls of the cabin next door. "You can't catch me!"

Luke hobbled along with the help of his cane to chase after the child, but his mind remained back with Ryan and Bree.

He was happy for them. He was. They'd all grown up together and Ryan Tanner was a good man. With *money*. His family owned the Triple T cattle ranch, largest in Fox Creek, maybe largest in all of Gallatin County.

But only six weeks had passed since their father had been injured in a fall from his horse and Luke, Bree, and Delaney had come home. Only six weeks since their grandmother offered them each part of the ranch profits if they agreed to stay. Six weeks since Bree and Ryan had reunited after years of being apart—long enough for Ryan to have a seven-year-old son.

And now, as of last night, they were engaged. How crazy was that?

There was no way *he'd* ever get engaged to someone after so little time together. At least they were planning to wait a year before going through with the actual wedding. Bree said she needed time to plan, but he hoped it also gave her enough time to make sure she was doing the right thing.

Of course, he had to admit she and Ryan seemed meant for each other. He glanced down at his leg. Maybe after he saved enough money and had the surgery he needed to carry his weight, he'd consider dating again. But not before then. Not until he was whole. The *last* thing he needed was for a country cowgirl to remind him with every soulful glance that he was damaged goods.

And not the hair-raising, high-flying, bronco-bustin' cowboy he used to be.

SAMMY JO MACPHERSON raised the brim of her straw hat to get a better look at the pair in front of her.

"You can't catch me." Meghan giggled again, her small body running easily through the open slats between the two-by-fours.

Luke grinned. "Oh, you don't think so?"

Meghan shook her head, making her ponytails swing back and forth. "Noooo."

Luke pretended he couldn't find an opening big enough for him to squeeze through the beams like she had, which made Meghan laugh so hard she almost fell down backward. Then he went through the opening for the door and she squealed and ran through the vertical beams framing the future bathroom.

Sammy Jo smiled, the longing in her heart doubling at the sight of them. Luke would make a good father someday. A man tough enough to jump onto the back of a wild bronc, but tender enough to give in to the whims of a toddler.

"Can I play, too?" Sammy Jo asked, her breath catching in her chest.

Luke turned his head, and when their gazes locked, the muscle along the side of his jaw jumped. "*Sammy Jo.* Aren't you a little old to play games?"

"Not if you're the one I'm playing with," she teased.

He gave her a puzzled look as if trying to figure her out. Then his expression relaxed and the corners of his mouth lifted into a welcoming grin. She smiled at him in return. She couldn't wait to spend the afternoon with him. Her cheeks warmed and her insides were already dancing around in anticipation.

Luke arched a brow. "Does your father know you're over here consorting with the enemy again?"

She laughed. "I'm a rebel. You know I don't have anything to do with my father's silly feud with your parents."

Luke glanced at his niece. "What do you say, Meghan? Should we let Sammy Jo play?"

Meghan looked at her and giggled. "You can't catch me."

"Oh, yes, I can, you little munchkin," Sammy Jo called out, and chased her through the open framework.

"Not if I catch her first," Luke countered, and dropping his cane, he leaned down and scooped the little girl up in his arms as she ran past.

"Aaaah!" Meghan squealed with delight. "Onkle Uke got me!"

"Lucky girl," Sammy Jo said, coming to a halt beside them.

Luke held her gaze for a fraction of a second, then released the squirming toddler and glanced at the cane, which lay on the floorboards between them.

Before he could ask, or do it himself, Sammy Jo bent down and retrieved the unique wood-carved stick he'd brought back with him from the Florida Keys. No doubt he'd fashioned it himself from a piece of driftwood.

"Here," she said, handing the cane back to him.

He hesitated, then reached out and took it. "Thanks."

"No problem."

But obviously, it was a problem for him. His smile disappeared and his expression sobered. And she was sure something other than the cane had passed between them. Something . . . cold.

"Do you want to talk about it?" she asked, placing a hand on his arm.

He pulled away. "Nothing to talk about."

"You know, there's a rehabilitation horse at the kids' camp where I work on weekends. They said I could bring him over and let you give him a try."

"I can't ride," he said, shooting her a sharp look.

"You could," she argued. "The horse lies down for easy mounting."

She followed his gaze across the yard to the staging area where Delaney was helping some of the inexperienced greenhorn guests mount up for a trail ride.

"No," he said, shaking his head. "I don't need special assistance."

"The horse is a real sweetheart. There's nothing to fear."

"I'm not afraid," Luke said, almost cutting her off. "I'm fine the way I am."

Sammy Jo found that hard to believe. Especially coming from *him*. Luke had been one of the best riders on the rodeo circuit before he left for the military. And over the last several weeks she'd seen the way he'd encouraged his sister Bree to get back up in the saddle again. She'd seen the envy in his eyes when he watched Ryan and the guests going on the mini-roundups ride out through the gate. And she'd seen the way he sat for hours in the stable, polishing the tack of his favorite horse.

He *must* want to ride again. All he needed was something to spur him into action.

A flurry of pounding hooves sped toward them, and Sammy Jo spun around and jumped when a runaway horse brushed its shoulder against the outside beam of the cabin they stood in. Her gaze fell upon the rider. A woman of medium build clung to the animal's back like a spider atop its prey. Except the woman didn't have any control. And Sammy Jo feared she'd soon be the real victim, not the horse.

"Help!" the woman cried. "He won't slow down!"

"Pull back on the reins!" Delaney shouted from across

the yard, but both horse and rider disappeared out of sight.

Sammy Jo squeezed through the open-slatted wood-work and stepped onto the dirt path that stretched before the cabins lining the river. *Someone* had to go after the pair before the Collinses' guest, who'd somehow man-aged to spook the horse, fell off and got hurt.

She glanced at Delaney, who still held the reins of two other horses tacked up for the group trail ride. Then she glanced toward Luke. For one intense moment, their gazes locked, and then, in the next instant, she knew.

It wouldn't be him.

LUKE WATCHED SAMMY Jo take the reins of one of the horses from Delaney's hands and swing up into the saddle.

"I'll get them," she promised.

Delaney nodded, and a moment later Sammy Jo took off past the trees in hot pursuit.

Luke scowled. She'd get them all right. Then she'd be back to talk about her new idea of a rehabilitation horse and pester him some more. The dark-haired menace was a year older, the same age as his sister Bree. And ever since he'd known her she'd been a tease, mocking and tormenting him every possible moment.

But what he didn't get was why she'd started *flirting*.

He found the new exchanges between them awkward and wasn't sure what she meant by it. Was this her new way of playing around? The result of transforming from a skinny, spitfire teen into a curvy, sweet-talking temptation?

Bree and Delaney were no help. When he'd asked his sisters what was up with the way Sammy Jo was acting lately, they'd laughed, as if it were all one big joke.

He had no doubt Sammy Jo had *something* up her sleeve—some kind of plan or hidden agenda. He just didn't know what it was.

With her stubborn "won't take no for an answer" attitude and a figure like hers, he was sure Sammy Jo could have any guy she wanted. So why wasn't she out pursuing someone else? What did she want with him anyway? What did she hope to gain?

The fact she lived on the ranch next door didn't help. Sammy Jo invited herself over all the time, and because she was best friends with Bree and Delaney, she thought she was part of the family. But he'd never considered her a sister. And he vowed he never would. Sammy Jo made him feel like he could never put his guard down. She was always trying to pull his strings and get him to do one thing or another.

Nothing had changed over the last seven years. After six years in the army and a year living in the Florida Keys, he'd returned to Fox Creek to find that even though his pesky next-door neighbor had grown up, she *still* refused to leave him alone.

First Sammy Jo had followed him around like a puppy and peppered him with questions about his leg. Then she manipulated him into being her partner for what seemed like a twenty-minute-long song at the barn dance, an awkward night for sure. And how she managed to enlist his help to catch a fourteen-inch rainbow trout in the river last week, he still didn't know.

But if there was one thing to be said about Sammy Jo, it would be that she sure *was* persistent.

SAMMY JO SQUEEZED her knees against the horse beneath her, urging him to pick up speed as they crossed the open field.

Unbelievable, but the woman atop the runaway horse ahead of her had managed to stay on. Probably because she had both arms and legs wrapped around the animal as tight as she could. Riding up on their left, Sammy Jo leaned over and grabbed the loose reins that had slipped from the woman's fingers and slowed both horses to a halt.

"You're okay," she assured the Collinses' guest, and handed her back the leather straps.

The startled woman, who appeared to be in her late thirties, nodded and sat up straight in the saddle, her eyes wide. "Thank you."

"You did a great job of holding on," Sammy Jo soothed.

"I—I—I . . ." The woman's voice faltered as the horse beneath her let out a loud snort. "I was afraid to let go."

"I'd say you are a natural," Sammy Jo continued, giving her a warm smile. "With a few more lessons you might be riding rodeo."

The woman returned her smile and Sammy Jo let out a sigh of relief. The last thing the Collinses needed right now was an unhappy guest. News of their previous ranch manager's embezzlement the month before had put their reputation on the line.

"I don't think rodeo's in my future," the woman assured her, "but I guess I *could* use a few more riding lessons."

When they returned to the stable across from the unfinished cabins, Delaney whispered, "Sammy Jo, I owe you."

"A bowl of hot buttered popcorn and a movie later?" she asked.

Delaney nodded. "Definitely."

Sammy Jo headed back over to Luke. He pretended to have his head buried in blueprints, but she'd seen him look at her as she and the woman she'd rescued rode up.

"How can I help?" she asked, glancing at the plans over his shoulder. "Do you want me to fetch your tool belt?"

"I don't need you to *fetch* me anything," he said and, using the cane, hobbled over to his tool belt and buckled it around his waist.

"Just trying to make you happy," Sammy Jo offered. Sidling up closer, she looked him straight in the face— her heart flipping over at the sight of those gorgeous hazel eyes—and asked, "How can we fix this?"

"Fix what?"

"You and me."

He gave her a wary look. "I didn't know we needed fixing."

Was he really going to pretend he was immune to her

advances? Because last month at the barn dance he didn't seem too immune. From the way he looked at her and said her name, and had drawn real close at the end of the evening, it seemed like it wouldn't be long before they'd become a real couple. Except . . . for some reason or another . . . they hadn't.

"Why won't you ask me out on a date?" she demanded.

The Adam's apple in his throat bobbed up and down and the muscle along the side of his jaw jumped, but he didn't say anything.

She leaned forward. "Well?"

He glanced away for a moment, then his face lit with amusement and he crossed his arms over his chest. "C'mon, Sammy Jo. We both know the only reason you're *interested* is to make your father angry. After all—what better way to get back at your dad than to date a *Collins*."

"That's not true," she protested. "My father has nothing to do with it."

"Oh, no?" Luke challenged. "Can you deny you wouldn't love to see the look on his face if he caught the two of us together?"

She hesitated and she could feel her face flush. "Of course I would. You know I think the feud he has with your family is outdated and silly. But that's not why I like you—and I'm not *pretending* to like you."

The expression on his face said he didn't believe her. "Look, Sammy Jo, we're just friends. That's *all*."

"We could be so much more," she insisted.

"You may be interested," he said, his tone resolute, "but I'm not."

He was wrong. He *was* interested in her. He just didn't know it yet. Her stomach twisted in knots and her eyes stung, but she raised her chin, determined not to let his words throw her off course. One way or another, she would make him believe her feelings for him were real.

Because she'd already decided that it was high time for her to settle down and get serious with someone.

And Luke was her man.

Chapter Two

SAMMY JO TOOK a knife from the butcher block and proceeded to chop the fresh zucchini, onion, tomato, and sweet red pepper spread across the cutting board. She'd picked up the vegetables at the local market earlier that day and had decided to make a nice green salad to go with the rib-eye steak and baked potatoes she was cooking for dinner.

It would just be her and her father tonight, but she'd soon be off traveling on the rodeo circuit and only popping in for a few days at a time. There wouldn't be much gourmet cooking until the end of the season and she planned to make the most of their last full week together.

Her father wouldn't be the only one she'd be leaving behind. She thought of her best friends, back from what seemed like the three corners of the earth: Bree from New York, Delaney from San Diego, and Luke from the Florida Keys.

This summer they'd all be living here in Fox Creek, while *she* was gone.

She sliced the onion harder than she'd intended and the juice sprayed up into her eye. Wincing, tears formed to blur her vision and she grabbed a dish towel to wipe them away. But the tears kept coming.

Why did they have to come back *now*? Why not a couple months ago when she had all the time in the world to spend with them? When she could have had more time to win over Luke and prove she'd changed?

It wasn't that she *needed* a man. She considered herself a strong, independent woman who was quite capable of taking care of herself. And she had, for seven long years while Luke wasn't around. But something had been missing from her life.

Someone to share it with.

The truth was, she hated being alone. Growing up an only child, she'd suffered terrible bouts of loneliness. That was probably why she spent so much time next door with the Collinses. Then after high school when Luke's father's impossible expectations drove him to join the military, she realized it was more than that.

She didn't need just a friend to cheer her on at the end of a rodeo show. She wanted someone to *love* who would love her in return. And after dating several different men, she realized none of them could capture her attention or make her heart race as much as Luke.

She'd always liked him, which was probably why she teased him so much when they were younger. But she didn't realize the extent of her feelings until after he was gone. She didn't know if it was his zest for life, his leadership skills, the crazy strategic plans he made, or his compassion for others, but when Luke walked into a room, the air always crackled with expectancy and excitement. Like anything could happen. Anything at all. And she loved dwelling upon all the possibilities.

Except she wasn't the only one. Even now there were other women in Fox Creek talking about him. Eyeing him up as he walked down the street. And it wasn't because Luke had come back injured, like he supposed, but because there weren't many single, handsome, awe-inspiring men like him around. Sammy Jo feared if she didn't act fast, another gal would snatch a marriage proposal out of him while she was away at the rodeos. And she'd lose him.

Like her father had lost her mother. All because he never showed how much he cared when he had the chance.

Sammy Jo didn't intend to leave behind any regrets.

After tossing the dish towel back down on the counter, a buzz jiggled inside the back pocket of her jeans. Retrieving her phone, she glanced at the caller ID and answered. "What's up?"

"Can you set an extra place at the table?" her father asked, his tone more cheerful than normal. "I invited a guest over for dinner. Hope you don't mind."

"No, I don't mind." Reaching into the burlap sack on the counter, she took out another potato and tossed it into the oven. "Who is it?"

"A surprise."

"You have a date." She pressed her lips together for a moment, thinking again of her mother, a woman who he hadn't yet officially divorced. "Is it that lady from the bank?"

"You'll see," her father said, his tone unyielding.

Sammy Jo's mother often told her she got her stubborn persistence from her father, and when dealing with him, she'd have to pick and choose her battles.

"Okay," she said, giving in. "But make sure your 'guest' knows that dinner is at six."

After Sammy Jo ended the call, she went to add a place setting in front of the seat at the table next to her father and hesitated. Her mother had left five years before, and now lived in Wyoming, but her parents had never filed divorce papers.

And she had no idea why.

Maybe her mother, who alluded to the fact she'd left because she'd felt unloved, still held hope that Andrew Macpherson could have a change of heart.

Sammy Jo scowled. There was no chance of that happening if he continued to date other women. He'd taken out Winona Lane five times over the last few weeks—twice to dinner, once to the movies, and two other times when she didn't know where they went and he refused to tell her.

The old matronly bat was assistant manager of the Fox Creek branch of Mountain View Bank and had lost her husband the year before. Word had it that she was interested in acquiring property. No doubt the woman saw both her father and the Macpherson land as a good investment.

Glancing out the window at the property next door, Sammy Jo wondered what Luke was up to at that very minute and sighed. Luke had made it clear he wasn't interested in dating so she didn't have to battle off any other contenders. *Not yet, anyway.* But that could all change in a heartbeat. After all, Bree had claimed *she* wasn't interested in dating either, but after reconnecting with Ryan, she'd had a change of heart.

What would it take to get Luke to have a change of heart toward *her*? While she might have the stubborn persistence of her father, she wasn't sure she'd inherited the patience of her mom. She couldn't wait years. She had to find a way to win Luke's heart *this* year, *this* summer, before either his father's high expectations drove him away again or he really did marry someone else.

But how could she do that while in the rodeo?

When her father arrived home it wasn't the banker woman, Mrs. Lane, by his side, or any other woman. It was a man, the transport driver for the auction house that took unwanted, low-bid horses to the slaughterhouse.

"Sammy Jo, you remember Harley Bennett?" her father asked as they entered through the front door.

She gave a slight nod. "We've met once or twice."

Harley removed his hat and came forward to shake her hand. "Thanks for the dinner invite."

Sammy Jo frowned. It wasn't *her* idea to invite him. She waved toward the adjoining dining room. "Have a seat. The steaks will be ready in a few minutes."

Returning to the kitchen, Sammy Jo clenched her teeth. It appeared she was about to suffer through another one of her father's business meetings. Andrew Macpherson worked for the county building department and was always meeting with local clients, even after office hours.

But why couldn't he have met the slaughterhouse accomplice in town at the café instead? Now she'd have to wear a polite smile and pretend that she was fine having this immoral person at her dinner table. Then again, would she have felt any different if Winona Lane had shown up instead of him?

She supposed not.

Stacking the steak and potatoes on a tray with the salad bowl, she delivered the meal and sat down at the table to join them.

"Harley, are you working on a project with my father?" she asked, careful to keep her tone pleasant.

He gave her a slow grin as he stuck his fork in a thick, succulent steak and transferred the double-portioned piece to his own plate. "You could say that."

"What are you building? Adding on to the slaughterhouse?" Okay, she did *not* have the patience of her mother. She shouldn't have said that.

Harley chuckled. "No such luck."

Luck?

"But I'm not here to talk about work," he continued.

She arched a brow. "No? Then why—"

Her father cut her off by clearing his throat. "I thought it would be nice for you and Harley to meet. You both have a lot in common."

Sammy Jo stared at her father, then cast a swift glance at Harley's beaming, brown-bearded face. "Is that so?"

Her throat was so dry she could barely get the words out and her stomach dropped down like dead weight on a fly pole.

Was her father trying to set her up?

The large, broad-shouldered creep her father had brought home let his eyes graze over her as he sat in a chair at the table. "I thought you and I could go out to the auction house this weekend and look over some horses together."

Never in a million years. "Sorry, but I'm off to the Great Falls rodeo."

"What about the weekend after next?"

"If I'm free," Sammy Jo said, lifting her chin, "I'll have *my father* call you. Now if you'll excuse me, I have to feed Tango."

"But you haven't eaten," her father protested.

Sammy Jo rose from the table. "I'm no longer hungry. Harley, I'm sure you'll enjoy the rest of the meal without me."

He placed a second potato on his plate and looked up. "We can grab some more food in town later if you like."

"No, thanks," Sammy Jo said, and shot a look at her father. "I've had enough for one day."

LUKE BROKE OFF a portion of hay from the bale in the back of the green gator. Then with the assistance of his cane, he hobbled over and tossed the thick square flake over the half door of the nearest stall. The horses greeted him with a series of snorts and soft whinnies, each eager for their morning feed. The horse in the next stall kicked at his door in impatience.

"Yeah, you're next," he told the sixteen-year-old gray gelding. Phantom had come to the ranch when Luke himself was a teen, and everyone considered the brute *his* horse, because he was one of only a few who could handle him.

But the horse had mellowed with age since he'd been away and was now used as a trail horse. Luke's father had said, "Phantom won't be giving anyone any trouble anymore."

That was okay, Luke supposed, for neither would he, with his leg the way it was.

He broke off another flake, tossed it into Phantom's stall, then leaned over the top of the half door and watched the gelding tear apart the pressed grass strands with his mouth. *Chomp. Chomp. Chomp.* The motion reminded Luke of younger days when his horse signaled his desire to run by champing at the bit. His gaze slid over the animal's shoulder toward his back, and the temptation to ride tugged hard. Did he dare?

Sammy Jo's uncompromising, self-assured voice broke into his thoughts as clear as if she were standing beside him. *"You could. The horse lies down for easy mounting."*

She was right. He *did* want to ride again. But on a rehab horse? What if he fell off and damaged his knee beyond repair? No, he couldn't do it, not at the risk of never walking without a cane again.

Besides, too much time spent with Sammy Jo, if he accepted her offer, would encourage her so-called "affection." And he wasn't willing to get involved with someone who might only want to take advantage of him.

Luke went into the kitchen of the main house for his own breakfast after feeding the rest of the horses. It smelled like vanilla. He glanced toward the stove where his eighty-year-old grandma stood stirring the contents of a large pot. "What are you cooking?"

Grandma turned to give him a wide smile. "Marshmallows."

His mouth watered just thinking about it. His grandma's homemade marshmallows were far more creamy, gooey, and tasty than any he'd ever eaten. There was only one word he could use to describe them. "Yum."

Meghan, who sat at the table between his sisters, Bree and Delaney, copied him and repeated, "Yum."

Delaney laughed. "I know, right? I haven't had any of Grandma's marshmallows in years."

"The guests love them," their mother said, whisking into the room and handing their grandma a bowl.

"First we've got to prepare the gelatin and cook the sugar mixture before we can whip them into shape and sprinkle on the powdered sugar. Any of you want to volunteer to help?"

"I can cut roasting sticks from the branches by the river, so we're ready to cook them over the bonfire tonight," Luke offered.

Grandma's white bushy brows drew together and she gave him a pointed look. "I meant help *making* the marshmallows."

Luke glanced at Bree and Delaney.

"Don't look at me," Del told them. "The friend I have in San Diego who agreed to take over the lease of my apartment shipped the rest of my things and the UPS truck should be here any moment."

"And Ryan suggested I interview a band to come play at our engagement party next month."

"Will there be dancing?" Delaney asked.

Luke hoped not. He'd barely survived dancing with Sammy Jo at the *last* barn party.

"Yes, of course there will be dancing," Bree said, her face aglow.

Delaney sighed. "I guess I'll have to find a date. But I really don't care for any of the locals. How am I going to find a handsome cowboy I *do* like all the way out here?"

Ma handed Luke a plate of bacon and eggs with jam-spread toast and he sat down at the table with them. "Why don't you go online and try Montana Mingle.com?"

"Sammy Jo has looked on there," Bree added.

Luke frowned. "She has?"

Bree nodded. "Yeah, but she said she couldn't find the right guy."

Was that why the dark-haired tease had taken to flirting with him? Because she couldn't find anyone else? He pushed down the sick sensation forming in his gut, realizing there was something worse than being used. It was being someone's "last resort."

"Seriously, where can I find a date?" Del asked, turning to wipe Meghan's jelly-stained mouth with a napkin.

"Ask the UPS man?" Luke teased.

Del swatted his arm with her hand. "Have you *seen*

the UPS man? No way." Then she smiled. "Maybe I'll get lucky and a handsome loner will decide to rent one of our cabins that week. A guy who loves animals as much as I do. Maybe a conservationist."

"What about you?" Bree asked as Luke was taking a bite of his food. "Why don't you try MontanaMingle. com?"

Luke shook his head. "I don't want to meet new people. I'm pestered enough by the ones I've already met."

"Sammy Jo feels the same way," Delaney assured him. "You can ask her to be your date for Bree's engagement party."

Luke set his jaw. "No."

"Sammy Jo came over late last night," Bree confided. "She was angry because her father tried to set her up with the horse auction transporter, a real loser of a guy. She says it's not the first time her father's done this to her either. Seems like her father's trying to marry her off."

Luke knew Sammy Jo had to have an ulterior motive for suddenly wanting to date him. It *was* to get back at her father. Bree's words just about confirmed it. He sucked in his breath, held it for a moment, then released the air slowly while trying to erase Sammy Jo's fun, flirty image from his mind. Yep, the curly-haired cutie couldn't be trusted. She was an expert manipulator, a spoiled only child used to getting her way.

Last month, Sammy Jo had tricked Bree into thinking she was hurt. He'd been in on the plan, along with Delaney and Ryan, but only because he agreed that Bree needed to get over her horse's death. It worked. Bree *did* start riding again after her mad dash on the nearest horse she could find to rescue her best friend from supposed life-threatening danger.

Bree had been mad at first, but had since forgiven them.

However, the incident had made Luke wonder if now it was his turn. If Sammy Jo had no qualms about deceiving Bree, how hard would it be for her to justify deceiving him?

He guessed he now had his answer.

All of a sudden the pantry door burst open and their two teenage twin employees, Nora and Nadine, rushed toward him, each taking one of his arms.

"We'll be your date for the engagement party," Nora exclaimed. "But first there's the big Fourth of July celebration, and—"

"We need someone to be our partner for the three-legged race," Nadine finished.

Luke glanced back and forth between them. "You only need two people for the three legged race, not three. You each have one leg free and tie your other two legs together to make the third."

The brown ponytailed twins stared at him, then chorused in unison, "You're *right!*"

Bree gave each of the sixteen-year-old girls a stern look. "What were you doing hiding in the pantry?"

"We needed bottle caps," Nora replied. "I saw on TV that if you glue a design inside a bottle cap, add a dab of clear coating, and then put it on a chain—"

"We thought we could help you, Bree," Nadine said, cutting her sister off in her excitement.

Luke smirked as Bree asked hesitantly, "Help me how?"

"We're going to help design boot bling jewelry for your new business!" they chorused again.

Grandma turned from the stove and waggled a crooked finger at them. "You better have left my bottled syrup unopened."

"We got the caps out of the garbage," Nora assured her.

"Yes," Nadine agreed. "The five-gallon recycling bucket."

Luke's ma pointed to the bottle caps in their hands. "I hope you're going to wash those first."

"But—" Bree's face took on a horrified glance as the twins ran from the room. "That's *not* the kind of jewelry I had in mind."

"You won't make much money with that," Del agreed.

"Speaking of money," Luke said in between bites of food. "Any news from the PI we have tracking down the Randalls?"

The last they'd heard, their embezzling ranch managers had been hiding out in Arizona. However, Susan and Wade Randall had still not been caught despite the efforts both the police and their hired PI had put into the search. The husband-and-wife duo had been at large for over six weeks, ever since mid-May when their father's fall from his horse put him in the hospital with a concussion and a broken leg.

Having been misinformed about the seriousness of his injuries, Luke, Bree, and Delaney had all flown home thinking the worst. They hadn't been planning to stay, but when the Randalls stole the money and it became clear Luke's and his sisters' assistance was needed to keep the ranch afloat, their grandma offered them each a portion of the ranch if they agreed to stay.

"Doug Kelly has a few leads so I hope to hear something good from him soon," Bree said, referring to the PI as she rose from her chair and took her plate to the sink. "Dad's given up on the sheriff's efforts. Can you believe it? After all his fuss about how he trusts the authorities to do their part, yesterday Dad actually admitted he was glad I hired the PI."

Their father wasn't one to dish out compliments or lend support, but since Bree had taken over management of the ranch she'd found a way to win the old man's respect. So had Delaney, mostly because she'd brought back an adorable granddaughter. But their father had always been hardest on him, maybe because he was his only son, and had always demanded more than Luke could give.

Now that he'd come home with a limp, and they'd had to hire Ryan Tanner to be head wrangler because he couldn't ride, Luke felt like it was even more impossible to please his father than before. But he would do what he could.

He pushed back his chair and thanked his ma for breakfast. "Got a full day of work ahead of me," he announced. "I best be getting to it."

"Luke," Bree called after him as he headed toward the door. "The father of the bride for the August wedding asked if we have a gazebo. He said the bridal couple would really love to get married in a gazebo."

He nodded, knowing they all had to do whatever it took to keep the Hamiltons and their one hundred guests from finding another venue. "They will," Luke assured her. "Tell him they will."

As soon as he could build one.

SAMMY JO ROUNDED the first barrel, already a fraction of a second behind where she wanted to be. She gave Tango an extra tap with the heel of her boot and pressed on. In professional barrel racing, an eighth of a second could make all the difference between a cash prize and going home with her pockets empty. But it wasn't Tango's fault. He'd been eager to leave the alley and take his turn in the arena. No, today the problem was her own. Her head . . . or maybe her heart . . . just wasn't in it.

She and Tango rounded the second fifty-five-gallon drum and her balance was off, making her trusty horse circle too wide. Another fraction of a second lost.

They approached the third barrel just fine, kicking up dust, but by then it was too late. Their completion of the clover leaf pattern had not beaten the top three competitors' scores. She gave Tango an affectionate pat on the neck as an apology for letting him down. For she knew, if it hadn't been for her sloppy cues, her beloved quarter horse would have won.

"Better luck next time," one her circuit buddies consoled.

Sammy Jo gave her a nod, and flashed a halfhearted smile. "Yeah, Tango will be raring to go at the next rodeo."

But would *she*? As her friend rode into the arena for her shot at the prized purse and accompanying buckle, Sammy Jo's smile slipped into a frown.

All her life she'd wanted to race barrels, and she had, winning many competitions and making it into the finals several times. But since the Collins siblings had returned to Fox Creek, her enthusiasm for the sport had waned. Instead of concentrating on the performance pattern, she'd been thinking of Luke and how his eyes used to twinkle right before mounting a wild bronc in the bull pen. How once in a while he would turn that twinkling gaze on her and how she wished he'd do it more.

She also thought of all the other women her age who were already married and brought their children to the horse camp where she worked a few days each week. Over the last year a creeping emptiness had taken root inside her and had only grown worse when Delaney returned with little Meghan, and Ryan asked Bree to marry him and be a mother to his seven-year-old son.

Sammy Jo had always considered her horses her kids. She'd had several of them over the years. But now she suddenly found herself longing for a child she could ride *with* and not ride *on*. And a loving husband to ride beside them.

A man of her own choosing. She shuddered as the image of the guy her father brought home for dinner came to mind. She'd thought her father had been bringing home a date for himself, not for *her*. Ugh.

After Harley Bennett left, she'd confronted her father in the living room.

"He's not the one who sells the mangy horses to the meat factory," her father argued. "He's just paid to transport them."

"No self-respecting cowboy could ever do that," she'd snapped back. "Driving the horses to their deaths makes him an accomplice in their murders."

"Strong words for someone who helped Luke Collins steal a crate of Thanksgiving turkeys and set them loose in a field full of hunters."

She shuddered. "That was a long time ago, and . . . that was a mistake. We thought we were saving them. We didn't know the hunters were there."

"I'll tell you what. You hanging around with that Collins kid is a mistake. Why do you think I brought Harley home? To get your mind off those no-good neighbors of ours."

"You admit you tried to set me up?" she demanded. "How could you! I'm *twenty-seven*, far too old to have my father pick out my dates, as if I *ever* needed your help in that department."

Sammy Jo would have left with her mother and moved to Wyoming, but her mom only had a tiny apartment with no acreage, and her father still had the barn where she kept her horse.

Saying goodbye had been one of the hardest things she'd ever done, but she and her mom kept in touch weekly via phone and computer, and they visited each other every couple of months. Still, she couldn't help thinking that if her father had tried harder to get along, her mother might have chosen to stay.

"I talked to Mom earlier," Sammy Jo informed him, throwing down the statement like a challenge for him to pick up.

Her father glared at her, then his expression softened and he cleared his throat. "How *is* your mother?"

"As well as she can be."

"Is *she* dating anyone?"

Sammy Jo scowled. "Of course not. I wish she would, but she won't, not while she's still married to you. You've been separated for five years. Why don't you make it official and get a divorce already?"

"We vowed on our wedding day we'd never divorce."

"But you're both miserable."

Her father shook his head. "I'm not."

"You are. I can see it in your face, and the way you talk, and the way you stare at her picture on the table beside your bed each night."

"How would you know—"

She waved his words aside. "Just like I see the way you look out the window toward the Collinses' property when you think no one is watching, with that same expression of regret. You are sorry you have an ongoing feud with them, aren't you?" Sammy Jo narrowed her gaze. "And the real reason you don't want me going over there is because you're jealous that I have a *good* relationship with the Collinses."

"I don't want to talk about them," her father said, his voice cold as his John Deere in winter. "Don't ever mention their name to me again in this house."

"But they're our neighbors," she said, trying to understand. "Why won't you tell me what happened between you and Jed and Loretta Collins? What is it you think they've done that would make you hold a grudge so long?"

"I said, I don't want you to talk about them," her father warned.

"I didn't say their name." She raised herself up on her tippy toes to look him straight in the eye and he looked right back.

"Subject closed."

Sammy Jo shrugged and turned away. "Okay, I'll see you later."

"You're leaving?" Her father's expression faltered. "At this hour? Where are you going?"

Sammy Jo glanced back over her shoulder as she headed toward the door. "Over to the *Collinses*."

Her father had called after her, "Don't forget you have to leave early for the Great Falls rodeo tomorrow morning."

As if she'd ever forget. She'd had this rodeo marked down on her calendar since the previous year. If there was one thing she *never* forgot it was the date of each rodeo. It was her dream, her life, her whole reason for being.

Until now.

LUKE SMILED A greeting at a few of the guests walking the path past the line of riverfront cabins. Everyone wanted to see how he was doing, and although he found some of the carpentry challenging, he was determined not to let it show.

Dropping a handful of nails into his shirt pocket, he hooked his hammer through his belt loop, and dropped his cane. Then leaning on his good foot, he took hold of the ladder with both hands and lifted his weak leg to stand on the bottom rung.

He winced as the pressure shot a painful twinge up to his knee. But with a small hop his weight shifted back to his good leg and the pain subsided. He drew a deep breath and repeated the process three more times before stopping to catch his breath.

Luke found if he leaned his hip against the upper rungs after each climb, he could utilize his good leg more efficiently. Keeping his eye on the two-by-four running across the top of the exterior cabin wall, he gritted his teeth and pulled himself up one more rung.

That would do it. After taking one hand off the ladder to swipe a bead of sweat off his brow, he retrieved a nail and his hammer. The top beam needed a little more re-inforcement before they could hang trusses for the roof. At that point he'd be forced to ask for help, but not before then. He was determined to do this on his own.

"*Luke!*" Bree's voice.

He turned his head to see his father and sister hurrying toward him, each wearing identical scowls.

"What the blazes do you think you're doing?" his father demanded.

"Exactly what I said I'd do," Luke told him. "Pulling my weight around here." *Literally.*

"This is crazy!" Bree exclaimed. "You're lucky you

didn't fall and break your neck. How do you think you're going to get down?"

Luke's gaze dropped toward their feet. "The same way I got up here."

The ladder slid sideways, due to the fact he was placing most of his weight on one side, and he had to quickly drop the hammer to grab hold of the top beam of the cabin wall with both hands. Then as if losing the tool wasn't bad enough, the entire ladder fell away beneath him.

"*Luke, hold on!*" his sister screamed. Then turning around, she called to Ryan, who had mounted his horse across the way.

It only took a few seconds for Ryan to ride up, rein his horse to the side, and grab Luke with one arm so he wouldn't fall. "I've got ya, buddy," Ryan said, his voice strained as he braced sideways to balance his weight. "You can let go."

Luke released his fingers from the top beam and Ryan lowered him to the ground onto his good leg as if he were some feeble old woman.

Heat flooded into his face as he then had to look his future brother-in-law in the eye. "Thanks for the lift."

Ryan slapped a hand on his shoulder and grinned. "Any time, my friend."

As Bree picked up Luke's cane and brought it over to him, his father shook his head and started grumbling under his breath.

"Stop being such a hothead and accept you can't do it," his father barked.

Luke held his gaze. "I can. None of this would have happened if you didn't come out here and distract me."

"We're still paying off my hospital bill," his father argued. "We don't need to pay off another one for you, too."

"I've got military health coverage," Luke retorted, although the coverage was *very* limited. "No need for anyone to have to pay for me." He picked up his hammer, intent on finishing his work, but his father wasn't finished with him.

"Your stubbornness is costing us precious time we don't have," his old man continued. "Either you hire an able-bodied carpenter to finish these cabins or I'll have your sister call someone."

Hire his own replacement?

"No need," said a stout, black mustached, craggy-faced man approaching with a clipboard in his hands. "Your building permits are expired. All work on this property must come to an immediate stop."

Chapter Three

EXPIRED? LUKE LOOKED at the date on the building permit attached to the outside wall. The man who had joined him and his father, sister, and her fiancé was *right*. The date read June 15 and today was July 5.

"My name's Frank Irving, county inspector for the planning department in Bozeman. We heard reports you've been building illegally."

"We didn't realize the permit was expired," Luke's father said, casting Luke a swift glance as if it was his fault.

Luke swallowed hard. Maybe it was. He should have checked the date before he took over the job their previous ranch managers had begun.

"You say you heard reports?" Bree asked the inspector, her tone filled with suspicion. "From who? Who reported us to the planning department?"

Frank gave her a haughty look. "I'm not at liberty to say."

Luke's father let out a growl. "The guests wouldn't report us, and since the Owenses aren't home, that only leaves one person I can think of."

"Andrew Macpherson," Bree said, nodding her head. "But why would Sammy Jo's father do such a thing?"

"Yeah, Dad," Luke said, turning toward his own father. "Why *would* he want to shut us down?"

Luke's father let out a low grunt. "He thinks I stole something from him a long time ago . . . before any of you were born. Something that he's never been able to get back."

"What's that?" Luke exchanged a quick glance with his sister, and winced when he realized they'd both chorused the words together like Nora and Nadine.

Bree smiled and they both leaned in for their father's answer.

"Your *mother*."

"You and Mr. Macpherson are fighting over Ma?" Luke gasped. "Is that what your feud has been about all these years?"

"The reason you two won't talk to each other?" Bree added, her eyes wide.

Luke realized with disgust that he and Bree really *did* sound like the twins, but he wanted to know the answers as much as she did.

His father let out another grunt, his way of affirming most questions. "Andy and I used to be friends . . . a long time ago. Andy had his eye on your ma but she chose me over him. Andy said he'd never forgive me and so far he's kept his word."

The building inspector chuckled. "It's not the first time I've had neighbors turn each other in. Happens all the time. But not usually because one is a jilted lover."

"But Andrew Macpherson is nearly sixty years old," Luke exclaimed. "Holding a grudge all these years seems childish. He can't still have any feelings for her."

"Why not?" Bree mused. "Maybe that's why Sammy Jo's mother left. Maybe she realized he'd never love her the same way he loved Ma."

"No one ever said he loved her," their father barked. "I don't think the guy knows what love is. He's just mad he didn't get what he wanted and I did. End of story."

"End of construction," Frank Irving said and, walking over to the cabin, he tore the permit off the wall and handed it to Luke along with a letter of cease and desist. "You'll need to reapply online and start the permit process all over again."

"But that could take weeks." Luke saw Bree's horrified expression and added, "Isn't there anything we can do to speed the process along?"

The inspector smirked. "Do you know anyone over at the building department?"

Luke tensed. He knew one, but the guy he had in mind could be as stubborn as his daughter and promised to be more of a hindrance than a help.

SAMMY JO HAD never been so happy to return home after a rodeo. The trip back had taken a couple days longer than she'd expected, due to a broken hitch the local garage couldn't fix until after the Fourth of July holiday weekend.

She unloaded her horse, put away her tack, and ditched the idea of getting something to eat so she could hurry over to see her friends. One friend in particular. *Luke.* So she could try once again to win his heart.

Hopefully he'd be more receptive than the last time. And no one else had gotten to him while she was away. She'd pulled her truck into the gas station in town on her way home to fill up and overheard a woman at the opposite pump say she'd decided to pay Luke a visit and bring him a batch of chocolate fudge brownies. Sammy Jo had been so rattled by the conversation that she didn't wait for the pump to finish but tore out the nozzle and drove home as fast as she could, knowing her window of opportunity was closing in with each passing day.

Sammy Jo found her reluctant hero by the unfinished cabins, painting the one that had been roofed and sided with a color that matched dark clover. Smiling, she noted he'd chosen to wear his olive drab T-shirt and mixed green camouflage pants from his military days. Smart man. Any drips or unintended splashes would blend right in.

Her pulse kicked into high gear as she walked forward, studying Luke Collins further with each step. His golden-brown hair used to be shorter, but since his return to Fox Creek he'd left it kind of shaggy so that it fell down over his eyes. She preferred a clear view of his face, but didn't dare offer to give his hair a trim. Not until he warmed up to her and allowed her to spend more time with him.

"How's it going?" she asked, drawing near.

Luke scowled. "The county planning department shut us down. One of our neighbors snitched on us, told them we were building with expired permits."

"One of your *neighbors*?" Sammy Jo asked, and felt her stomach contract. She and her dad were the only neighbors the Collinses had right now, and it wasn't her. "Oh, no. My dad? Are you sure?"

Luke dipped his brush in the bucket of paint by his feet and gave her a quick glance. "Yeah."

With an inward groan, Sammy Jo's thoughts flew to her father. Why did he continue to cause trouble between her and the ones she loved most? He certainly wasn't helping her to win Luke's favor.

"I'd reapply for a new permit right now," Luke continued. "Except it's late and the building department doesn't open its doors again till tomorrow. I figured if I can't continue to build, at least I could paint."

She grabbed the extra brush lying on the tarp he'd spread on the ground. "Let me help. It's the least I can do."

Luke shook his head. "No, I've got it handled."

"I want to. *Please.*"

Sammy Jo went to dip her brush into the paint, but he pulled the bucket away from her and set it on the ladder beside him.

"I didn't mean to lay a guilt trip on you," he said, his tone softening. "We all know you don't agree with your father."

"I still want to help," she argued, waving the brush in

front of his face. "Why is it so hard for you to let anyone help you?"

"You're not just anyone."

Sammy Jo tilted her head to the side to catch his eye, arched her brow, and gave him a big smile. "No, I'm not. Glad you noticed." Then she frowned. "Wait a minute. What do you mean by that? You'll let others help you but not me? Why?"

He hesitated and for a moment she didn't think he would tell her. Then he pinned her with a sharp look. "You don't know what you're doing."

Not one to let anyone intimidate her, Sammy Jo raised her chin and stood her ground. "I know how to paint."

"That's not what I meant."

Was he referring to the way she made him feel? If that was the case, then he was wrong. She knew *exactly* what she was doing. But was it having the effect she wanted?

Luke's body tensed the way it always did when their conversations turned personal. Okay, so maybe he didn't feel the same as she did, not yet, but she wouldn't let that discourage her.

Smiling, she took the clean brush she held in her hands and swept the soft bristles across his shoulder and down the length of his fine muscled arm. "What *did* you mean?"

"Don't play games," he choked out, and glanced away from her.

She stepped around, bringing them back face-to-face. "I'm not. I just want to spend time with you. There. I've said it. What's wrong with that?"

"Your motives."

Sammy Jo froze as he met her gaze, and it seemed as if he could see right through her. But could he see the love she had for him swelling her heart? Sometimes when they stood this near she thought her chest would explode with the emotion she fought so hard to restrain. But if she gushed like a schoolgirl and told him how she really felt, he'd never believe her. Not that he did now. And she'd only shown him a quarter of the affection she'd been hiding.

"Okay," Luke relented, "you can help. But keep your eyes on the job."

"Where else would my eyes be?" she teased.

Luke shot her a look of amusement, but didn't reply and she didn't dare push the subject any farther. Determined to show him she could be of value, she shot out her arm to retrieve the bucket of paint he'd placed on an upper rung of the ladder.

Except Luke reached for it at the same time and the double movement made the bucket wobble, tip, and then . . . dump the five gallons of thick, clover-green liquid right over both their heads.

Sammy Jo let out a screech, jumped back as the bucket hit the ground to avoid another splash, and brought her hands up to her face to keep the paint from streaming into her eyes. The chalky latex enamel substance smelled as bad as it tasted and she had to spit several times to get the wretched stuff off her lips and out of her mouth.

She glanced down at her white T-shirt and denim cutoffs coated in green, as were her arms, legs, and what used to be her blue canvas shoes.

Then her hands flew to the top of her head where gobs of the green goo weighted down her long dark curls and left them hanging limp over her shoulders. She tried to separate the icky green strands with her fingers and let out another cry. Returning her hair to its natural color would be no easy task. No easy task at all! Maybe next time she'd think twice before offering to help for the sake of spending time with him.

She glanced at Luke, also covered in green, except she'd been right—his clothes hid the paint better. Holding her breath, she waited for his reaction. Would he be mad? Blame her for wasting the gallon of paint?

No . . . he grinned. As if this was funny. As if . . .

"Did you do that on purpose?" she demanded.

"Of course not," he said, inspecting the new color of his cane. "If I had, I would have stepped back so the paint didn't get *me*."

"Then why are you laughing?"

"I'm not." He broke into another grin. "Although you *do* look a lot like the wicked witch from *The Wizard of Oz*."

Sammy Jo sucked in her breath. "And you look like a cow has spewed all over you with a whole day's worth of green cud!"

This time Luke *did* laugh. He laughed for several long seconds, harder than she'd ever heard him laugh since he'd been back home.

"You know that Emerald Isle shade becomes you," he teased. "Matches your eyes."

"Not funny," she shot back. "How am I going to get all this paint out of my hair?"

"You can't. You'll have to cut it all off."

The thought of styling a bald head didn't hold much appeal. She'd rather sport her clover green curls until the color grew out, although that image, too, was almost enough to bring her to tears.

Then his amused expression made her realize he wasn't serious and she pointed her finger at him. "Now who's playing games?"

Luke shrugged. "It'll wash out with a good shampoo. You'll just have to scrub real good. For now, we can rinse off with the hose in the wash room."

She patted the front pocket on her denim shorts. "I hope the paint didn't go through to my cell phone. What if I lost all my contact numbers? Or my photos?"

"Would be a shame," he said with mock concern.

Luke did not appreciate the finer aspects of having multiple apps available at one's fingertips 24/7. A fault she could easily forgive him for if he'd only pick up the phone to call her for a date.

A real date. Not just hanging out at the barn, or attending a rodeo together with the rest of their friends, or even roasting marshmallows by the fire with his sisters. But one-on-one time with just the two of them.

Luke led her toward the open double doors of the stable to the large cement wash room where they usually gave the horses a bath. When she envisioned a date, this setting had never come to mind either.

"Stand over the drain and I'll hose you down," he said, turning on the water.

She took her phone out of her pocket and set it on a

shelf holding the horse shampoo, a sponge, and squeegee. Then stood ready to embrace the oncoming shower.

"Tip your head back and close your eyes," Luke instructed.

"So you can kiss me?"

"No," he said, shaking his head. "So I can do *this*."

The water burst out of the end of the hose and Sammy Jo squeezed her eyes shut to avoid the fresh onslaught of paint running off the top of her head.

This was a disaster! This was not what she'd had in mind when she'd come running over here today. This was . . .

She felt his hand cup the back of her head and his strong fingers tangle in the back of her hair. To help rinse the paint out, she supposed. But the sensation sent tingling shock waves of awareness down her spine and she wished she could open her eyes, just for a moment, to see the look on his face. She tried, but it was impossible with the thrust of the torrent.

When the water stopped, Sammy Jo found parts of herself still green, but at least the main bulk of the paint had washed away. She pasted on a bright smile and said, "Your turn."

But instead of letting her touch him the way he'd touched her, Luke set his cane to the side, leaned against the wall, and used one hand to hold the hose and his other to scrub.

Sammy Jo's spirits plummeted. "You don't want my help?"

He chuckled as if she'd said something funny. *"No."*

Fine. Be that way. Sammy Jo retrieved her phone and was about to call Bree to bring her a towel when Luke gave a sharp whistle.

She turned toward the door to see who he'd been signaling, and caught a glimpse of the Walford twins as they were about to enter one of the other cabins.

"Hey," he called to Nora and Nadine. "Bring those towels over here."

The girls came running, then stopped in their tracks, their mouths falling open when they caught sight of them.

"You can't use these towels," Nora exclaimed, her arm protective around the stack of clean white folded terry cloths she carried.

"No, absolutely not," Nadine agreed. "You'll turn them green and Bree will—"

"Make us do the laundry," Nora wailed, cutting her sister off. "And the last time we did laundry, the washer overflowed!"

"I'll take full responsibility," Luke assured them. "Now give us the towels. *Now.*"

Sammy Jo watched Nora and Nadine exchange glances, then the sixteen-year-old twins threw the towels toward them and scurried away, chattering like chipmunks.

"Guess you'll be leaving now, too?" Luke asked once they'd dried off. "You'll want to go home and get a real shower and change of clothes."

Was he trying to get rid of her? "Yeah," Sammy Jo said, trying to swallow her disappointment. "I guess so."

An awkward silence followed and as he picked up his

cane, she added, "But I could come back later to tell you more about the rehabilitation horse they have at the kids' camp where I work."

"Not interested," he said, slinging his green-tinted towel around his neck. Then he took her towel from her hands and dabbed at her cheek.

She assumed she still had a green smudge he was trying to wipe off, but she didn't care about that. All she knew was that Luke's face was incredibly close to her own, and he had the most amazing long-lashed hazel eyes, a small endearing crook in the bridge of his nose, and enticingly firm lips, which parted slightly and—

"Don't look at me like that," he warned.

Heat rushed over her face and she felt too guilty to play innocent so she remained silent.

"Enough is enough," he continued, his voice turning edgy. "Bree told me about the guy your father brought home for dinner and I know you'll do whatever you think you must to get your father off your back."

"Yes, I will, but—"

Luke gave her a stern look. "You won't use me to get back at your father."

"Of course not," she said, and placed a hand on his arm to keep him from leaving. "But let's talk about this."

Shaking her hand off, Luke gave her one last glance as he walked out the door. "I said *no*."

WHEN THE DOORS opened the following morning, Luke's father accompanied him into the Department of Planning and Community Development set on making sure their new permits were filed.

Luke would have preferred to have made the trip on his own, but his father had argued that he couldn't drive a street-legal automobile with a bum leg. Luke disagreed. He could maneuver their all-terrain utility cart around the ranch just fine. Even if he did have to use his left foot instead of his right to step on the gator's gas pedal. He was certain if allowed to drive the pickup he could do the same.

His father cast him a sidelong glance as they waited for the elevator to take them to the second floor. "You've got the blueprints?"

"Right here," Luke said, patting his backpack.

"And the new permit application?"

"Every detail is filled out and ready to go." Luke wished he could have taken the stairs, but once again, it was his injury that kept them together.

"Can't have anything holding us up," his father continued.

"Yeah, I hear you. Loud and clear."

His father hesitated, and a bead of sweat ran down the side of his face. "I'm not sayin' I don't trust you, it's just that—"

"Yeah, what?" Luke demanded.

"We need to be ready."

He *was* ready. Even if the planning department was not. When they entered the permit office, Luke scanned the empty room and pushed the bell on the front counter. "Hello?"

Other than the rhythmic drum of a copier spitting out paper and the aroma of fresh brewed coffee, it didn't seem like anyone else was there. Seconds later, a tall, thin man with gray hair, white sideburns, and a peppered mustache came out of a corner office and stiffened as they recognized one another.

"Can I help you?" Andrew Macpherson asked, his tone sharp.

Both Luke and his father hesitated, but it was his father who spoke first. "We need to speak to Ted Gurgens."

"Ted isn't in," Andy replied.

"When will he be back?" Luke asked.

Their neighbor tapped the wall calendar beside them with the tip of his pen. "He's on vacation for the next three weeks."

"Three weeks?" Luke's father exclaimed, his voice thunderous. "We can't wait three weeks. Who's in charge of filing permits while he's away?"

Andy leaned over the counter, his face smug. "*I* am."

The hostility between the two rivals raised the hairs on the back of Luke's neck and he knew he'd have to act as the go-between. He laid the rolled blueprints and accompanying paperwork on the counter. "We need to file new permits for our building projects. Will you help us?"

"Of course." But as Andy took their check for the application fee, the smile Luke and his father received wasn't reassuring.

Two days later, when Luke called to inquire on the status of the permit, their neighbor informed him that because the office had been closed the previous Monday for the Fourth of July, the planning department was behind. They hadn't even looked at it. Another three days passed and when Luke followed up he was told the engineer had misplaced the plans. A third call promised Luke and his family they might have to wait up to two full months before being issued a new permit.

Two months would be too late. If Collins Country Cabins couldn't provide the two extra guest lodgings required for the August 6 wedding, the Hamiltons would drop their many thousands of dollars into another venue.

Luke thought of the numbers Bree had calculated their family would need to keep Collins Country Cabins afloat. And there was no doubt about it. They *needed* that money.

He'd asked his mother if she'd talk to their neighbor, thinking if Andrew Macpherson still harbored feelings for her, he might give them a break. But his mother refused and warned Luke never to bring up the subject again.

Luke had promised his family he'd get those cabins built no matter what, and the churning in his gut kept him awake two more nights before he decided to enact a plan that would at least give them a chance.

Sometimes, if the enemy got the upper hand, one had no choice but to call for reinforcements. And in this particular case, Luke could think of only one person with the influence, persistence, and stubborn willpower to convince Andrew Macpherson to cut the red tape and push their permits through the appropriate hoops.

If only she'd agree to help.

SAMMY JO CLAPPED her hands together and cheered as the ten-year-old girls she'd been teaching to ride rounded the dusty arena. "Great job! Now give your horses a pat and bring them down to a walk to cool off."

She'd loved every minute of teaching the various age groups at the kids' camp how to ride over the last few months. Their jubilant laughter, excitement, and eagerness to learn reminded her of her youth when she, Luke, Bree, and Delaney would go on trail rides and participate in the western games at the fairgrounds together. Here, she was surrounded by people, a part of a team, while riding on the rodeo circuit often had her competing *alone*.

"You're a great teacher," the thirty-six-year-old owner of the camp said, eyeing the girls' progress with appreciation.

"Thanks, Jess." Sammy Jo helped her collect the bright orange cones they'd set out in the arena for the girls to circle. "I wish I could stay and work here all summer."

"So do I," Jesse Rinehart said, her tone wistful. "I have a favor to ask. I know you'll be away at rodeos on the weekends, but do you think you can still help me out during the week?"

Sammy Jo picked up the last cone and hesitated. "I'm already helping out at the Collins ranch a couple days a week. I wouldn't have any days off."

Jesse bit her lip. "You'd still have your evenings free."

"I don't know," Sammy Jo said, shaking her head. If she worked seven days a week she'd make a lot of money doing what she enjoyed, but . . . she wouldn't have much time to spend with friends . . . or to make Luke fall in love with her.

"Think about it?" Jesse asked, her expression hopeful.

Sammy Jo nodded, although she knew if she were to accept this job, she'd have to sacrifice something else.

Something important.

KEEPING A FIRM grip on his cane, Luke walked into the Happy Trails Horse Camp looking for Sammy Jo. But the place looked overrun with children of all ages and their various western mounts. How would he find her?

He passed five girls who looked to be about ten or eleven wearing the green Happy Trails camp T-shirt with white lettering and matching silhouetted horse head logo.

"Have you seen Sammy Jo Macpherson?" he asked, searching each of their faces for some kind of lead.

"She's still in the arena working with Jesse," one of the girls volunteered.

Who was Jesse? A child, a horse, another trainer? He gave the girl a nod and continued toward the white fenced enclosure, hoping if Jesse *was* a trainer, the person in question would be female. When he asked Sammy Jo to help, he sure as heck didn't want to have to do it in front of another man. Especially if the dark-haired vixen demanded he seal the deal with a kiss.

Sammy Jo's familiar tinkling laugh caught his attention and he spotted her inside the fenced enclosure wearing the same green Happy Trails camp T-shirt as the kids. She *was* with another male cowboy—except the young partner's height only came up to her waist. A dark-chestnut quarter horse stood beside them and Sammy Jo was passionately giving the boy instructions on how to ride in simple, easy-to-understand terms.

Luke stood transfixed, unable to pull his gaze off her. Sammy Jo's face positively glowed every time she laughed or smiled. And her exuberance was not only captivating, but contagious. A crowd of other children had gathered around to watch and Luke found himself drawn forward as well. There was no mistaking the fact she cared for these kids. So how was it he had trouble deciphering how she felt about him?

He thought back to the day the bucket of green paint had spilled over top of them. She wasn't glowing with enthusiasm that day, but the memory brought a smile to *his* lips. He was still smiling as he made his way into the arena, then stopped short when the horse suddenly kneeled down in front of them, and let the young cowboy climb onto the soft, saddle pad strapped to its back.

"Is that—" Luke stared as the horse shifted its weight, and stood up to full height.

"The rehabilitation horse I was telling you about," Sammy Jo said with a nod. "Impressive?"

Luke didn't answer. His body had stiffened so much he couldn't tell his good leg from his bad. Yes, the feat was impressive and he was sure the horse helped numerous people with disabilities. But he didn't come here to watch her work or to rehash their argument over using the rehab horse.

Tipping his hat toward her in greeting, he glanced

around at all the kids and wondered how to best explain the reason he *was* here. "I . . . uh . . . came over to see what you do on the days you aren't helping us."

He figured he should ease into it since Sammy Jo had already shot down both Bree and Delaney when they asked her to help the night before. Sammy Jo had told them she didn't feel comfortable getting in the middle of their parents' feud, but Bree thought her friend might be holding out until *he* asked her.

Sammy Jo's mouth curved into a saucy grin. "You came all the way out here just to see me?"

"I did."

She gave him a puzzled look, then glanced around as if expecting someone to be with him. "How did you get out here?"

"Ryan was on his way home and offered me a ride."

"I finish work in about five minutes," she told him. "You could have waited until I got back home and used the gator to drive next door to see me. Why are you really here?"

"I couldn't wait," he choked out, his voice hoarse, but sincerely honest. "Sammy Jo, we need your help."

"*We?*" Motioning for an older woman with a brown ponytail to come take her place, Sammy Jo left the boy, the horse, and other children behind to follow Luke out the gate.

"Look," she said, hooking her thumbs through the belt loops on either side of her patched denim cutoff shorts. "You know I feel like I'm a part of your family. I love you all, I really do. But I won't get between you and my father. Remember, I'm the one who has to live with him, not you."

"That's why you're the best one to persuade him to issue us the building permits."

"He's not the only one who works at the building department," Sammy Jo argued. "You act like the decision is solely up to him, but it isn't."

Luke swallowed hard. He needed her on *his* side, not her father's. "He has influence," he said, trying to keep his tone light. "Your father could speed up the process. Instead, he's made it clear he's going to delay our permit as long as possible."

"He did?" Sammy Jo's expression softened and her green gaze locked with his in that special way that always stole his breath whether he wanted to admit it or not.

"What do you think?" Luke challenged.

She let out an exasperated sigh. "Of course he did. My father has been whistling about the house these last two weeks as if he's the happiest man in the world."

"Help us," he said earnestly, "and you'll make *me* the happiest man in the world."

Her dark brows drew together into a tight scowl. "After I got that bucket of paint dumped over my head I vowed I'd never help you again."

"That's one promise you will never keep." He drew closer and brushed her cheek with the back of his hand. "Because you weren't made that way. I see that now. You love helping others. That's what you do. You're also very convincing. I was hoping you could use some of your special persuasive powers to convince your father to speed the permit process along?"

She let out a laugh and rolled her eyes. "You think I have 'special persuasive powers'?"

"Definitely."

"Except they don't appear to work on you." She frowned. "You want my help, but you won't even ask me out on a date."

Luke shrugged. "I'll take you anywhere you want to go." Then he grinned. "If you drive."

"You'll take me out on a date if I go against my father?"

Luke shook his head. "I'm not asking you to go against him. Just soften him up and convince him this may end the silly feud once and for all."

Sammy Jo's expression perked up. "You really think it will?"

Luke shrugged. "Who knows?"

She hesitated. "I don't think I can change his mind. He's been awful stubborn lately."

"And you're not? If anyone can change his mind, it's you."

"You'll really take me out on a date?"

"Whatever it takes."

"I'm tempted. But now that's not enough."

Not enough? What more did she want? A kiss?

His gaze dropped to her mouth. She did have a set of full, inviting lips . . . and he'd wondered more than once over the last couple weeks what they might taste like, despite his misgivings.

He hesitated, his heart pounding, then drew his head closer and asked, "What will it take to make you say yes?"

"A fair trade," Sammy Jo announced, pulling back. "I'll *try* to get my father to push your permits, if you'll *try* to get on the rehab horse."

"The *rehab horse*?"

"Yes."

"You call that a fair trade?"

Sammy Jo smiled. "I do."

He stared at her, stunned. He thought for sure she'd demand a date or kiss, but *why the horse*? What did she have to gain? "I told you I can't ride."

This time she gave *him* an earnest look. "Have you tried?"

"No, but one fall and, instead of using a cane, I could end up in a wheelchair the rest of my life."

"Doubtful. They make prosthetic legs now all the time."

"Not something I would look forward to," he assured her.

"I don't want you to get hurt," she explained. "But I do want to see you happy again."

"You think riding a horse will make me happy?"

"Whenever you think no one is watching I see how you look at the other riders, longing to tear out into the fields with them at breakneck speed, with an excited, half-wild look in your eye and that wide goofy grin."

"No."

"No?" She put her hands on her hips and gave him that adorable stubborn tilt of her chin. It was clear she was enjoying this. Enjoying having the upper hand and making him eat humble pie.

He couldn't start a feud with her. He needed her. He needed to help his family. As co-owner, he needed to make his guest ranch work.

"Please, Sammy Jo. Let's be honest and make this easy on each other. You want to use me to get your father off your back so he won't set you up with any more creeps. I want to use you to soften your father up so he'll issue our permits. It's a win-win for both of us and we both get what we want. What do you say?"

"I want you to try the rehab horse."

Luke glared at her and she glared right back. She wasn't going to lay off the horse issue. She would hold on and fight him until she finally got her way. Just like she always did. But isn't that why he was making her the deal in the first place? Because she was persistent?

"Okay," he agreed. "But you've got to 'try' to convince your father to give us the permits *first*."

Chapter Four

SAMMY JO WASN'T sure she'd made the right decision. Instead of having Luke try to ride the rehab horse, she could have pressed her advantage. She could have demanded a kiss.

"What do you think it would be like to kiss Luke?" she asked Tango as she ran a brush over his thin palomino summer coat.

The horse didn't answer but gave a loud snort. Then he continued chewing the patch of green grass in front of the tack shed as if he wasn't interested. But she was.

If Luke kissed her, would it be hot and hungry? Slow and soft? Hesitant at first, then more insistent? She smiled as she dwelled over the countless possibilities. If only she'd asked . . .

Then she remembered why she hadn't and her shoulders slumped. Luke had *expected* her to ask. She could tell by the way his gaze kept drifting toward her mouth.

Except he didn't look too sure about whether he wanted to.

Despite her pleasant romantic daydreams, the reality was that if she'd asked for a kiss, Luke would have given her a fast, stiff, brotherly peck. And if she'd insisted he prolong the kiss, she knew his heart wouldn't be in it. What an awkward disaster that would be. Not the best way to make him fall in love with her. No, what she needed was time. The more time they spent together, the more likely he'd *want* to kiss her. Then someday, when their lips finally met, they'd *both* be happy.

Luke had jerked back in surprise when she'd insisted he try to ride the rehab horse. Obviously he hadn't seen that one coming. But she got him to agree and that was all that mattered. Now she could look forward to spending several long days with Luke as he discovered he *could* ride, and he *did* want to kiss her.

Sammy Jo took a hoof pick out of Tango's tack bucket and gave him the cue to pick up his foot by leaning into his shoulder and running her hand down the length of his leg. But instead of complying, Tango pulled away from her.

"Hey, boy, what was that all about?" she asked, running her hand down his leg again.

The area just above his hoof was warm and slightly swollen. Gently, she lifted his foot to take a look beneath and, sure enough, he had a pea-sized abscess. The good news was that it was draining. The bad news was that she'd have to soak his foot in Epsom salts and they'd have to back out of the rodeo that weekend.

Maybe she could spend the extra time with Luke?

The familiar rumble of her father's truck pulled into the driveway. Good. She wanted to talk to him about the Collins building permit to uphold her end of the bargain.

Except . . . her father wasn't alone. This time he *did* bring that banker woman, Winona Lane, with him. And another truck, a brown Ford with a deep V-shaped dent above the left rear wheel well, pulled into view behind them. Harley Bennett's truck. He was pulling a brown horse trailer and Sammy Jo could see through the side window slits there was a single horse inside.

"Oh, no," she told Tango with a groan. "Looks like I won't be able to talk to my dad about the Collinses anytime soon."

She let her palomino friend go back to grazing, and looked around for a bucket to fill with water and the salts for his hoof soak, then realized her father wasn't taking his company into the house. He was leading them toward *her*.

"We have a surprise for you," her father announced, a proud eager grin spread across his face. "Mrs. Lane has agreed to sell us her barrel-racing champ, Black Thunder."

Sammy Jo glanced at Mrs. Lane, who affirmed what he said with a nod and a smile, then her gaze flew toward the dark horse Harley Bennett was unloading from his trailer.

"But—" She looked back at her father, who had come to all her competitions while growing up but had never been interested in riding too much himself. "I don't need another horse."

"Tango's age may be catching up with him. I heard you didn't even place in the top three at the last rodeo."

That wasn't Tango's fault, it was hers, but instead of telling her father that, she said, "Tango has a hoof abscess. I'm sure that's why we didn't place. It might have already been bothering him."

"See?" her father exclaimed. "Another reason you need a second horse—in case one is lame. Now you'll never have to miss another rodeo."

He had a point. Every rodeo she passed up meant less money in her pockets and she needed to be able to support herself and save enough for her own house someday.

"At least take him for a quick ride to try him out," her father insisted.

Thunder had beautiful conformation. A quick ride wouldn't hurt. It would be fun to see what kind of speed and pivotal turns the supposed "champion" had.

"All right," she agreed. But then after Harley brought the horse's tack out of the trailer and she saddled up, Tango let out a soft whinny that shot a pang of guilt straight through her heart. "Don't worry, Tango," she called over to him. "You're still my best boy."

Her ride around the orange barrels strategically placed in the open field beside the river affirmed it. Although Thunder had Tango's talented ability, Sammy Jo didn't have the same bond with him as she did with her own horse. Bonds like that took months, sometimes even years, to develop. But when two hearts finally shared that special connection . . . it was worth every moment of the wait. And with that realization came another. She now knew what it was she had to do.

"I appreciate the offer," Sammy Jo told her father's

entourage upon her return. "But I don't have time for another horse. I've been overwhelmed enough as it is. Jesse Rinehart, the owner of Happy Trails Horse Camp, asked if I could continue to help out over the summer even though she knows I've been going to the rodeos on weekends, and during the week I help out the Col—"

"You'll have to tell the Collinses you need to focus on your priorities," her father said, and Mrs. Lane and Harley nodded in agreement. "Let them find someone else to give their guests weekly lessons."

Sammy Jo shook her head. "They need me."

"You can't do everything."

Was that what this was all about? Her father's way of getting her to stop spending time at the Collinses'? How could he do this to her? First he'd brought Harley over, hoping to distract her, and now a horse?

She dismounted, handed the black horse's reins back to Harley, and drew in a deep breath to steady her anger.

"Well?" her father asked. "What do you think of Thunder?"

"He's a fine horse," she told him. "One who deserves to be ridden. But it won't be by me."

"But he's the best barrel racer in the county," Winona protested, her face aghast.

Sammy Jo would have argued in Tango's defense but didn't want to offend the woman any more than necessary. "Mrs. Lane, the truth is, I've decided I'm not going to compete in any more rodeos this year."

"What?" her father demanded. "You're not serious!"

She lifted her chin and looked him in the eye. "I am."

Taking her arm, he pulled her out of earshot of the others. "You haven't missed a year in over a decade."

"Well, then, maybe it's time," Sammy Jo said, keeping her voice low. "There's more to life than rodeo."

"A year ago you would have sworn differently."

"You're right," she agreed. "But now things have changed. *I've* changed. I want . . . more."

"It's because of those Collinses, isn't it?" he demanded. "You'd give up rodeo to be with them?"

"Yes, I would. Because I care about them, and since their previous ranch managers left town with their money their guest ranch is struggling."

Her father smirked. "Nothing you do will be able to help them. You'll just be wasting your time."

"Why?" she challenged. "Did you delay the filing of their building permit on purpose?"

This was *not* how she'd envisioned the conversation when she'd rehearsed it earlier that day. However, she couldn't back down now.

"I may have misplaced their paperwork for a few days," he admitted.

"But it's filed now?" she pressed, hoping to be able to give Luke the news.

He hesitated. "Well, not yet. I still need to go over the fine print and make sure all is in order."

"When? By the end of this week?"

He inclined his head, ever so slightly.

"Give me your word."

"I give you my word, the Collins permit will be filed by the end of the week," he said, then frowned. "But that doesn't mean they'll get a new one. Their application still has to go through several of our departments."

"I understand," she said, and smiled. "Thank you, Daddy."

"You shouldn't be thanking me," he scolded. "You should be riding rodeo."

"And *you*," she said, reaching up to give her father a quick kiss on the cheek, "should be making friends, not enemies."

"The Collinses and I will never be friends," he warned.

"Why?" she pleaded.

"I don't want to talk about it," he replied.

Sammy Jo noted his troubled expression and didn't press him further. She'd already won one battle today, and for now, that was enough. She'd have to discover the details behind his feud with Jed and Loretta Collins some other time. Or else maybe . . . it would be a good question to ask Luke.

LUKE WITHDREW SOME of his savings at Mountain View Bank to buy the lumber he'd need to build the gazebo. Then noticed the assistant manager giving his ma a hard time.

"Not many people keep a safe deposit box in Fox Creek," Mrs. Lane drawled. "What do you keep in there?"

"That's my own business," his ma said, her voice rising—a sure sign she was agitated.

"Jewels? A few gold coins, maybe?" Mrs. Lane pressed.

Luke stepped forward. "We don't have all day," he told

the middle-aged woman. "Open the vault so my mother can access the box and we'll be on our way."

"Well, you could say 'please,' " Mrs. Lane shot back. "No need to be rude about it. Just wanted to satisfy my curiosity, is all. I've been working here over twelve years and see your ma come in every two weeks to take a peek in that box of hers, but I never see her take anything out."

"That's to keep it safe," Luke's ma said, her face creased with worry. "Some things are too valuable to keep at home."

"Now you've really got my curiosity cranking," Mrs. Lane said, and laughed. "Follow me. I'll open the vault and won't say another word. Maybe another day you'll finally tell me what you've got hidden in there."

Luke doubted it. His mother didn't even tell *him* what she kept in her private box. And she'd had it as long as he could remember.

As Mrs. Lane led his ma toward the door to the vault, Luke went out and sat in the passenger seat of his family's parked pickup and waited for her return.

Glancing around, he realized Fox Creek hadn't changed much over the years. The same two-block strip of stores lined both sides of the street with Ralph's garage on one end, and the historic Fox Creek Hotel on the other. The bank lay smack-dab in the middle, on the corner next to the sheriff's station.

A cowboy with a straw hat and trophy-sized rodeo belt buckle exited the bank and pocketed a wad of green bills. When he looked up, Luke recognized him and gave a slight wave.

"Luke Collins, The Legend of Fox Creek," A.J. Malloy greeted in his familiar easygoing tone.

Luke smirked. "I haven't been called 'The Legend' since high school."

A.J. let out a hearty chuckle. "Remember the time you left your keys in the truck outside the café and that bully, Harley Bennett, drove off with it? You ran three blocks to catch up with him, jumped into the back, and punched him through the window to make him pull over."

Luke remembered all right. Except it hadn't been his truck but Sammy Jo's and she'd been the one who had left the keys in the ignition. He'd acted, not to save Sammy Jo like some damsel in distress but because her truck was his and Bree's only ride home and he had a job to do that night. The carpenter up the road had promised to pay him a hundred dollars if he showed up to lend a hand on the Johnson house at five o'clock. And he'd needed that money to help cover his entrance fee at the next rodeo.

"And the time you led us out to the range to rope that wild mustang?" A.J. continued. "You jumped on his back and it's a miracle you didn't get thrown off and break your . . ."

"Yeah, good times," Luke said, sliding his cane unseen under his seat.

"What are you up to now?" A.J. asked. "Still in the army?"

Luke shook his head. "Got out last year. Spent some time in Florida, but now I'm part-owner of my family's ranch."

"Going to compete in any of the local rodeos this

season? I'd hate to lose the prize purses I've been winning over the last few years but I'd sure love the competition."

Luke hesitated. "No, not this year. Too much work to do."

"Too bad," A.J. said with drawn-out regret. "I saw Sammy Jo Macpherson at the rodeo in Bozeman a couple weeks back. But she must have been having an off day. Her scores weren't even high enough to get her into the top three and we know she's better than that."

"Yep, she's a top-notch competitor, hard to defeat," Luke agreed. *Especially when she is fixated on getting her own way.*

A.J. double tapped his hand on the rim of the open truck window and shot him a grin. "Hey, me and some of the other guys are meeting up at the café later tonight before we head off to the next rodeo in Helena. You want to come?"

And listen to them brag about their latest scores and meanest ride? Again, Luke shook his head. "Maybe next time you swing into town."

"They'll be disappointed The Legend turned them down." A.J. hesitated, as if hoping he'd change his mind. Then stepped back. "Well, hey, good seein' ya."

Luke nodded. "Yeah, you, too."

A.J. had been his partner in crime as they'd picked the lock on Mrs. Owens's shed and raided the ice box to steal some of her homemade popsicles when they were ten.

At fifteen, they'd advanced to midnight tractor races down the stretch of dirt roadway leading to the grave-yard. They'd charged spectators five dollars to watch, enough to fund an illegal fireworks display the residents of Fox Creek would never forget.

Then at eighteen, they'd entered the exciting, fast-paced world of rodeo bull riding. A world where their fortunes could change in a mere eight seconds.

A world which Luke still lived for but no longer belonged in.

He thought about his promise to Sammy Jo and wondered if it was possible for him to ride again . . .

Possible that one day he'd walk unaided . . .

Possible he'd once again be the man he used to be.

"Look, it's Sammy Jo," a jubilant ten-year-old called out.

"Sammy Jo, are you going to help us out today?" another girl asked, her expression hopeful.

"Yes," she answered, smiling at each of them. "Just as soon as I talk to Jesse."

"Here I am," Jesse called as she came from the main house carrying several quarter-inch-wide strips of colorful ribbons. "Didn't expect to see you today. Aren't you heading off to the next rodeo?"

Sammy Jo shook her head. "I quit. I decided I'd rather be here and work with the girls."

Jesse wrapped her in a hug. "I know that decision must not have been easy, but I'm sure happy to have you with us."

"I just have one favor to ask," Sammy Jo said, and clasped her hands together in front of her.

Jesse gave her a nod. "Ask me anything."

"Can I borrow the rehab horse for a few days? The friend I told you about has agreed to give him a try."

"Luke?" Jesse's smile widened. "Finally persuaded him, did ya? Yes, you can take Prince for the next two weeks, but then I need him back. We've got a new little boy whose leg is amputated at the knee coming to ride him."

"Thanks, Jesse."

Later that same afternoon, Sammy Jo greeted Delaney and her daughter, Meghan, as they came to the camp for a visit. "You like?" she asked, waving her hand toward the hitching post where eleven middle-grade girls were braiding ribbons into the horses' manes and tails.

"Pretty," Meghan said, pointing.

"Yes, the girls are making all the horses look pretty," Sammy Jo told her.

"Thank you for inviting us," Delaney said, holding her daughter's hand as she led her around. "Meghan loves seeing all the kids."

"So do I," Sammy Jo admitted. "It brings back the fun memories we used to have decorating our horses for shows."

"Maybe Meghan will be in a horse show one day," Delaney said, smiling. "She's already riding my grandma's miniature pony, Party Marty, on short rides to and from the garden. Of course I'm right with her the whole time." Then Del gave her a wink, leaned toward her, and whispered, "So what's up? I could tell by your text that you had something important you wanted to talk about."

Sammy Jo laughed. Of course Del had seen right through her invite and sensed an underlying purpose. Delaney Collins had always been intuitive that way.

"Okay," she told her friend. "I made a deal with Luke and he's agreed to give the rehab horse a try."

"I heard all about it yesterday," Del said, and rolled her eyes. "At breakfast, lunch, and dinner."

Sammy Jo hesitated. "So . . . he's thinking about it. Okay, mental preparation is good. But the question is . . . what can I do to make the experience easier on him?"

Delaney sat Meghan on top of a large wooden barrel and let one of the older girls braid pink ribbons into her daughter's hair. Then Del said, "Luke doesn't like being told what to do. Maybe when you're giving instructions, word it so he thinks he's figuring it out on his own."

"Good advice," Sammy Jo agreed, and then let out a sigh. "You think he'd like me better if I wasn't so aggressive?"

"A woman has to be aggressive to get anywhere with Luke these days," Del encouraged. "But it'll take time for his head to make the mental shift required to switch you from the role of friend to fiancée."

"I *know*," Sammy Jo crooned. "I've been trying to learn how to cook, bake, clean, mend clothes, can vegetables. What else do you think I could do to prepare to become domesticated?"

Delaney laughed until tears formed at the corners of her eyes. "Sammy Jo, no offense, but I don't think you're meant to be that kind of housewife. And Luke wouldn't want you that way either."

Sammy Jo bit her lip. "Are you sure? I could have your grandma teach me to make her homemade marshmallows . . ."

"Her marshmallows are the best," Del said, "and it

might be a good idea to learn how to make them, but you know what my grandma would say?"

Sammy nodded. " *The way to a man's heart is to be yourself.*' But what if being myself isn't good enough?"

At first Delaney didn't answer and her face took on a haunted look. Then she confided in a soft voice, "I asked myself that question every day for several months after Steve and I divorced. Then I realized if he couldn't appreciate who I was, I was better off without him."

Sammy Jo's throat grew uncomfortably tight as she thought of life without Luke. While he was away, her days had been filled with activity but none of it made sense . . . until his return. It was their shared enthusiasm that brought everyday conversations to life. Their challenges and dares that changed common tasks into an adventure. And their awareness of each other's emotional "triggers" that turned ordinary moments into something breathlessly profound.

Smiling, she realized she'd been wrong to let her mind disperse doubt. Because in her heart she just *knew* she and Luke were meant to be together. The same way she looked at these horse-crazy, fun-loving, enthusiastic young girls and knew she wanted children of her own someday.

Luke *had* to feel the way she did.

LUKE LOOKED AT the dark chestnut quarter horse Sammy Jo had brought over to his family's guest ranch in her horse trailer.

"He doesn't even know me, how is he supposed to trust me?" he demanded.

"Prince is very well trained," Sammy Jo assured him. "He'll bow down for anyone. And he might not know you, but he knows and trusts me. I've been working with him for years."

In the past, Luke had always been the first one to sign up for any new crazy adventure, always believing he could do most anything. But after a couple of his friends in the military were killed in what was supposed to be a routine helicopter training exercise and he later tore his ACL in the motorcycle accident, he'd been forced to come to grips with the fact that he *wasn't* invincible. None of them were. And if he wasn't careful he'd end up in a coffin like his buddies.

"You *did* talk to your father?" Luke asked, stalling for time.

She nodded. "Yes, I did."

"And what did he say about expediting our permits?"

She gave him an agitated look. "I'll tell you *after* you keep your promise. Now give Prince the cue by saying, 'Bow.' "

Luke stiffened. "You already ran through the procedure once, you don't need to tell me again. I heard you the first time."

Sammy Jo bit her lip, then stepped back and nodded. "Of course. If anyone can do this, it's you."

Her sudden, submissive tone filled him with remorse. "Sorry, Sammy Jo. I didn't mean to bark at you. Jeez, I sound like my father more and more every day."

"You're nothing like him," she said loyally.

Luke held her gaze. "I'm afraid I am."

His father often sent confusing messages. Some days it seemed as if he truly cared, and other days not so much. Luke didn't want to send any confusing messages to Sammy Jo. He wanted to be as up front, straightforward, and honest as he could.

"A deal is a deal," he told her. "So here goes." Then he turned toward the horse beside him and said, "Prince, bow."

The horse pulled his left front leg in, then dropped his head and shoulders low to the ground so that the saddle was only a few feet off the ground. Luke placed his weight on his good leg, grabbed hold of the saddle horn with his left hand, and hesitated. Should he drop or hold on to his cane?

Sammy Jo lurched forward. "I can take—"

"No."

She stepped back, again biting her lip as if she realized she'd said too much, or regretted saying anything at all.

Here he was, making her feel bad again. "I meant," he said, forcing a grin, "I've got it handled."

"Of course you do," she agreed, her eyes wide. She looked as if she were holding her breath and her knuckles were white as she clasped her hands in front of her. Probably praying this worked, although he still had to figure what she hoped to gain from it all.

"Go big or go home" had always been his motto, so he dropped his cane on the ground and prepared to mount. Tightening his hold on the saddle horn, he used his upper body strength to brace himself. Then he lifted his leg over the horse and winced as a sharp pain shot through his knee, up his leg to his head, and burned behind his eyes, nearly blinding him. For a moment all he saw was stars.

Then the pain subsided and his vision cleared. He gave the command, "Up!" and the horse rose to his full height in one swift, smooth move.

Luke gasped, his stomach tight, as he realized . . . he couldn't use his injured leg to press against the horse's side to keep himself balanced. If he hadn't grabbed on to the horse's mane and readjusted his weight at the last minute, he might have fallen off.

"Are you okay?" Sammy Jo asked, her voice filled with concern, then she cupped her hand over her mouth. "Of course you are. You've got it handled."

She didn't sound as confident as her words implied. Luke frowned. "You're not going to tease me and say I look ridiculous like when we were kids?"

"Of course not," she said, as if appalled by the notion. "You can trust me."

He doubted that and frowned again as Sammy Jo's behavior continued to confuse him. Then the horse took a step forward and he had other things to worry about. Like how to stay balanced when using only the pressure from one leg. He wobbled back and forth as the horse took another few steps, and three thoughts raced through his head.

First . . . he was *riding*. Second . . . his knee didn't bother him nearly as much as he thought it would. Third . . . he was *free*.

The view from the saddle sent his pulse skyrocketing. The sun appeared to shine brighter, the tree line looked greener. He glanced at Sammy Jo, even more beautiful than moments before with that incredulous look on her face, and he grinned. Then his gaze was drawn back to the wide golden fields stretched out before him, beckoning him . . .

"Luke, *don't*!"

Sammy Jo's call came too late. He'd been too impulsive, too eager. Too excited by the prospect of flying over those fields that he'd forgotten the fact that one fall could damage his knee beyond repair.

The minute he'd clucked his tongue for the horse to move into a jog, he'd realized his mistake. He bounced back and forth and the mere inches he raised out of the saddle seemed like several feet. As if he were at a rodeo on the back of a bucking bull.

And the fall seemed just as far and hard. He let out a *"Yow!"* as another bout of pain shot through his knee when he tucked his body in and rolled. Dust clouded around him, shot up his nose and into his mouth. He leaned over and spit on the ground beside him to get the dry, earthen taste off his tongue and then sneezed.

"Luke!" Sammy Jo plopped down on her knees beside him and she placed her hands on either side of his face, cupping his cheeks. "Look at me. How's your head? How's your knee? Where does it hurt?"

"Everywhere." Lying flat on his back, he looked up at her, too stunned to think of much beyond the pain, except he kind of liked the idea of her fussing over him. Then he sat up and glanced around. "Where's my cane?"

"Over there," she said, and pointed to the spot. "I'll run and get it."

"No," he said, tucking her hand in his arm. "Let me lean on you for support and I'll get it myself."

Sammy Jo's mouth fell open as if to protest, then she put her arm around him to help balance his weight.

She was warm and soft; her hair smelled of roses. And for the first time since his neighbor had started to lavish him with attention, Luke allowed himself to enjoy it.

At least until he regained his senses.

Chapter Five

SAMMY JO STOOD by the jewelry stand in the corner of the Collinses' guest registration office admiring Bree's handmade leather and bead boot bling. Her friend had always loved fashion and had worked herself up to fashion retail assistant at a prominent store in New York before moving back to Fox Creek.

Her sister, Delaney, loved animals and photography, and had placed some of her nature prints on postcards, which were displayed in a spinning rack beside Bree's jewelry.

Their grandma's basket of homemade oatmeal and lavender soaps claimed a shelf in the corner, along with her canned homemade jams and pickles, and small bags of homemade marshmallows.

"Have you had many sales?" Sammy Jo asked, pointing to all their homemade items.

Bree sat at the desk and turned her head away from

the computer screen to glance her way. "Yes, the guests love them. First they buy for themselves and then they buy more as souvenirs to take home to all their family and friends."

"I wish I could make something to sell," Sammy Jo said, walking over to take a seat beside her. "But I'm not very creative."

"You're talented at other things," Bree told her, and scowled at the computer screen. "I wish I had your techie computer skills. Do you think you could help me?"

"For a price," Sammy Jo teased.

Bree nodded. "Name it."

Sammy Jo smiled. "Your grandma's homemade marshmallow recipe? I figure if I want to become Luke's wife, I'll want to learn to make his favorite treat."

Bree broke into a smile. "Luke's wife," she repeated. "Yeah, how's that coming along?"

Sammy Jo took the computer mouse, glanced at the screen, and with a few clicks made some adjustments to the financial sheets her friend had been working on to get rid of some funky formatting. "Luke got on the rehab horse yesterday and . . . oh, Bree, you should have seen the way his whole face lit up. Then he looked at me . . . and it was almost as if . . . as if he could love me."

"Are you sure that's not just what you *wanted* to see?"

"Why?" Sammy Jo's heart skipped a beat. "Did he say something about it?"

"Well . . . not about you exactly." Bree bent down and scooped her new black-and-white puppy into her lap. "Luke came in the house, his face covered in dirt, and said, 'I'll never get on another wobbly wheelchair horse again!'"

Sammy Jo frowned. "Wheelchair horse?"

"His name for the rehabilitation horse," Bree explained.

"He *has* to get on him again. In fact, I was hoping we could train Luke's horse, Phantom, to bow so he can get on."

"That's a great idea!" Bree agreed. "Delaney can help out too, and we can take turns when Luke's working so he won't even know."

"And when Luke's ready," Sammy Jo continued, excitement bubbling up within her now that she had Bree's support, "we'll surprise him."

Ryan's seven-year-old son, Cody, ran into the office, followed by two more of the black-and-white border collie puppies. The boy gave Bree a quick hug, then took the puppy she had and set it down with the others. "I'm going to take Boots out to play with Oreo and Lucky."

The empty hole in Sammy Jo's heart widened as she watched the look of affection pass between Bree and her soon-to-be son. "You're the one who's lucky," she whispered in Bree's ear. "Lucky to have Ryan and Cody and . . ."

"A whole pack of dogs to go along with all the horses and cattle?" Bree joked as Cody ran back out the door.

Sammy Jo nodded. "At least you won't ever have to worry about being alone."

Bree smiled. "No, I definitely won't. And you're right. I *am* lucky—to have a friend like you. Will you be my maid of honor at my wedding?"

"Of course!" Sammy Jo exclaimed, clapping her hands. "Unless I'm married to Luke before you marry next summer. Then I'd be your *matron* of honor."

Bree laughed. "Then we'd *both* be lucky!"

LUKE TOSSED ANOTHER log on the evening campfire and a flurry of sparks flew into the air. "I'll tell you what," he told Ryan and Josh Tanner. "Sammy Jo says the horse was trained, but I've ridden unbroken broncs who were smoother than her trick-bowing beast."

"She should have known better," Ryan agreed, his tone anything but serious as he lent mock support. "Women only *think* they know everything."

Josh grinned. "You got that right."

"A man knows whether or not he's healed enough to ride," Luke continued, using the tips of his cane to stir the coals. "A woman can't make those decisions for you."

"Yeah," Ryan said, his smile broadening as he adjusted his chair to lean out of the way of the smoke. "They certainly can't."

Josh smirked. "You got that right."

Luke frowned. They wouldn't think it was all so funny if *they'd* been in his position. He sat back down beside the two jokers who had come to visit the humble abode he'd set up on the other side of the Collinses' property. "And you can't let them follow you around or tell you what to do."

"I told Bree we need to make decisions together," Ryan said, and chuckled. "Except for the wedding plans. I gave her full rein to go ahead and do what she wants with that."

"Some decisions don't need a man's input," Josh said with a nod.

"And some do." Luke leaned forward and eyed his friends. "Sammy Jo said her father agreed to file the permits."

"Great news," Josh exclaimed.

"Yeah, it is," Luke said, stretching out his bad leg so it wouldn't stiffen. "Guess who I saw in town the other day when I went to buy some lumber for the gazebo? A.J. Malloy. Haven't seen him in ages."

"Heard he got himself a big glass case to put his trophies in," Ryan said, and then gave Luke a sidelong glance. "Heard he also has his eye on Sammy Jo."

"Good for him." Luke's jaw tightened. "Does she know?"

Ryan shrugged. "You want me to ask Bree?"

"No! Why would I care? Women are nothing but trouble."

"That's what I told Ryan," Josh teased, "but instead of listening he dropped down on his knee and proposed."

"Won't happen to me," Luke told him. "I'd rather wrangle cattle than wrangle myself a wife."

Ryan's amused expression fell from his face. "That reminds me. While I was leading the guests on the weekend cattle roundup, someone mentioned seeing a strange man outside their cabin . . . wearing a black ski mask over his face."

Luke sat up straight. "Again?"

Ryan nodded. "Your father thinks it could be some local teens playing a prank."

Luke hesitated. "Or someone else our ranch managers hired to wreck our business. A few weeks ago when Mrs. Owens was arrested and admitted she'd been an accomplice, she said she wasn't the only one."

"We'll help keep an eye out," Ryan said, nodding to his younger brother, Josh. "And so will Dean and Zach."

Having all four of the Tanner brothers on their side would ease his family's nerves. They were the best wranglers in Fox Creek and their cattle ranch was only fifteen minutes away if a problem should arise.

"My family would appreciate it," Luke said, his gut twisting from the thought of having to deal with more trouble. "The more eyes, the better."

SAMMY JO STOOD on one side of the rehab horse while Luke stood on the other. "Please, Luke," she coaxed, her patience wearing thin. "Give him one more try."

"You said your father would file our permits by the end of the week, but instead he gave our family a call and said we forgot to sign the forms in one spot."

"Did you?" she challenged.

"No. I went over each line and made sure everything was filled in. When my dad went in to sign he noticed one of the pages in our original submission had been replaced."

They must have been mistaken. "What proof do you have?"

"No proof," Luke told her. "I just know. So did my dad, and apparently some bitter words were exchanged."

Sammy Jo sighed. "That's probably why my father kept silent last night during dinner. Tonight I'll try to talk to him again about issuing your permits, if *you* get on the horse."

Luke shook his head and glanced across the field toward the Collinses' main cluster of buildings. "No time. The lumber arrived for the gazebo and I need to work."

"What about later?" she pressed.

"Me and the guys are going to keep watch for prowlers."

"Wouldn't it be better to chase away prowlers if you were on horseback?"

She had a point. She knew it, and by the way Luke set his jaw, she could tell *he* knew it too.

"One more try," he said, his voice low.

Sammy Jo smiled and handed him the reins, then stepped back to allow Luke to take charge and do it on his own. Except she wasn't one to stand by and watch, and began to fidget in place.

As Luke commanded the horse to bow and Prince knelt down, she wanted to run forward and take his cane. When the horse rose onto all four feet, she wished she could have tightened the girth around the horse's underside to make sure Luke didn't fall off again. And when Luke winced, she would have given anything to kiss away every ounce of his pain.

"Hurts worse than last time," he said through gritted teeth.

"Give it time to subside," Sammy Jo advised.

Luke's face paled and he winced again. "You know I'd love to ride. But this . . . isn't working."

A few teenage guests drew near and one of the boys pointed at him, snickered, and said something to the others. Something like, "Watch him fall off."

"We don't need an audience," Sammy Jo said, waving them on. How dare they mock her beloved Luke! If only they knew what a town hero he'd been in the past. The Legend, people called him. Mostly because he was the most impulsive, reckless, daring cowboy in town. Some of the older folk called him wild, but she thought he was . . . amazing. For many of those same reasons. A kindred spirit.

At least he *used* to be.

"That's okay," Luke said, glancing toward the teens. "I'm done here."

She opened her mouth to argue, but realized he'd already commanded the horse to bow. First Luke's good foot touched the ground. Then he slid his injured leg off the horse and yelped in pain.

"You're probably still sore from that fall you took the last time," she assured him. "We'll try again next week after you heal."

"Don't you understand?" Luke said, giving her a look of disbelief. "My leg isn't ever going to heal. Not without surgery."

She met his gaze head-on. "So get the surgery."

"I'm working on it." He glanced away and she got the feeling there was something else he wasn't telling her.

"Don't you have insurance?" She drew forward as if to take the reins from his hand, then took his hand in hers instead.

He glanced down at their entwined fingers, but didn't pull away. "My military coverage only covers a portion of the cost."

She gasped. "That's why you accepted your grandmother's offer and are working so hard to make the ranch a success, isn't it? To get the money you need for your surgery."

He hesitated. "Yeah, that's part of it."

"And the other part?" She held her breath. Did he stay because of *her*?

"My family might not always get along, but we're family, and . . . they need me."

"And?" she pressed. "What else?"

Luke shrugged. "I didn't have much else going for me in Florida."

"No girlfriend?"

Luke grinned. "I had a few. One of them had the best lips for kissing, soft wide lips that—"

"I do *not* want to hear about other women you've kissed," she spat out harsher than she'd intended.

His mouth curved up into another grin. "Why not? You want to know about everything else."

"You're not funny."

"No, most women tell me I'm sweet."

"Teasing me like this is not sweet," she said, a lump rising in her throat. "Why would you even *want* to tease? I thought you were in pain."

"I am, but teasing you is a good distraction."

"Sweet words from a sweet-talkin' cowboy," she drawled, and with jealousy still eating at her, she turned away.

A hand on her shoulder turned her back. What did he want now?

"Sammy Jo." For a long moment he just gazed down at her with those mesmerizing hazel eyes. Then the sexy Adam's apple in his throat bobbed up and down as he swallowed, and he said, "There were no other women."

"You didn't kiss—"

He shook his head and, reaching forward, placed his finger against her lips. "No, not for a long time."

Her breath caught in her chest and she broke into a smile. "Now *that*," she told him, "is the sweetest thing I've ever heard."

LUKE COULDN'T SLEEP. He rolled over in his sleeping bag and stared up at the moonlit peak of his triangular tent.

When he'd first arrived back at the ranch he'd stayed in the main house with the rest of his family. For about a week. That's about all he could handle before their chatter, checking in, and constant invasion of his privacy got to him. Then he'd moved out and set up camp on the opposite side of the property with the help of the motorized gator that he'd learned to operate with one foot.

Except it wasn't his family that kept him awake this night. It was Sammy Jo.

He'd teased her, thinking she didn't really care for him the way she let on. Then when that genuine look of jealousy, anger, and . . . hurt crossed over Sammy Jo's features . . . it made him think that maybe . . . she *did*.

What then?

Most of his life she'd been the next-door menace he couldn't escape. Even after he'd left town, she'd filled his return visits with dread. Not because she wasn't good-looking, because . . . God knows she was. Her dark curls had grown out into longer waves while her slim form had developed all the right curves.

And it wasn't her personality, because he admired her extroverted, fun-loving ways, her skill at persuasion, courage in the arena, and even more . . . her loyalty to his family despite her father's opposition.

But what haunted him the most was how she could tease him like a bothersome little brother, and then . . . become attracted to him, as if he was *not*. What changed? Had she simply grown up?

In the past she'd always made a point to remind him he was younger, as if that one year made all the difference in the world. Since he'd come back she hadn't mentioned it once.

Sammy Jo had always made it clear she would rather hang out with his sisters than him, and groaned whenever they had to bring him along on their adventures. Now she sought him out first whenever she came over, instead of Bree or Delaney.

She also used to put him down for things he couldn't do. Like the time when he was twelve and tried to pop the clutch on his father's pickup so he could drive into town for the rodeo. He'd been grounded for another offense and forbidden to go. Then when the entire stick shift pulled out of the casing and he crashed into the side of the barn, he'd found himself in double trouble. And

Sammy Jo had laughed and told him he would have had better luck if he'd borrowed her Barbie bicycle. He'd been mad at her for over a week for saying such a thing.

True cowboys rode horses, he'd thought, not bicycles. Especially not bicycles meant for girls.

He'd been wary of her suggestions ever since. So naturally, when she said she liked him and wanted to spend time with him, and hinted she might even like him to kiss her . . . he'd had a hard time trusting her.

He kept waiting for the other shoe to drop, the stinging reversal, the next retort out of her mouth that would confirm she could never be interested in someone like him.

But then the look on her face when he'd made up the bit about kissing another woman flashed into his head again. No matter how he tried to dismiss her expression from his mind, or discount the emotion he'd heard in her voice, something deep inside kept niggling at him.

Something that said her feelings toward him were real and sooner or later he'd have to tell his own secret. Over the last few weeks he'd been looking at *her* in a whole new way, too.

After fluffing the pillow beneath his head, he rolled over, and chuckled to himself in the dark.

He'd thought of Sammy Jo as self-centered and manipulative, but after he'd seen her working with the kids and saw how she'd given up a date to help him ride, he wondered if maybe *selfless* or *encouraging* would be better words to describe her.

He supposed he'd also traded in the notion that

Sammy Jo was a bothersome annoyance because the truth was . . . her flirtation made his heart beat twice as fast and he now looked forward to their conversations when she came around.

And if she really did have feelings for him? Then that meant she did *not* consider him a last resort or want to *use* him. It meant she admired him, thought him worthy, maybe even worthy enough to kiss.

If he chose to go that route.

Two consecutive shots pierced the still air, the first disrupting his thoughts and the second making him bolt upright in his sleeping bag. The thunderous sound of racing hooves followed and Luke scrambled out of his tent, his hand on his pistol.

Who would be out shooting at this hour? On their property?

Scanning the moonlit landscape, he spotted four silhouetted riders on horseback not more than a hundred yards away. They'd come from the direction of the cabins and were headed toward the distant tree line.

More prowlers? He and the Tanner brothers had ridden along the border before sundown and hadn't seen anything suspicious. Adrenaline surged through every part of his body, bringing him fully awake. He'd jump on his horse right now and chase after them in a heartbeat . . . if he could.

Instead, he clenched his hands into fists and watched them disappear. Next he found his flashlight and aimed the illuminated beam toward his watch. It was 2:35 in the morning, not the same time as the other two sightings.

Grasping his cane, he climbed into the gator, revved the motor, and made his way back to his family's house as fast as he could.

When he arrived, he found his entire family outside milling about the main courtyard with a crowd of troubled guests.

"I'm not staying here another minute," one man said, turning toward his wife. "Let's gather our things and get out of here before those men come back."

"We're leaving, too," said another family. "This is no place for kids. Some vacation! You'll be hearing from my lawyer."

"I want my money back," a woman demanded, shaking her fist in front of Bree's face.

"We *all* want our money back," cried out a man behind her.

Luke's gaze swung toward the Walford twins, who stood beside him, squealing they'd been attacked.

"Tell me what happened," he said, shining the light so he could see their expressions.

Nora used frantic hand gestures to illustrate her experience as she spoke. "Instead of going home we stayed overnight in one of the guest cabins. We were sleeping and—"

"There was a crash," Nadine said, cutting in.

Nora nodded. "Then another."

"And then another and another!" Nora exclaimed. "Each one coming closer and closer."

"Louder and louder," Nadine added, waving her arms.

"Then someone broke our cabin window," Nora continued. "We got up and turned on the light and there was glass all over the floor."

"That's when we saw the blood," Nadine told him.

Luke's stomach dropped. "What blood?"

Both the twins pointed toward their toes and chorused in unison, "From our feet!"

"We'd stepped on some of the glass when we sprang out of bed," Nora explained.

The teenagers showed him their cuts and Luke was relieved to see they were minor. "Did you see who broke the window?"

"No," Nadine said, her eyes wide. "But someone else did. There were four riders on horseback. And they had guns."

Luke recalled the shots he'd heard back at his camp and the hair on his forearms stood on end. He glanced around at the other faces in the crowd to make sure everyone was accounted for. Hard to tell with some of the guests walking back toward their cabins, and others just coming out.

"They rode real fast," Nora said, her voice rising. "And smashed the back window of every cabin as they went."

"Then what happened?" Luke demanded.

The twins looked at each other and back at him and said together, "They rode away!"

Luke left them and wove through the crowd to find Bree.

"Ryan will be here soon," his sister told him. "And the sheriff. The gunmen must have used the butt of their rifles to break all the windows. Dad thinks they did it to scare everyone away. Probably also why they fired those shots into the air. I'm just thankful no one got seriously hurt."

"Someone *did*," Luke said, his chest tight.

Bree gasped. "Who?"

"Us." He motioned toward all the guests who were carrying suitcases out of their cabins and heading toward the parking lot. "Not only will we have to refund their money, and try to put a stop to potential lawsuits, but we'll have to pay to replace all the windows."

Bree cringed. "We'll also need to repair our reputation."

Luke wasn't sure Collins Country Cabins' reputation had ever been repaired from the previous month when their ex–ranch managers hired their vindictive neighbor, Mrs. Owens, to sabotage them.

"We'll get through this," he said, not only to assure his sister, but to assure himself. "We found out who was responsible last time and we'll find out who's behind this, too."

"Luke," their ma called, coming toward them. "Thank God you're here. I was worried those men might come up on your camp and catch you alone. It's not safe out there."

"Seems I'm safer than you are," he countered.

"Please move back into the house?" Ma pleaded.

"No," he said as the sheriff's car pulled into the driveway. "It will be easier for me to catch these guys if I stay out in the field."

"You think you're going to catch them?" Bree asked, and glanced down at his injured leg. *"How?"*

Chapter Six

THE FOLLOWING MORNING, Sammy Jo pulled back on the reins and slowed Tango to a stop in the middle of the field, not far from Luke's camp. A second later, Bree and Delaney halted their own horses beside her.

"What's up?" Bree asked as Sammy Jo slid out of the saddle. "Do you see something?"

Bending down, Sammy Jo retrieved the small, metal, cylindrical item that had caught her eye and held it up. "Rifle cartridge."

Bree nodded. "Our intruders fired two consecutive shots in the air. The first cartridge had to drop out of our shooter's rifle right here before he could fire off the second round."

"Unless two men each took a shot," Delaney pointed out, "instead of one man firing both."

Sammy Jo shook her head. "Either way, Luke said he heard the shots and then saw them run past his camp, which would place the men here when they fired."

"If they waited until reaching the field to fire, that must mean they didn't intend to harm anyone, just scare them," Bree said, giving her new mare, Angel, a pat.

"It worked." Delaney sighed. "Every guest packed up and left, leaving us with an empty guest ranch in the middle of summer for the first time in . . . well, forever."

"A new week's worth of guests will show up soon," Sammy Jo assured them.

Bree winced. "Not if news of what happened spreads."

Sammy Jo hoisted herself back up into the saddle. "Let's continue on. We know there were four men from the four different sets of tracks. They entered through the Owenses' vacant property, cut across toward your guest cabins, then came through here. I'd bet their tracks lead straight out the back of your property into the hills."

She was wrong. Minutes later when they stopped again, it was because they'd followed the soft hoof prints from the intruders' horses straight toward Sammy Jo's own property line.

"They cut my fence!" she exclaimed, inspecting the damage. "The same way they cut the Owenses' fence line. Straight up between two posts so they could pull the wire away and ride right on through."

Bree took the lead as they galloped across Sammy Jo's property, then slowing a third time, she pointed. "I don't think they were headed toward the hills. I think they were headed toward the road."

Sure enough, the trail of scuffed dirt ended at the pavement. When they'd set out on the trail ride they'd assumed since the men had been on horseback that they must be from a nearby ranch. But now . . . it was possible the men had a horse trailer waiting for them, to drive them away.

"Oh, no!" Delaney cried. "Now how are we supposed to find out who they were? If they left in a horse trailer, it could have been *anyone*."

"Not anyone," Bree said, raising her chin. "Whoever it was, we know they had to have a trailer large enough to transport four horses."

"What if they had two smaller ones?" Del argued.

"Two might have been too noticeable. I think Bree's right." She pointed toward the bend in the road shaded over with a grove of aspen. "They probably had a driver waiting for them, someone who parked a single trailer there, out of sight. Then when the other men rode up they could have easily loaded the horses and driven away."

"You think there were that many of them involved? Five men?" Bree's mouth fell open. "Who do we know who has a group like that who also owns a trailer large enough to transport multiple horses?"

Sammy Jo froze as the answer slipped easily to the forefront of her mind.

"I have an idea," she told her friends, "but before we go pointing fingers, *I have to talk to my father*."

SAMMY JO SCANNED the interior of her house wondering how she could make it look more romantic. Her father would be home from work any minute, and for her plan to work, she needed to make him believe she was besotted with a new beau.

Of course, she *was*, even if her intended didn't feel the same way. Not yet. She thought of the tenderness in Luke's voice when he told her he hadn't dated—or kissed—anyone in a long time. If that wasn't a reason to dance, then she didn't know what was!

She twirled and dancing made her think of music. Yes . . . of course. Turning on the stereo, she inserted a CD titled *Country's Most Romantic Hits*, and moments later the room was filled with the rich, melodious sound of a country crooner.

Sammy Jo twirled again and touched the soft, velvety petals of the red roses she'd purchased in town. She signed the attached card with *"To my beloved sweetheart, Sammy Jo, from the one who adores you with all his heart."* At least that's what she'd always dreamed some sweet-talkin' cowboy would say to her one day. Then she placed the fragrant flowers in a vase on the dining room table where her father would notice them as soon as he walked in.

Next, she dipped into the box of chocolate-covered cherries and popped one of the rich, fruity delicacies in her mouth. As long as she was buying, she figured she might as well pick out her favorite. No real beau ever had.

The door opened, her father walked in, and stopped up short. "What's all this?"

Sammy Jo smiled, heaved a great dramatic sigh she'd seen actresses do in movies, and flounced toward him the way she'd practiced. "I guess I'm officially off the single market."

Her father still didn't move, but stood where he was by the door. "What do you mean?"

She gave him another smile. "You don't have to worry about fixing me up with one of your clients for a date anymore."

"You're dating someone?" The look he gave her was incredulous. Didn't her father think she was capable of finding a man on her own?

She raised her chin. "You could say that."

"Who?"

The question shot out of his mouth faster than a bull from a bucking chute, exactly as she anticipated. "I'm not sure you'll approve, but who I date is my business. I'm twenty-seven, not sixteen, and I can date whoever I want."

Her father set down his briefcase and stepped forward, his face lined with concern. "I still think I have a right to know who my daughter is dating."

"Why is that?"

His expression turned dark and he scrunched his nose in obvious disgust. "Because there's only *one guy* I know of who could bring that big of a smile to your face and if you're dating *him*—"

"Who, Daddy?" she asked, keeping her tone as sweet and syrupy as her chocolate-covered cherries.

Here it comes, she said, inwardly bracing herself.

"It *is* him, isn't it?" he demanded. "If Luke Collins lays a finger on you—"

"Better him than that last guy you tried to fix me up with."

"Harley Bennett? What's wrong with him?"

"Four horsemen sabotaged Collins Country Cabins

last night," she told him. "The intruders cut our fence and rode across our property as they made their escape. I believe your precious Harley was one of them."

Her father frowned. "Why would you say that? What proof do you have?"

"He hangs out with those other wretched men from the auction house and he has a trailer large enough to load four horses and make a clean getaway."

"Now you're jumping to conclusions," he stated, his voice matter-of-fact.

"So are you, when you think you can dictate who I spend my time with."

"Anyone but a Collins," he warned.

She sighed for effect, hoping he'd take the bait. "Okay, Dad, I'll make you a deal . . ."

LUKE FINISHED NAILING together the floorboards for the gazebo, glanced across the front lawn of the eerily vacant guest ranch, and saw Sammy Jo, dressed in her usual V-neck T-shirt and cutoff denim shorts, headed his way.

His pulse automatically kicked up a notch and he couldn't help but anticipate where their conversation might lead this time. Maybe she'd ask more questions about his past relationships? Or try flirting with him again? Call him a sweet-talkin' cowboy?

Stopping directly in front of him she crossed her arms over her chest and announced, "I talked to my father."

"Did you ask him about our permit?" he asked, trying to sound casual.

"Yes, I tried to reason with him, many times, but—"

"But?" He looked straight into her emerald green eyes, admiring their beauty . . . as if he'd never seen them before.

"It didn't work. He's as stubborn as a mule."

"What? You were the best on the debate team in high school. No one could defend themselves against your quick wit and smart replies. How could you not convince him?"

For a moment Sammy Jo just stood there staring at him with a surprised look upon her face as if he'd never paid her a compliment. Maybe he hadn't.

"I didn't say I was finished," she said, her face turning red. "When he couldn't be reasoned with I decided to appeal to his emotions."

"How?" he asked, his gaze dropping toward her mouth.

"I said that he could stop trying to fix me up with other men because you had expressed romantic interest, and if he didn't approve your permits, that you and I would start dating."

"What?"

Sammy Jo frowned. "I thought you said you were willing to do whatever it takes."

He *did* say that.

"Is the thought of dating me that horrible?"

No. Not anymore. He grinned.

"Is it?" she demanded, hands on her hips. *Nicely curved hips.*

Luke pulled his attention back to the matter at hand.

Then couldn't help himself. He grinned again. "It's just awkward, you know. I've known you since we were kids."

Sammy Jo's mouth formed an adorable little pout. "Well, what matters is that my father believed me . . . and it made him mad."

"I bet it did."

Luke had only been in Sammy Jo's house once. She'd wanted to show him and his sisters her new Breyer horse figurine collection in her bedroom. But her father had come in, lifted him by the ear, and steered him toward the door with a warning never to return.

"After I threatened to date you," Sammy Jo continued, "my father said he'd seriously see what he could do to get your building permits approved. But I think if I brought you home for dinner, it would clinch the deal."

It sure would.

"You haven't said much," Sammy Jo commented, the confidence on her face fading. "What do you think?"

Luke tried to imagine the look on her father's face when she brought him through the door and let out a chuckle. "What time's dinner?"

"Six o'clock. And, Luke?" She held his gaze a moment, then warned, "Act like you love me."

SAMMY JO HAD faced a number of opponents in her life from top of the line rodeo contestants to overly aggressive men who didn't know how to keep their hands to themselves. But never had she felt this nervous. Maybe because she'd never seen her father angry except when talking about the Collinses and knew she was about to get a front row seat when Luke arrived in less than fifteen minutes.

Her palms damp, she brushed them over the front of her denim shorts for the fourteenth time and took the round, ceramic pan of shepherd's pie out of the oven. The dish filled with savory ground beef and a mixture of fresh vegetables covered with piped, gently browned mashed potatoes was her father's favorite. She'd thought the meal might soften the blow of dining with a Collins, but she also hoped she might prove her cooking skill and show Luke what he could look forward to . . . when they married someday.

Now that she'd quit riding rodeo, she had more time to win Luke's favor without having to worry he'd find another woman during her absence. But that didn't decrease the urgency of her mission. She'd always valued independence as much as Luke did, but the more time they spent together, the less she wanted to be apart. She'd spent enough time on her own. Now what she wanted most was to build a future *together*.

And while she expected them to be equal partners in the household, her attempt to improve her domesticated skills had taught her something new about herself—she actually *loved* cooking! Maybe one day soon she'd be able to cook a meal for just the two of them, or maybe they could cook together and have a "cooking date." She'd heard Luke's grandma say his skills in the kitchen weren't half-bad.

Of course she'd have to put her plans to date Luke

on hold until the Collinses' building permit process was over to keep her word to her father . . . or else find a way to get Luke to propose *without* dating him first. Challenging, but not impossible.

The anxiety in her stomach continued to churn. Why did getting herself hitched have to be so complicated?

Her father's words echoed in her head. *"Anyone but a Collins."*

Except she didn't want just anyone. She wanted *Luke*. And she'd known it since the day he'd valiantly chased after the high school bully who'd stolen her truck, and returned her ride. After that, her entire perception of Luke Collins's character and good looks had changed, and now that she had marriage on her mind . . . there was no one else who would do.

She placed the dish on a hot plate on the dining room table next to her vase of roses. The night before, she'd caught her father looking at the attached card she'd placed on the flowers and heard him groan. Would he ask Luke about them?

Maybe she should have told Luke that he was supposed to be the one who "adored her with all his heart." Another wave of queasiness rolled over her stomach. What if her father didn't buy the fact Luke was interested in her? What if Luke didn't play his part?

Her father walked into the room and hesitated. "The table is set for three."

"Yes, we're having company tonight," Sammy Jo informed him. "I hope you don't mind I invited a guest."

"Depends on who—"

The back door opened and Luke Collins walked in as if he'd been there a million times without need of a welcome. Assisted by his cane, he strode forward, gave her father a nod, then came right up and delivered a kiss to her cheek.

Sammy Jo stared at him in shock, her gaze taking in the light dancing behind his eyes, his amused grin . . . and the fact he'd dressed up in his Sunday best. His blue plaid Western-style shirt was clean and crisp, his denim jeans so dark she wondered if he'd remembered to cut the tag off from the store, and his black boots were so polished they looked like they'd never stepped foot on anything but pavement.

She glanced down at her own attire and wished she'd thought to wear something different. Then she closed her gaping mouth and remembered *she* had a part to play, too.

"Thank you for the flowers," she said, nodding toward the bouquet on the table and silently willing Luke to take the hint.

He leaned forward, glanced at the tag, and let out a small chuckle. "I'm glad you liked them, 'sweetheart.'"

Sammy Jo's cheeks flamed and, glancing at her father, she wondered if her cheeks were as red as his.

"You have no business in this house," her father choked out, his eyes on Luke.

"Of course, I do," Luke said, his voice full of confidence. "Sammy Jo invited me. And look what she's made. My favorite—shepherd's pie."

Her father's gaze darted to the dish on the table. "She made that for *me*."

"Well, now I'm sure there's enough to go around," Luke said, taking a seat. "Right, Sammy Jo?"

She glanced from him back to her father. "Uh . . . right."

"You see, that's what I love about your daughter," Luke said, tucking a white napkin in around his neck. "She's always doing whatever she can to please others." He looked at her father and frowned. "Mr. Macpherson, don't you agree?"

Sammy Jo saw her father's jaw working and imagined he was grinding his teeth back and forth as he decided what to do.

"Sammy Jo is all I have and I will not stand by and see her get hurt," her father warned.

"Neither will I," Luke promised, and taking her hand, he pulled her down onto his lap and gave her another kiss on the cheek. "She's something mighty special."

Sammy Jo had never been on Luke's lap. She'd never heard him sweet-talk this way. And she hadn't seen him take charge of a situation like this in a very long time. Her heart beat rapidly in her chest, stealing her breath and leaving her light-headed.

"Daddy," she said, sliding off Luke's lap to a chair of her own. "Aren't you going to sit down?"

Her father hesitated and for a moment she thought he would flee the room. Or else haul Luke out of the chair and throw him out of the house. Then Sammy Jo saw him glance again at the shepherd's pie and to her surprise . . . he *did* sit down. As if there was no way Luke was going to eat her cooking without him.

"Now, Andy, about our permits," Luke said, talking to her father as if they'd been longtime pals. "When do you think—"

Her father cut him off midsentence. "You'll have them first thing in the morning."

LUKE WHISTLED TO himself over the hum of the gator as he drove back over the property line to Collins Country Cabins. He couldn't get the look on Sammy Jo's face out of his head. He didn't know who had been more surprised when he pulled her down onto his lap—her . . . or her father.

But the romantic ruse had worked. If her father kept his word, and Luke believed he would, by this time tomorrow he'd have the building permit in his hands and finally be able to resume construction on the two unfinished cabins.

His thoughts drifted back to the way Sammy Jo's hair had smelled like roses when her soft curves plunked down on top of him. Then he recalled the words on the card she'd written to herself and shook his head with a laugh.

"To my beloved sweetheart."? What self-respecting cowboy used words like that anymore? It sounded like something his grandpa would have said to his grandma back before he died when Luke was ten. And what was up with "*from the one who adores you with all his heart*"?

After the tasty but awkward meal had been finished, Luke had given Andrew Macpherson's hand a firm shake and said, "Nice doing business with you."

Andy had let out a low grunt, similar to those his own father issued now and again to show dissatisfaction. Then Luke had taken his leave, with Sammy Jo following him out the door.

"You did it," she said, her eyes shining. "You really acted like you loved me and you played the part so well!"

He'd decided to have a little fun and set out to tease her using the term she'd written on the card. "Sweetheart—"

"*Beloved* sweetheart," Sammy Jo had corrected, breaking into a smile.

He'd smiled in return. " '*The one who adores you*' was happy to oblige."

"With all your heart," she'd corrected again. "You're supposed to say '*with all my heart.*' "

Luke had never heard anything so ridiculous in all his life, but he'd just overcome a large hurdle to his family's success, so he decided spouting a couple lovesick words to appease Sammy Jo couldn't hurt.

"With all my heart," he repeated, but couldn't stop himself from grinning as he said it.

Then they both had laughed and for a moment everything seemed like old times because Sammy Jo had once again convinced him to do something there's no way he'd ordinarily do.

Except this time, he'd enjoyed it.

"RYAN, DO YOU think you can give me a hand with something?" Luke asked a short while later before dusk.

They stood by the outdoor pasture housing a few of

the horses. Luke's horse, Phantom, was in there . . . along with Prince, the rehab horse Sammy Jo had left behind . . . in case he changed his mind and decided to give riding another go.

"Sure, what is it?" Ryan asked, setting the tack for his own horse aside.

"Could you spot me for a few minutes?" Luke nodded toward the rehab horse and Ryan followed his gaze.

"Want me to bring him out for you?"

"No," Luke said, unlatching the gate. "I've got it handled. Just need someone to pick me up off the ground in case I get bucked off again."

"Yeah." Ryan grinned. "I heard about the last time you mounted up. Seems to me that horse should be in a rodeo instead of lolling around out here."

Luke ignored the friendly jibe. "Just be there, okay?"

"Sure thing," Ryan agreed.

Luke wished what he was about to do was a sure thing as he took the horse out of the pen and tacked up. When he was ready, he commanded the rehab horse to bow and braced himself against the pain he knew would come when he placed his injured leg over the lowered saddle. If only he could ride . . . The few moments of victory he'd experienced when he'd mounted up twice before had been taunting him ever since.

"Hold on with your good leg," Ryan instructed, "and use the cane to press against the opposite side to maintain your balance."

"Gotcha." Luke nodded as the horse rose up beneath him.

"How does it feel?"

Luke winced and took a couple of deep breaths. "Not so bad now that I'm on him. I think it's that initial bending of the knee to get on that really gets me."

"That's what I've heard from other guys with knee injuries," Ryan said, leaning against the fence to watch.

Luke rode a few loops around the outside of the fenced pasture, then said, "Okay, that's enough."

"But you've only been on ten minutes," Ryan said, glancing at his watch.

Luke nodded, his muscles taut. "That's enough."

LUKE WAS INSIDE the main house around eleven p.m. sneaking a few more of his grandma's homemade marshmallows before he left to go back to his camp for the night when he first heard the ruckus.

Cows bawled in the distance, and closer to the house, the horses neighed and kicked against the inside of their stalls so hard it sounded like a series of gunshots.

His father joined him by the door. "What's going on?"

A rumble sounded behind them as both Bree and Delaney flew down the stairs, their faces filled with alarm.

"I saw it from the upstairs window," Bree shouted.

"Saw what?" their father demanded.

"Intruders?" Luke asked.

Bree shook her head, her eyes wide. *"Fire!"*

Chapter Seven

THE GOLDEN FLAMES lit up the darkness as the extra bales of hay stacked against the outside wall of the hay barn continued to burn. Luke thought of all the work they'd put into fixing up their family's guest ranch and all their hopes for the future riding on its success. They couldn't lose it all now.

Ma called the fire department but they couldn't wait for the hose trucks to arrive or it would be too late. They had to put out the blazing bales before the whole barn burned and they lost a serious amount of money tied up in hay. There was also the chance the fire could eat up the ground and place the horses and guest cabins in danger.

Delaney left Meghan, who had awoken with all the noise, in the care of their grandma and ran toward the stables to lead the horses toward a safer pasture.

"Don't forget Sammy Jo's rehab horse," Luke called to her. "He's in the end stall."

She glanced over her shoulder and nodded, her face filled with both determination and terror. No doubt after she'd saved all the horses she'd also try to save every other animal within a half-mile radius. Then they'd have an assortment of injured raccoons, rabbits, possums, and squirrels to care for.

Meanwhile, the flames were climbing higher.

Their father hopped on his John Deere tractor and tried to pull some of the burning bales away from the barn before the fire spread to the walls and roof. Bree ran for a hose, and Luke made his way toward another, although not as fast due to his injured leg. Dragging the long hose from the house over to the hay barn proved even more difficult and by the time he got there the flames had jumped in height.

Backing the tractor away and parking at a safe distance, his father jumped off and ran toward him. "I'll take over here," his father said, grabbing the hose from Luke's hands. "Go back to the house and stay with your ma."

Go back? Luke scowled, and indignation soured his stomach. "I can help," he argued. "You need me."

"I *need* you to stay with your ma," his father insisted.

A roar of spitting gravel sounded behind them and they both turned to see Ryan's truck come up the driveway. Once parked, all four doors of the extended cab flew open and Ryan and his three brothers—Dean, Josh, and Zach—jumped out.

"We've got plenty of help," Luke's father said with a nod.

"But I—"

"Luke," his father said, his voice stern. "There's nothing you can do."

There was plenty he could do. Just because he was injured and needed a cane to walk didn't mean he was useless. How *dare* his father treat him like an invalid when the welfare of their ranch was at stake.

Luke glanced back at the house. Ma and Grandma stood outside, huddled with the wide-eyed Walford twins, little Meghan, and Ryan's son, Cody, who had spent the night to be close to Bree. Is that all his old man thought he was good for? To watch over the women and children?

Luke had no intention of following his father's orders. He might have trouble with a hose and a shovel, but he could at least *fill* water buckets . . . even if he couldn't carry them. He took a step toward a nearby spigot, then stopped and turned around when he heard his mother scream.

Ma?

His gut slammed into his chest as he watched her knees buckle. A second later she doubled over, as if in pain, and Grandma put an arm around her. But his mother shook it off and screamed again, holding her face in her hands.

At first Luke thought she'd been burned by a wayward, high-flying burning ember. But as he took in her condition, it appeared her distress was purely emotional. He decided he better check on his ma first, just to be sure, then he would go back and help the others.

"*Nooo!*" his mother wailed as he drew closer. Her body trembled and her face took on an expression of pure fright. "*No fire! No fire! No fire!*"

"Ma, it's all right," Luke assured her. "It's only a few hay bales."

"*Jed?*" she screeched.

Luke laid a hand on her shoulder. "Dad's okay."

"No, he's not," Ma protested, her eyes wide. "Have you seen what fire can do?"

She lurched forward as if to run after him and Luke dropped his cane to grab her around the middle. "You can't go out there."

"I can't let him die!" Ma shouted, and let out a series of shrieks as she kicked at his legs and pulled at his arm with her fingers in an attempt to free herself.

Luke held tight, trying to balance their weight with his good leg and make sure neither one of them got hurt. Not an easy task. His mother was stronger than she looked. Maybe his father had anticipated her reaction? Is *that* why he had sent him to stay with her?

"Loretta, calm down," Grandma soothed. "Jed's in no danger. See? Those Tanner boys already have the fire under control. And as for the hay, well, there's no sense cryin' over what you can't change."

But his mother didn't calm down. Her face paled and her eyes took on a wild, haunted look as she continued to fight, scream, and . . . *wail*.

Luke's father must have heard her because a few minutes later he hurried over and took her into his arms. "It's okay, Loretta. I've gotcha. You're safe now."

Ma continued to tremble, but she nodded she understood, and let him lead her into the house.

Luke blew out a long breath and took the opportunity to join Bree and the Tanners by the smoldering embers, determined to do whatever needed to be done next.

"Not only are we out a full week of money from losing this week's guests," Bree said with a gut-wrenching catch in her voice, "but we've now lost a quarter truckload of hay."

Delaney ran toward them, her face crumpled into an expression even more troubled than Bree's. "That's not all we've lost."

SAMMY JO LIFTED her headphones off her ears. She'd been lying in bed, listening to her country tunes, hoping the music would help put her to sleep. Then she thought she heard something. A truck? Was it her father coming back from his date with that banker woman? Lately, Winona Lane seemed to have her dad wrapped around her little pinky finger, a fact she'd conveniently left out when she talked to her mom on the phone earlier that day.

Through the window Sammy Jo could hear Tango cry and she stuck out her head to listen. Both Tango and her mother's old mare, who kept him company, were pacing around their paddock and neighing to the Collinses' horses in the next field.

She frowned. Delaney usually kept the horses in at night. The horses cried out again. Something wasn't right. Grabbing a flashlight, Sammy Jo made her way to the door, stepped outside, and smelled . . . *smoke*.

Whipping out her cell phone she quickly sent Bree, Luke, and Delaney each a text. She waited a few moments, but no one replied. Not a good sign. She thought about tossing a halter on Tango and riding him bareback over there to see what was going on, but Tango didn't like smoke and she didn't want to traumatize him. She'd go on foot.

Using her flashlight to light up the well-worn path, she ran as fast as she could, thankful she'd had the sense to pull on her boots before leaving the house. However, she *was* still in her blue camisole top and matching smiley face pajama short bottoms. Not that it mattered. Not if there was a true emergency.

The foul-smelling charcoal odor grew stronger the closer she got to the property line and she wrinkled her nose. The place reeked. And where there was smoke, Luke's grandma would say, there was usually fire.

Seconds later her light fell upon a pair of wide thick treads and she stopped up short. They were *fresh* . . . and hadn't been made from any of her or her father's vehicles. She followed them through the broken wire fence that had been cut by the Collinses' intruders the week before, her stomach tight.

Had the intruders come back? Started a blaze? She sucked in her breath and ran faster. What if someone got hurt? Luke? His limp didn't allow him to run very fast. What if he tried to play the hero and got too close . . . and . . . and . . . *Oh, God.*

When she came around the cabins she could see the blackened wall of the hay barn, the smoke spiraling up from the charred ground, and the hoses. Her gaze darted toward the four Tanners, then spotted Bree and Delaney beside them. But where was Luke? The others appeared distraught. She continued forward, and experienced a few more seconds of agonized panic before Luke stepped out from behind the other men blocking her view. She swallowed hard.

He was all right.

Luke's gaze locked with hers, and the hard lines of his face softened as she went to stand at his side. "I smelled smoke," she explained, then glanced around at the others.

Bree nodded. "Yes, we lost several bales of hay but it seems the fire was a decoy. While we were busy putting out the flames, the arsonists made off with six head of cattle from the back field."

Oh, no. Cattle cost money, a large amount the Collinses probably didn't have, not since their ranch managers siphoned the majority of it into their own accounts.

"They left through my property again," Sammy Jo informed them. "I saw the tracks. Must have been a truck pulling a cattle trailer."

"Do you think we should cancel the incoming guest reservations?" Delaney asked.

"For how long?" Luke shook his head. "We don't know if or when they might come again. It could be next week, next month, or next year."

"Luke's right," Bree agreed. "And in the meantime, if we don't have any guests we don't have any business. We could go bankrupt if we wait around. But we can get the sheriff and his men to patrol the area."

"So will we," Ryan said, and nodded toward his brothers. "We'll round up the cows from the field each night and put them in the corral. That way they're in one spot."

"Bring in the horses each night, too," his older brother Dean suggested, "and lock the barn up tight."

"We'll divide up into pairs and take turns watching over the corral in shifts," Luke agreed. "At least for the next week."

"I'll help, too," Sammy Jo volunteered.

"Then you'll be with me," Luke said, giving her a look that demanded no argument. Then he pointed a finger at his sister. "Bree, you and Ryan take another shift. Dean, Josh, Zach, two of you can be together and one of you can keep watch with Delaney."

"That will be me," Zach said, giving Del a wink.

Delaney rolled her eyes but didn't protest. She and Zach were both the youngest, and having been in the same grade at school together, they were friends.

Sammy Jo hadn't expected Luke to pair up with her. Now that they'd convinced her father to issue Luke's family the permit, the two of them weren't *supposed* to spend time alone together. Part of the deal was that she and Luke wouldn't date. She cast him a sideways glance and in a soft voice asked, "Why me?"

Luke leaned over and whispered in her ear, "You wear cute pajamas."

Then he grinned, tipped his hat toward her, and walked toward his family's house, glancing over his shoulder at her as he went.

AFTERWARD SAMMY JO returned home and her father met her at the door. "Where have you been?"

"Someone set the Collinses' hay bales on fire. Bree said her ma was really upset."

"Loretta wasn't hurt, was she?" her father asked, his tone turning anxious.

"No, she wasn't near the flames."

Her father let out a sigh of relief. "That's good."

"Dad, we have a problem. The intruders cut our fence and drove through our property on their way out to get to the main road. I had headphones on at the time, but did you hear them?"

Her father's eyes widened. "No, I just got home five minutes ago. I had a date with Mrs. Lane."

"You were out pretty late, don't you think?" she asked, raising a brow. Then continued. "I think we should repair the fence. And maybe put up a few more wood posts to make it harder to drive through."

Her father nodded, and narrowed his gaze. "I agree. No one should be trespassing through our fields. First thing tomorrow I'll place an order at the hardware store. And a call to the sheriff."

"How about a call to Mom?" Sammy Jo suggested. "I talked to her this morning and she said it would be nice to hear from you now and then."

Her father let out a soft grunt. "I'll let her know you're okay, but I don't think you should be going outside anymore after dark."

Sammy Jo opened her mouth to protest, but he put up

his hand and continued. "It's not safe. Who knows what these people will do next?"

LUKE LAY ON his back looking up at the stars through the open tent flap near his head and listened to the chirping of bugs, frogs, and other whatnot. And thought of Sammy Jo . . . and the fact his performance at dinner hadn't been a *total* act. Of course, none of it mattered now. They'd promised her father that if he took the deal, they wouldn't date.

Yep, Sammy Jo would pester him no more . . .

Which is why he chose her as his watchdog partner. When it came right down to it, he found the thought of a day without Sammy Jo coming over to "help" didn't sit well in his gut. He'd grown used to seeing her sparkling green eyes and wide teasing smile as she tried to persuade him to do one thing or another. And he wasn't ready to give it up.

After only a few hours' sleep, Luke rose at sunup and drove the gator across the fields toward the main house to see who could drive him to Bozeman to pick up the promised building permit. He found most of his family in the kitchen, sitting around the table, nibbling on a few pieces of toast.

"No one had much of an appetite for anything else," Grandma said, placing a small bowl of blueberries on the table in front of Meghan. "Except her, of course."

"Onkle Uke, you want boo-berries?" his niece asked.

He reached into her bowl and then popped one into his mouth, making her smile. "Thanks, Meggie."

"Luke, please move back into the house," his ma pleaded. "I don't like thinking about you all the way out there on the other end of the property . . . all alone. What if you're attacked?"

"Ma, I'm trained for attacks. After serving in Iraq, I'm sure I can handle a few Montana cattle rustlers."

"You had full use of your leg in the military," his father reminded him. "Your mother might be right."

"I am *not* moving back in," Luke said, his voice firm.

"We're not sleeping here anymore either," Nora announced, coming through the doorway with her sister. "Every time we do—"

"Something bad happens!" Nadine exclaimed. "Like this morning."

"What happened this morning?" Luke asked, jerking his head toward them in alarm.

"We were walking from our cabin toward the house," Nora said, her eyes wide. "And then we looked down and—"

"Saw our new bottle cap boot bling was covered in ash!" Nadine wailed, pointing to their feet.

Nora nodded. "From now on we sleep in our own beds and we'll drive back and forth each day from home."

"I was up at the crack of dawn going over the financial numbers on the computer," Bree said, glancing around the table. "And if the people who booked the August wedding cancel on us, I don't think Collins Country Cabins can survive."

Luke grabbed the keys to the family's red ranch truck off the counter. "Good news. Our building permit should be ready this morning. Who can take me into town to pick it up?"

Ma shot out of her chair. "Me. I need to go into town, too."

"Loretta, are you sure you're up for it?" Luke's father asked.

"I *need* to go into town!" she repeated.

Thirty minutes later, Luke followed his mother into the bank. After signing in, a courteous bank employee led her into the vault where she rented a safe deposit box. However, a minute later his ma returned to the lobby.

"My key isn't working," she explained, the same horrified expression from the day before on her face.

"I'll get the assistant bank manager," the bank teller told her.

"I don't like that nosy woman," Ma confided in a whisper. "Luke, will you come back there with me?"

At first Winona Lane made a stink about Luke accompanying them. But after his ma signed an additional form allowing him access, the woman had no choice but to allow him through.

The vault wasn't very big, then again, neither was their town. The room was roughly the size of a four-by-six closet with the main safe at the back and the walls on either side lined with safe deposit boxes.

"I don't understand," Ma said fretfully. "Why wouldn't my key work?"

"Could be you've used it so much the cut has worn down," Winona told her. "But don't worry. I have a master key to open it for you."

When the box opened Winona peered inside, then frowned. "There's another box."

Luke's ma took out the rectangular metal box and hugged it. "Yes, there is."

"A box inside a box?" Winona exclaimed. "Why?"

"It's fireproof," Ma said, and took another key from her purse to open it.

Winona peered over her shoulder, and when Luke's ma turned to look at her, the woman jumped back. "Just curious," the woman apologized.

Luke didn't blame the woman. He was curious, too. Ma often talked about her "valuables," but no one except his father seemed to know what they were.

"Mrs. Lane," his ma said, giving the assistant manager a big fake smile. "Could you please escort my son to the lobby?"

Winona lifted her nose in the air as if insulted, then glanced at Luke and nodded. "Very well, Loretta. Let me know when you're done."

His ma only took ten minutes to look at her "valuables" this time instead of thirty, and came out looking a whole lot more relaxed than when she went in.

"I want to apologize for flipping out when you tried to hold me back yesterday," Ma said as they got back in the car. "I saw the flames and . . ." She drew in a deep breath and turned to look at him. "I remembered the fire that burned my house down when I was ten. It was during the summer near Billings, and it had been dry. The wildfire started near our house in the middle of the night and took everything . . . including my parents."

Luke gasped. "That's how Grandpa and Grandma Newton died? You've never said much about them."

"A firefighter pulled me out of the flames and I was airlifted to a hospital where I was treated for minor burns. Then I lived with an aunt in Fox Creek until I married your dad. Your father, he always promised to keep me safe."

Luke now understood his father hadn't been belittling his ability to help with the fire. He'd given him the more important task of keeping his ma safe in his place.

"Sorry, Ma, I didn't know." He wondered what else he didn't know about his parents. Glancing at his ma as she turned the key in the truck's ignition, he asked, "What's in the locked box at the bank?"

Ma smiled and stepped on the gas. "My inheritance."

SAMMY JO FROZE. She had no idea Luke and his ma would be back so soon. She and Bree had taken Phantom into the arena to work with him and Luke walked up just as she issued the command for his horse to lower its upper body.

"What's this?" he demanded.

"Luke, I thought it was a good idea, too," Bree said, stepping between them.

"Teaching my horse to bow?"

"Don't worry," Sammy Jo assured him. "He's not getting it."

Luke grimaced. "Phantom was made to gallop, not bow like some circus animal."

"Like you?" Sammy Jo challenged. "That's how you feel, isn't it? That if you can't ride fast, you won't ride at all?"

"When are you going to take your rehab horse home?" Luke shot back. "He's just takin' up space hangin' around here."

Luke stalked off, hobbling with his cane as he moved toward the gator, the one device that still gave him the most mobility.

"We're not giving up," Bree said, gesturing for her to give the command again.

"Not in a million years," Sammy Jo agreed.

Sammy Jo was still thinking about her session with Phantom that afternoon while fixing the fence broken along the Macpherson-Collins property line. They didn't use ropes or any special devices to force the animal down into the correct position like others did. Bree insisted only on natural horsemanship techniques that focused more on developing a bond of trust between the animal and trainer. However, they *did* stoop to using a little bribery with carrots.

As Sammy Jo slipped on a pair of work gloves, she realized she wouldn't be doing any of this if she had still been riding rodeo. The time she now spent with her friends, the girls at the horse camp, and with Luke . . . had all reaffirmed that when she'd decided to stay home this summer, she'd made the right choice.

She also had time to fix fences. Her father kept his word, like always, and had the new wood posts and wiring delivered from the hardware store. He'd also promised to help her fix the fence after work, but Sammy Jo hadn't wanted to wait. She was perfectly capable of fixing it herself, and after her spat with Luke, she needed to do something to vent her frustration.

If only she and Bree had found more time to train Phantom before Luke discovered what they were doing. Then maybe he wouldn't have reacted with such disgust.

Taking a shovel she dug into the hard, dry ground and, after the fifth scoop, realized the job was going to take longer than she thought. She wiped her gloved hand across her brow, eyeing the stack of six-foot posts that needed to be stuck two feet under, then spun around toward the distinct rumble of a tractor heading her way.

It was the Collinses' green John Deere and Luke sat in the driver's seat. Maybe he was coming to apologize? Luke pulled up beside her, shut off the engine, and climbed out, hopping down using his good leg.

"Bree told you what I was doing this afternoon, didn't she?" Sammy Jo accused.

Luke shook his head. "I could see what you were up to from the cabins. Thought you could use a post hole digger."

"You want to help me?" Sammy Jo drawled. "Now *that's* a switch."

"The new guests are busy checking in and I thought I'd get out of their way," Luke said, ignoring her sarcasm. "Besides, it's our fence, too. It borders both properties."

"Don't worry about it. I've 'got it handled,' " she said, using one of his own quotes against her.

Sammy Jo stuck the blade of the shovel into the

ground and placed her foot on the shoulder, ready to continue digging, but Luke stopped her by grabbing the shaft. "Look. I'm sorry about . . . earlier. I shouldn't have got so mad you were working with Phantom."

"I'm doing it for you," she said, meeting his hazel-eyed gaze.

"I know." Luke cleared his throat and his fingers slid a few inches down the handle of the shovel to cover her own. "Your father kept his word. I got the building permits this morning."

Sammy Jo nodded. Her fingers tingled beneath his warm hand, and she scarcely dared to breathe as she tried to figure what to make of it. "My father may be feuding with your parents, but he's a good man."

"I don't think he has anything against my ma," Luke said, and narrowed his gaze. "He was pretty sweet to her when she went into the planning department. I think my father's the main one he has a problem with." Then Luke chuckled and added, "Besides *me*. He definitely has a problem with me."

"Yes, he does," Sammy Jo agreed, and relaxed as they shared a laugh. "He wouldn't like it if he knew you were out here helping."

"It's *not* a date," Luke said, his voice warm, his look soft.

"No . . . it's not." Sammy Jo smiled as Luke continued to look at her, as if . . . as if . . .

His thumb rubbed over her fingers, then he dropped his hand from hers and moved back toward the tractor.

"Back up while I dig the holes, then we can put in the posts," he called over his shoulder.

Sammy Jo did as he said, and had to admit using the tractor's attached auger to drill the needed depth was better than digging by hand. Of course, working with Luke beat working alone any day, too.

After he finished, they placed each post in the ground, repacked the dirt to hold them steady, and stretched the thick, white, vinyl-covered wiring across the posts in three rows.

"When my father found out about the tracks across our field, he said he'd like me to stay in at night," Sammy Jo said, watching for Luke's reaction.

The muscle along his jaw jumped, then pulled tight. "You won't be able to help me keep an eye on the cows?"

"Of course I will," she said, thrilled that he really did want her there. "I'll just have to climb out through my bedroom window so my father doesn't see."

Luke grinned. "You used to do that quite a lot, didn't you?"

Sammy Jo tossed the remaining wire on the ground and laughed. "Like the time we had a marshmallow war and we used those homemade plastic tube marshmallow shooters?"

"We had twenty kids running around the fields that night," Luke said, giving her a mischievous look.

"First your guys in front launched the attack, then you yelled that silly code word that meant, 'Get down!' " Sammy Jo reminded him. "After they ducked, you had the guys behind them stand up and shoot a second wave over their heads. The opposite team was pelted until we surrendered."

"Yeah," Luke said, moving closer, "and you told me I'd never be a real military captain because I was too immature."

"Because you shot sticky marshmallows into my hair," Sammy Jo complained. "It took three showers to get it all out."

Luke reached his hand and pulled one of her long, dark, curly locks forward, letting it run through his fingers. "Served you right for not being on my team."

Sammy Jo stared up into his eyes, shocked by the tenderness she saw in his expression, and her heart slammed into her chest. "I—I would have given anything to be on your team."

Luke rested his hand on her shoulder and tugged her toward him ever so slightly. Then he lowered his head and Sammy Jo gasped, her heart jumping up and down inside her rib cage like a caged frog on the Fourth of July.

Was Luke Collins about to *kiss* her?

He didn't say anything for several long moments. He just stood there gazing at her as if studying every feature on her face. Then the corners of his mouth jerked upward into a half grin and he asked, "Would you like to come over to my camp?"

Sammy Jo nodded, not trusting her voice to speak, and Luke led her toward the tractor.

"Hop aboard, sweetheart," he teased, taking her hand and helping her up.

"Where should I sit?" she asked, glancing around the cab and noticing the single seat.

Luke looped an arm around her waist and pulled her toward him. "Right here on my lap."

His arm tightened around her as they drove and Sammy Jo's imagination went wild with possible scenarios of what she had to look forward to when they arrived.

Not one of them even came close.

"Someone slashed your tent," she said, staring at the green canvas that had been torn to shreds. "And broke your flagpole."

Actually, it looked like a tornado had leveled the place flat. The stuffing had been pulled from his pillow and sleeping bag. The rocks that had formed a ring around his campfire had been tossed in different directions. His clothes had been ground into the dirt. Even his cooking utensils had been smashed.

"Luke," she said, grabbing hold of his arm. "Why would someone do this?"

His muscles went rigid beneath her grip. "Because I'm too close to their path."

Chapter Eight

After driving back to the main house to report the damage, Luke had helped the others assigned to keep watch that night even though it wasn't his turn. Then he'd slept a few hours in an outside hammock until his grandma woke him for breakfast.

Tonight, Delaney and Zach would take the early shift and he and Sammy Jo would take over at two a.m. and patrol the area till dawn. But for now, the day was still young, so Luke salvaged what he could from the remains of his camp.

He didn't own much, but the wreckage still filled six large trash bags he'd brought with him from the main house. The most disappointing was the loss of his olive-drab military duffel. The bag had been his personal suitcase over the last year and had held one personal memento in one of the pockets that he was sad to let go.

One of the men who had mutilated his camp must

have taken it, because although he searched, he couldn't find it anywhere.

No matter. He'd get by. *"No sense cryin' over what you can't change."* Wasn't that what his grandma always said? He still had his health, *for the most part*, his family, and . . . *Sammy Jo*.

He'd come close to kissing her the night before, but if he had . . . it would have changed everything. Never again would she be just a neighbor or friend of his sisters, but like an identifying brand that could never be removed, she'd be . . . *his*.

Because as innocent as a kiss might be . . . Sammy Jo would never let him forget it for as long as he lived.

Luke drew in a deep breath. Perhaps he should be grateful the slashed tent saved him from making a mistake he couldn't change. For if they had spent any more alone time together, who knows what could have happened?

Which reminded him, they'd be alone again . . . tonight. He'd picked Sammy Jo as his partner so he could make sure nothing happened to her. She could be overly confident and impulsive at times and it often landed her in a heap of trouble.

Like it did to him.

He shook his head, realizing that in some ways, they really were too much alike. Not only did he need to watch out for the cattle rustlers, and Sammy Jo's safety, but he would also have to watch out for himself, and make sure *he* didn't do anything rash tonight either.

Piling the trash bags into the back of the gator, Luke

left the empty field and motored past the line of guest cabins. A flurry of new guests were moving about. Some hung out by the river. Others talked to his father next by the corral. And a few more gathered by the garden around Grandma and Meghan, petting the dappled gray miniature pony, Party Marty.

Luke entered his family's house, climbed the stairs, and took a small bag of personal belongings up to his old bedroom. He could pick up a new tent, but figured it might be safer for his family and the guests if he stayed closer until the crooks were caught.

He opened the dresser drawer and grinned. There, among a few other childhood items, sat his famed plastic marshmallow shooter, one of his best Christmas presents ever. The double-barreled, pump-action gun stored up to twenty mini-marshmallows per magazine for a total ammo capacity of forty, and shot up to thirty feet. Best of all, it required no batteries.

He thought back to the time he'd armed himself with a big bag of his grandma's mini-marshmallows, and climbed up the water tower. He'd stayed up there for nearly an hour shooting marshmallows off in every direction. Until the sheriff caught him. Some of the townspeople had complained it looked like it had been snowing in July.

He placed his stuff away and moved toward the windows to check on his escape routes. The trellis outside the window by his bed still looked sturdy enough and the angled roofline that acted as a slide out his other window remained clear and ready, if needed.

He doubted he'd be using them, especially in his condition with his leg the way it was, but out of habit he always looked at his options whenever he moved into a new location. There was nothing worse than being trapped in a small space with no way out. Perhaps that's why he preferred the open field.

"Looks like we have a full house," Luke joked later that afternoon when he entered the enclosed front porch they'd turned into a main office.

"Yes, lots of guests and—" Delaney looked at him, grasped his meaning, and gasped. "You moved back in?"

Luke nodded. "For now."

"That will ease Ma's fears," Delaney said, smiling.

"But not the fears of our employees," Bree said, coming in from outside. "All three of the ranch hands I hired last month just quit."

Luke shrugged. "They were terrible. We might be better off without them."

"It will mean extra shifts for the rest of us," Bree assured them. "On top of our night watches."

Nora and Nadine opened the screen door and came in behind her, each wearing identical scowls showcasing their mood.

"We need to talk to you," Nora said, directing her attention to Bree.

"Yes, we do," Nadine agreed.

"What now?" Bree demanded. "Have you decided to quit, too?"

The screen door opened a third time and a tall, sturdy

kid with short cropped hair as dark as Sammy Jo's entered the room.

"Can we help you?" Luke asked, assuming he was a guest.

The young guy nodded. "I'm ready to work."

"Who's he?" Nora and Nadine chorused, starry-eyed and mouths hanging open.

Luke shot Bree a questioning look. Had his sister already hired someone new?

"Devin Williams," she introduced. "He'll be helping Luke with the cabins so we can get them finished in time for the August wedding."

Luke did a double take. "What?"

The young cowboy ignored his reaction and instead tipped his hat in greeting toward the twins. "Do you ladies work here, too?"

Nora jabbed her sister in the ribs with her elbow and both of the ponytailed sixteen-year-olds looked at each other, cast a quick glance at Bree, and then chorused again, "Yes, we *do*!"

The young cowboy smiled at them and turned toward Luke. "I'll meet you outside?"

Luke gave him a hesitant nod, and after the guy left, Nora and Nadine both let out a high-pitched squeal, hurting his ears.

Then the girls high-fived themselves. "Score for the Walford twins!"

"Now do you see what you've done?" Luke asked, catching his older sister's eye.

Bree nodded and cringed; Delaney laughed.

"He's so *dreamy*," Nora exclaimed. "He's—"

"*Dreamy Devin*," Nadine said, cutting her off.

Both broke into a fit of giggles and hurried out the door, most likely to go running after the poor kid.

Luke smirked. "How old is he anyway?"

"Dreamy Devin is eighteen," Bree teased. "And he's experienced in roof work."

"At eighteen?" Luke scoffed. "How experienced can he be?"

Bree shrugged. "Devin says he's been working with his father in construction since he was a kid."

"He's still a kid right *now*," Luke pointed out.

Bree pursed her lips. "He has a driver's license, can climb, and can pound nails with a hammer. What else do you want?"

His sister was good with numbers and balancing the books, but she didn't know construction. Still, she was right. Even if the newcomer had just a little skill and half a brain it could work.

As long as the kid followed his directions.

SAMMY JO ROLLED her eyes as she held her cell phone to her ear. "Mom, I know what I'm doing."

"You can't force someone to love you. Believe me, I know."

"I don't plan to force him, just *convince* him. There's a difference. Look, I gotta go. I'll talk to you again tomorrow, okay?"

After a quick goodbye, Sammy Jo sent a text to Bree

and Delaney, two she could count on to be happy for her instead of being such a worrywart, like her mom.

He almost kissed me, I know it! Sammy Jo told them by typing in the letters on her touch screen.

Silence.

A minute later Bree texted back. *Luke?*

Yes, Luke. Who else? Sammy Jo punched back.

I believe you, Delaney joined in, and sent her a smiley face.

Why wouldn't she believe her? Did they think she was making it up? That she was imagining things? Another message popped up.

Be careful tonight, Bree warned.

Were they still talking about Luke? Did his sisters agree with her mother and think she'd end up with a broken heart, too? Or did she mean be careful if they ran into the bad guys? Either way, her answer was the same.

Not worried, she sent back.

Putting her phone back in her pocket, she glanced up and surveyed the camp full of eager, smiling children learning to ride their horses in the various arenas. They weren't afraid of failing or getting hurt. They were going after what they wanted with gusto!

And so would she.

She *would* get a kiss. She *would* marry Luke. And together they *would* have a house full of their own children.

They *would*.

LUKE MET SAMMY Jo by the corral where Ryan had placed the remaining cattle for the night.

"Any trouble?" he asked.

"Nope." She smiled. "I greased my window earlier today so when I raised the screen it wouldn't make a sound. My dad will never suspect I'm gone."

Luke chuckled. "Hope not, or we'll have more than cattle rustlers to deal with."

"I guess Zach and Delaney didn't have any trouble during the first watch?" she asked, settling in beside him in a small grove of trees.

"Nope."

"I brought you something," she said, handing over a canvas bag.

"My duffel!" Luke said, careful to keep his voice low. "Where did you find it?"

"Halfway across my yard." She pointed to the zippered pocket in the front. "Who's that in the photo?"

Apparently she'd looked through the bag's contents. "Those are the guys I served with over in Iraq," Luke told her. "We took that picture together right before I got out and came home."

"Do you still keep in touch?"

Luke's jaw tightened as he shook his head. "No."

"Why not?"

"They're all dead."

Sammy Jo gasped. "Oh, no. I'm so sorry."

Luke drew in a deep breath and swallowed the knot that always formed at the back of his throat when he thought of them.

"My term was up," he said, reliving the memory like he'd done countless times before. "And I flew home for

Bree's birthday party. A week later, when I went to Florida to see another friend, I heard the news."

Sammy Jo didn't say a word but took his hand in hers and gave it a reassuring squeeze.

"The official story is their helicopter crashed during a routine training exercise," he continued. "Others believe they'd been on a recon mission to recover a shipment of supplies that had been dropped in hostile territory. All I know is that if I'd still been there, I would have been with them."

"That's when you had your motorcycle accident," Sammy Jo said, "isn't it?"

Luke nodded. "I wasn't in the best frame of mind. The front tire of the motorcycle hit some gravel and swerved out. I couldn't maintain control and my left knee went down. Ended up with a few cuts and bruises, and . . . I tore my ACL."

"But you said it could be fixed with surgery," Sammy Jo reminded him.

"Maybe." Luke swallowed again. "Then again, the doctors could knock me out and I might not ever wake up again, like my three good friends in the picture."

"Luke Collins," Sammy Jo demanded in a stern whisper. "Are you telling me you're afraid of being put to sleep? Is *that* why you've been stalling?"

He flinched as she hit on the truth.

"You're one of the bravest, wildest, risk-taking cowboys I've ever met. How could you let a little medical sleepy juice scare you away from an operation that would allow you to regain the full use of your leg?"

Luke swallowed hard. "One of the guys you saw in the photo . . . the one on the left, his name was Greg Quinn. They found his body among the wreckage. But he didn't die in the crash. His family had been told he was going to be all right, just as soon as they removed a damaged kidney. Then they gave him an overdose of meds to put him asleep for the procedure and . . . he never woke up. He was pronounced dead later that same day."

"I'm so sorry," Sammy Jo whispered, placing her hand on his arm.

"So I guess I'd rather take my chances on my own terms," he continued. "Rather than rely on someone else."

She hesitated, then in a small voice that tugged at his heart, she said, "Sometimes having someone else to rely on isn't so bad."

Luke grinned, thankful he could share this conversation with her. Thankful she was so compassionate. Thankful to have her by his side. "I'm beginning to see that."

A stream of moonlight filtered through the leaves above and illuminated her face—her sparkling eyes, her pert little nose, her wide mouth with her full lips.

"Oh, no," Sammy Jo said, glancing up at the sky. "They'll be able to see me, won't they?"

"Not if you move closer to me," he said, putting his arm around her and pulling her into the shadows. He didn't expect her to protest, and she didn't.

Luke cleared his throat, relishing the warmth she provided even though he didn't need it with the higher than normal midsummer temperature.

"Guess who I saw when I went to pick up the building permit at your father's office?" he asked. When she shook her head, he continued. "A.J. Malloy. He said he's building a new stable for his rodeo champion."

Sammy Jo laid her head back on his shoulder and looked up at him. "He's all talk, talk, talk."

Luke shrugged. "Ryan says the guy has his eye on you."

"I assure you," Sammy Jo said, and laughed. "The feeling isn't mutual."

"Why not?"

"Because," she told him, her voice turning silky soft. "I've got my eye on someone else."

Luke grinned. He'd hoped she'd say that. More heat flooded over him along with a surge of adrenaline the likes he hadn't felt in a long while. However, this wasn't the time or place for either of them to lose focus. He cupped her chin and turned her head toward the corral. "You're supposed to have your eye on the cows."

Sammy Jo sucked in her breath and pointed. "Luke, what's that?"

His gaze shot to the open field beyond the corral and he heard the faint drum of the truck's motor the same time he saw the dim headlights.

Sammy Jo jumped up and whipped her cell phone from her pocket, then tossed it to Luke. "Call 911," she said, moving away from him. "Then call your family and the Tanners and let them know what's going on."

"Where are you going?" he hissed.

"I'll be right back," she told him. "I just want to get close enough to take a look at their license plate."

He stumbled as he leaned on his cane for support and tried to hoist himself onto his feet. *"Sammy Jo!"*

She ran over to the paddock in front of them, and pulling a halter off the gate, she went in, slipped the straps over the nose of the nearest horse, and hopped on bareback.

"No!" he shouted, scrambling toward her.

She wasn't looking at him, but was focused on the men getting out of the truck in the field opposite the corral about five hundred yards away.

They'd miscalculated which direction the cattle rustlers would come from. Both times before, they'd entered from the Owenses' vacant property and exited out through Sammy Jo's toward the road. This time, however, it appeared they'd done just the opposite, which put Luke and Sammy Jo quite a distance from where they'd wanted to be.

Luke squinted and could just barely make out her silhouette as she wove in and out along the tree line. But then her horse let out a high-pitched neigh, and one of the dark figures in the field shouted a warning to the others. A second later, a small beam of light flashed toward her, and with a sickening sensation tightening his gut, Luke realized Sammy Jo had been caught.

For a second, fear for her life knocked the breath right out of him. Then his gaze fell on the rehab horse not twenty feet away.

Without thinking of anything except Sammy Jo, he half ran, half limped forward, grabbed Prince's halter, slipped it on, and commanded him to bow. A sharp twinge ripped through Luke's leg and shot up his side as he swung onto the animal's back, but he clenched his teeth and ordered the horse to stand.

For there was *nothing* he wouldn't do for her. Not in days past, not now, or in the foreseeable future. And there was nothing that was going to stop him from making sure Sammy Jo did not get hurt.

SAMMY JO FOUGHT back as three of the black-masked men pulled her off the horse and pushed her to the ground.

"Your daddy wouldn't like it if he found you out here," one of them drawled, grabbing hold of her wrist.

Sammy Jo's heart raced. They knew her father. Then again, everyone in this small town knew who both she and her father were. Still, it proved they were locals.

She'd caught a glimpse of the truck's plates and, sure enough, it was the truck that belonged to Harley Bennett, though she couldn't be sure if he was the one talking to her. All of their voices came out muffled from beneath the black hooded ski masks.

"What are we going to do with her? Take her with us?" the man in the driver's seat asked.

"I don't know. This wasn't part of the plan," said the guy who held on to her.

"Well, make up your mind," said one of the other three who loaded six of the Collinses' cows into the back of the cattle trailer. "We don't have all night."

The thunder of hooves froze everyone in their tracks.

"What's that?" one of the rustlers by the cows called out.

"*Someone's coming,*" the driver warned.

The rustlers spoke among themselves so fast Sammy Jo couldn't figure who was saying what, but the words she made out filled her with hope.

"What if it's him?" asked one.

"Who?" asked another.

"*The Legend,*" a sharp whisper shot out.

"Impossible. Heard that cowboy's now a cripple with a cane. There's no way he can ride."

Sammy Jo jerked her head toward the intensifying sound, and wondered if she dared use the distraction to jump up and attempt an escape.

A second later her captor shoved a rifle against her chest, and she didn't dare move.

LUKE USED THE cover of darkness to his advantage as long as he could by staying within the tree line like Sammy Jo had tried to do. Then he urged his horse forward and rode into the open at a full gallop.

After one bloodcurdling glimpse of the rustler who threatened Sammy Jo, Luke swung his cane and knocked the gun away from the man's hands with a sharp *thwack*. Then Luke dropped the reins, and slid off his horse like he'd done a thousand times during his rodeo days, and wrestled the man to the ground like a bull.

"I thought you said he couldn't ride," a distant rustler's voice shouted as Luke drew back his arm and punched the man beneath him.

"Move out! Now!" called another voice.

The man beneath Luke pushed him aside, rolled, then got up on his feet. So did Luke. The man stood halfway between him and the truck, and for a moment Luke thought the rustler meant to come after him and return the punch.

Then the trailer behind the man pulled away and after a brief hesitation the rustler turned, ran, and jumped into the back of the pickup.

"Luke?"

Hopping on his good foot, Luke spun around and Sammy Jo ran toward him. She appeared unharmed, except for the tears streaming down her face and the fact she trembled from head to toe. His heart wrenched as her vulnerable gaze met his and he suddenly realized he was trembling as well.

Then in one, swift, fluid motion he scooped her into his arms and seared her with a kiss so hot it could have melted the ground beneath them. Warning bells went off in his head, but the burst of adrenaline pumping through his veins robbed him of all thought except the fact she was safe . . . and her lips held the faint taste of strawberries.

As his breathing slowed, the image of the gunman holding a rifle to Sammy Jo's chest shook him to his senses and he pulled his mouth away from her.

"What did you think you were doing?" he demanded.

"*Me?* What did you think *you* were doing?" she countered, her incredulous expression boring into him. "You could have hurt your leg even worse than before. You could have—"

He cut her off with another kiss, except this time it was a little softer, less demanding, and held more promise.

Sammy Jo's hands wrapped around the back of his neck, and when the second kiss ended she smiled up at him. "What are *we* doing?"

Luke held her gaze for a brief second and said, "What we've both wanted to do for a while now."

"*You've wanted to kiss me?*" she asked.

He nodded, and grinned, then dipped his head to kiss her sweet, tender lips . . . one more time.

Chapter Nine

LOOKING BACK, SAMMY Jo saw she'd been foolish to take the horse. She should have gone on foot. But she'd been afraid she wouldn't get there in time to see the rustlers' license plate. And although she was certain that one way or another she could have escaped her captors on her own, she was perfectly content to let Luke take the credit.

Especially after he'd mounted the rehab horse and endured the pain she knew he must have suffered on her behalf. Her heart *still* pounded from seeing him ride in like a white knight to "save" her.

She smiled, and her mind dreamily relived the scene again and again. Never had Luke looked more dashing, more heroic, more fully alive, than in that moment. And afterward, when they kissed . . . and his arms held her close . . . the accompanying burst of sensations that shot through her body, igniting all her senses, confirmed more than ever that she'd been right—Luke *was* her man!

"Miss Macpherson, do you think this is funny?" the sheriff questioned. Sheriff McKinley and his deputy had arrived close to three a.m. to take their statements and write a report.

"No, of course not," Sammy Jo said, dropping her smile. Heat rushed into her cheeks as she realized the two officers had been staring at her. "My mind wasn't on the rustlers. I was thinking of something else."

Luke glanced her way and grinned, as if he could guess what that "something" might be. Was he reliving the kisses they'd shared, too? She had wondered if he'd back away from her in front of his family, but he continued to hold her hand with everyone present. And from the direction of Bree's and Delaney's wide-eyed gazes, it was obvious her friends had noticed.

Focus, she told herself, *right now we have rustlers to catch*. "I saw their license plate," Sammy Jo announced, and dropped Luke's hand to scribble the digits on the deputy's notepad. "The truck belongs to Harley Bennett."

"Harley called in a few minutes ago and reported his truck stolen," the sheriff informed her.

"Of course he did," Sammy Jo said. "He's trying to avoid being arrested."

"He said about two hours ago he woke up and thought he heard a noise outside. He didn't think too much of it at first and fell back asleep. Then when he awoke a second time, he went out, found his truck missing, and called the station."

"I suppose his truck just happened to be hooked up to the cattle trailer at the time, too?"

The sheriff nodded. "Yes, he did say that."

"You don't believe him, do you?" Sammy Jo pressed. "Can't you see he's guilty?"

"Not without proof," Sheriff McKinley said, glancing around the room at each of them. "We can point fingers all night, but without any kind of hard evidence, I can't make any arrests."

"What *can* we do?" Bree demanded.

"We can remove the hay from the hay barn and lock the cattle inside at night," Luke suggested.

"What if the rustlers steal our hay or light it on fire again?" Bree argued.

"Better to lose the hay than the cows," their father stated, backing Luke.

"We'll need to keep all the horses inside their stalls at night, too," Delaney added. "And install security cameras on each of the main buildings."

"A security system will cost more money," their ma fretted.

"Money well-spent," Grandma Collins countered. "We need to do whatever it takes to stop these scoundrels, right, Luke?"

He nodded. "Whatever it takes."

A vibration in her pocket alerted Sammy Jo she had an incoming text and she withdrew her cell phone and glanced at the screen.

Where are you?

With an inward groan, she said, "I have to go. My father has discovered I'm not home in bed, and I really do need a few hours' sleep before I have to work."

"No sense sleeping now," Jed Collins grumbled. "Luke and I should get started moving that hay." Then he hesitated, glanced at Luke, and added, "If you're up for it."

Luke's expression hardened. "I'm fine. Let's get started."

Sammy Jo turned toward Luke, expecting him to do or say something. Maybe kiss her goodbye?

But his father motioned him toward the door and Luke moved to follow.

She stepped toward him. "Luke?"

He glanced back at her over his shoulder.

"We'll talk later?" she asked, hating the desperation in her voice.

He gave her a partial grin and said, "Yep."

His one-word answer wasn't very satisfying, but there was nothing else she could do for now. She'd just have to keep reliving the kiss in her mind and be satisfied with the progress she'd made so far. The three kisses they'd shared would surely lead to many more, and in another few months?

Why, he might even *propose*!

LUKE FROWNED AND cast his father a sharp glance as they walked down the path toward the hay barn. "I rode."

His father nodded. "I heard."

"Soon I'll be able to help Ryan lead the weekend roundups and you won't have to treat me like an invalid anymore."

"I wouldn't have asked you to help with the hay if I

thought you were an invalid," his father muttered, his tone gruff with annoyance.

Luke stopped walking and clenched the handle of his cane. "I just don't live up to your expectations, is that it?"

His father took a few more steps, then stopped, turned around, and faced him. "You're a man, of course I expect more from you than your sisters."

"I've always worked twice as hard as anyone, even *you*."

"Then you left me to do all the work myself so you could go off and do your own thing," his father said, narrowing his eyes. "This is supposed to be a family business."

"Families are supposed to trust each other and treat each other with respect. I figured if you meant to keep ordering me about, I might as well join the army."

"I never wanted you to leave," his father spat. Then he scowled. "I jus' wanted to make sure you grew up to be responsible, make the right decisions, so you could run the whole ranch on your own one day."

Luke hesitated. "Me? Run Collins Country Cabins on my own? What about Bree and Delaney?"

His father dismissed them with a wave of his hand. "I always knew Bree would move to the city and follow her dreams to have a big fancy career. I didn't expect her to come back, but now that she did, it hasn't changed anything. She'll marry Ryan and they'll have their own ranch to worry about."

Luke hadn't given Ryan and Bree's engagement much thought, but realized his father was right. Even though

Grandma had given each member an equal share of Collins Country Cabins, Bree's work here would most likely be temporary. After she was married and became Cody's new mom full-time, she might even have babies of her own. And with horses to train and the Tanner cattle ranch to help run . . .

"What about Delaney?" Luke asked. "She has nowhere else to go. Her ex-husband isn't even paying child support for Meghan. She needs this ranch to work even more than the rest of us."

"A temporary situation," his father assured him. "Delaney's a sweet, young, beautiful girl with her whole life ahead of her. It won't be long before some handsome cowboy strolls into town and turns her head. Then she'll be married and taking off to care for her own horses, or open an animal rescue center, or launch a 'save the bears' campaign. She's always been more interested in the wildlife outside, rather than the people inside this place."

"That's true," Luke admitted.

"And when Grandma's gone and your ma and I can no longer care for the guest ranch, who do you think we'll want to take over?" his father demanded.

Luke stared at him, unable to believe his father had wanted to prepare him and not punish him. "I didn't think you'd *ever* let anyone take control of the ranch."

His father scoffed. "Well, after you left, I gave partial control to Susan and Wade Randall and look at the mess that made. I trusted them and they nearly destroyed us." His father chuckled. "I figure you can't do much worse."

This time when his father cast the insult, Luke knew

he was joking and he grinned with him. "No, I reckon not."

Then his father did something he'd never done before. He laid a hand on Luke's shoulder, looked him in the eye, man-to-man, and said, "I trust you."

Luke nodded, not trusting himself to speak. He'd never imagined he'd be having this conversation, or if he had, that it would turn out this way.

After a long moment, he swallowed the lump that had risen in the back of his throat, and said, "Thanks, Dad."

SAMMY JO CROSSED the Collins-Macpherson border and frowned. She'd expected to see her new gate or another piece of the fence cut, run down, or destroyed. Instead, she found everything intact except the gate had been left open, and the padlock—unscathed—now hung loose from the latch. But if she and her father were the only ones with a key, how had the rustlers managed to open it?

When her house came into view, she saw her father waited for her outside and she raised her brows. "Did someone steal your keys?"

"No," he said, his tone full of disgust. "I'm outside because I wanted to keep a lookout to make sure you got home safe."

"Then how did the rustlers open the lock on the gate?"

He narrowed his gaze. "Rustlers? What are you talking about?"

She bit her lip. She should have thought ahead before she'd spoken. Now she'd have to tell him what happened.

Or at least part of it. She'd keep the details of her capture and Luke's magnificent, romantic rescue to herself so she wouldn't alarm him any more than necessary.

"Five men drove off the road and crossed through our property to steal six more of the Collinses' cows. Somehow they opened the new padlock we put on the gate. I have my key right here," she said, patting her jeans pocket. "Where's yours?"

He patted his own pockets, front and back, and gave her a puzzled look.

"It's missing?" she asked.

He hesitated. "I thought I had them in my pocket, but let me check the house."

After they both searched every countertop, drawer, nook, and cranny, Sammy Jo placed her hands on her hips and said, "I think the rustlers stole your keys. Where were you the last time you had them? Did you leave them on the picnic table outside?"

"No. They never left my side. Except when—"

"Yes?" she prompted.

Her father frowned. "I let Winona drive my truck into town because she was having car trouble and said she needed to pick up a new battery."

"It was her!" Sammy Jo exclaimed. "I knew something wasn't right about that woman."

Her father reached into the pocket of one of his lightweight jackets hanging on a peg by the door, and when he pulled his hand back out, he held up his key ring. "I think you owe Winona an apology. I have them right here."

Sammy Jo scrambled to come up with an explanation.

"She must have got an extra key made when she was in town and then gave it to the rustlers."

"Why on earth would she do that?" he argued.

Wasn't it obvious? "Because she's *in on it*! Winona Lane is working with the cattle rustlers."

"Samantha Josephine!" her father thundered. "How dare you toss accusations like that at an innocent lady."

"She's not here," Sammy Jo pointed out.

"Yes, but I am," he said, his tone indignant. "And I happen to care about Winona very much."

"You hardly know her. You've only been dating for, like, what? Two months?"

"Your friend Bree got engaged after only knowing that Tanner fellow six weeks."

Sammy Jo gasped. "They've known each other all their lives, and you are not thinking of asking that banker woman to marry you, are you? Because, in case you have forgotten, you're still married—*to Mom*."

She and her father stared each other down for what seemed like several hours. In reality it probably lasted only a few short seconds.

"The rustlers may have got hold of the keys somehow while they were in Winona's possession," Sammy Jo conceded.

"They could have manipulated her without her even knowing what they were doing," her father agreed, then his stubborn expression changed to one of worry. "I hope she's not in any danger. Maybe she should have her nephew stay with her."

"Who's her nephew?"

"A.J. Malloy."

Sammy Jo remembered Luke questioning her about him. She'd even thought Luke sounded a little jealous when he said A.J. was interested in her. She often ran into the cowboy on the rodeo circuit and he seemed like a nice guy, just not her type. She didn't think A.J. was the type to steal the Collinses' cows either, but the rustlers had called Luke by his old nickname, "The Legend," so it had to be *someone* they knew.

She'd talk to A.J. Malloy and see if he could have been one of the men who had captured her. But for now, she whipped out her cell phone to talk to Luke—and warn him that his past rodeo pal could be a prime suspect.

LUKE STARTED THE tractor and helped his father transport the hay from the barn to an area along the edge of the parking lot. They'd thought the location would be safer than any other since it was closer to the house and easier to keep an eye on.

Once the barn was empty, they pulled tarps over the hay to protect the bales from unfavorable weather and secured the tarps with a few heavy rocks. Luke had always worked hard before, but after his talk with his father, he worked with renewed vigor and saw the ranch in a whole new light. Collins Country Cabins wasn't just his family's guest ranch. It was his future. And these intruders, or rustlers, or whoever they were . . . were messing with it.

Ryan had called and offered to lend them some of the Tanners' cows for the weekend roundups, but Luke's father had said no, worried they might be stolen, too. For now, they'd preserve the dozen Black Angus they had, and once the rustlers were caught, they'd buy some more.

His cell phone buzzed, and when he checked his messages, he saw he'd missed a few. Five to be exact. All from Sammy Jo.

For a moment he just stared at her name on the caller ID.

Nothing about the night before had gone as planned. He'd never intended for the rustlers to come from the opposite direction. He'd never planned to mount a horse and ride out to face them alone. And he certainly hadn't planned on kissing Sammy Jo.

He thought of the way her soft lips had felt against his own and he grinned. One thing was for sure. He'd never think of Sammy Jo Macpherson as just "the girl next door" ever again. He'd never again eat a strawberry without thinking of her either. She must have had on some sort of girlie strawberry lip gloss, but whatever it was, it had only made kissing her even more pleasant.

Spontaneous, but definitely . . . pleasant. He grinned again, thinking of the first fiery kiss they'd shared. And the slower, shy second, and then the timeless third.

Afterward Delaney had taken the horses back to the fenced pasture and Bree had brought the gator out to the field so he wouldn't have to walk all the way back to the main house. He'd been thrilled to ride, but once he got off, his legs were so sore he couldn't get back on. Not then. But maybe later this day or the next, he'd give it another go.

Because riding again had been a lot like kissing Sammy Jo. Now that he'd done it, he never wanted to stop.

Chapter Ten

"WHAT DID HE say after he kissed you?" Jesse asked, her eyes wide. "Did he tell you he loved you?"

"No, not exactly," Sammy Jo said, dropping her voice into a whisper when a few of the girls from camp walked past and giggled.

"But you could see it in his eyes, right?" the camp owner pressed, her face rapt with attention.

"If you must know," she confided, her face flooding with warmth at the memory, "it was the way he held my hand afterward, and refused to let go."

"That's a good sign," Jesse agreed. "When are you going to see him again?"

"I don't know," she confessed. "Maybe tonight after I finish up here."

Sammy Jo didn't normally gush about her romantic encounters when working with Jesse, but she needed to tell someone. She couldn't possibly keep all the emotions bubbling up inside her to herself. And Bree and Delaney had not been as enthusiastic as her employer to hear their brother was a good kisser.

"Oh, Jesse, if only you could have seen him ride in to save me!" Sammy Jo crooned. "It was so intense! And none of it would have been possible without the rehab horse."

Jesse's smile waned. "How's the training with Luke's *own* horse coming along?"

"Okay, but it's going to take a while."

"Yes, it usually does." Jesse glanced away and when she faced her again it looked like the woman had bit into a sour grape. Except they hadn't been eating; they'd been cleaning tack, with no food in sight.

Sammy Jo frowned. "What's the matter? Did a bug fly into your mouth?"

Jesse laughed and shook her head, then pressed her lips together, and winced again. "I hate to tell you this, but I need you to bring Prince back here to the camp."

"*What?*" Sammy Jo couldn't breathe. *Oh, no, not now.* "You—you said you didn't need him another whole week."

"I know, I'm so sorry, but I got a call from a disabled woman who's coming out to see Prince later today."

"*Today?*" Sammy Jo repeated.

Jesse nodded. "Do you think you could take the trailer over to the Collinses' and have Prince back here by five?"

"How long will she need him?"

"She may buy him," Jesse informed her.

Sammy Jo gasped. "For how much?"

"For more than either you or Luke can afford," Jesse assured her. "I'm sorry, Sammy Jo. I know how long it's taken you to convince Luke to mount up, and now that he's made such tremendous progress—"

"It was never about just the ride," Sammy Jo protested, her stomach turning.

Jesse gave her a sympathetic look. "It never is."

Sammy Jo knew she couldn't argue any further; after all, the horse wasn't hers. She should be thankful Jesse had let her borrow the rehab horse in the first place. *But Luke had finally got on and ridden!*

Her thoughts returned to the previous night when Luke had come galloping in with his hair flying back, his eyes on fire. He'd been bold and confident and filled with *passion*! She'd hoped the horse would enable him to realize it wasn't his injury holding him back, but his own crippling beliefs.

But what would happen now if she took the horse away? The back of her throat closed tight and her heart skipped a beat. Would she ever see that wonderful, larger-than-life, vibrant side of the man she loved again?

LUKE DIDN'T LIKE using cell phones and cared for them even less once he finally had time to read the series of text messages Sammy Jo had sent warning him his friend couldn't be trusted.

He eyed the new teenage boy his sister had hired and narrowed his gaze. Trust had to be earned and he couldn't trust this newcomer any more than he could trust Sammy Jo's father, Winona Lane, Harley Bennett, or even his longtime rodeo pal, A.J. Malloy. Any one of them could have had access to the key that opened the Macphersons' gate.

"Where did you say you were from?" Luke asked, staring up at the eighteen-year-old on top of the unfinished cabin.

"Butte."

"And where did you learn construction?"

Devin hammered another beam in place, then reached into his tool belt and pulled out a few more nails. "I told you—from my father."

"What is his name, and why aren't you working for him now?" Luke demanded.

"His name was Mike Williams and I'm not working for him now because he's dead."

Luke blew out his breath, hoping it would release some of the frustration building within. "Sorry."

"Look, I'd rather you judge me on my work than who I belong to or where I come from," Devin said, narrowing his gaze in return. "Is that too much to ask?"

The young cowboy had attitude. Too much attitude, thinking he could fly up the ladder and start working without consulting him on how the trusses should be laid out. The boy was a hothead and would end up in a heap of trouble if he didn't look out. You couldn't just ride into a situation without knowing what lay ahead.

"Before you go making a mistake that costs us money, let me tell you how I think it should be done," Luke warned. Then he jumped back, startled, realizing he sounded exactly like his own father.

"I can do this without you," Devin retorted. "I don't need your help."

Luke stared at him a moment . . . then grinned, realizing the boy was just like *him*. And because Luke had resented his father for the way he spoke to him, he'd failed to see the man actually cared. He didn't want this young cowboy to suffer the same fate without just cause.

After all, he could be innocent. And if he was one of the rustlers, he wasn't the one he fought. His face was unmarked, and the rustler Luke had punched would be sure to have a bruise along his right cheekbone.

"No, I reckon you don't need my help," Luke admitted, lightening his tone. "If you've got that handled, then I guess . . . I'll get back to finishing things down here."

Devin tossed him a puzzled look as if he were crazy, then went back to hammering.

Luke picked up a piece of trim and was about to nail it alongside the cabin door when he turned and noticed a group of teenage girls coming toward them in one of those confounded girl huddles. The loud bangs must have drawn their attention, but no doubt the young cowboy on the roof was what held it.

They glanced up at him, glanced at one another, and giggled, the same way Sammy Jo and his sisters used to do . . . whenever they were interested in someone. It used to annoy him to no end.

"Can I help you ladies?" Luke asked, careful not to annoy their new guests into leaving like their last set.

One of the girls stepped forward. "We're part of Travel Light Adventures," she told him. "Our group is having a bonfire tonight in the pit outside our cabins and we were wondering if your partner up there on the roof would like to join us."

Luke realized the hammering had stopped, and when he glanced up, he saw Devin wave to the girls and grin. "I would love—"

"Sorry, he's not allowed to socialize with the guests," Luke said, drowning out the rest of the boy's reply.

The girls let out a series of disappointed groans, Devin shot him an indignant look, and seemingly out of nowhere the Walford twins raced toward him and latched on to each of Luke's arms.

"Thank goodness, you took care of them, Mr. Luke," Nora exclaimed. "They've been following poor Devin around all day and—"

"Won't leave him alone!" Nadine wailed, her eyes wide.

"I'm sure Devin isn't too bothered," Luke assured them.

"We're just looking out for him," Nora continued.

"Yeah," Nadine agreed. "Looking out for his best interests."

"Which would be?" Luke asked, following their dreamy-eyed gaze up to the rooftop.

"Devin told us that he can't be bringing any girls home or his cousin A.J. wouldn't like it," Nora explained. "And we don't want his cousin to get mad at him and—"

"Kick him out," Nadine said, her face full of worry, "or then he'd have to move back to Butte and we wouldn't be able to see—"

"Wait a minute," Luke said, holding up his hand. "Are you telling me that kid is the cousin of A.J. Malloy?"

Both the girls nodded and Nora gasped. "You know him?"

Luke ground his teeth together. *Oh, yes, he knew him.*

Dropping the trim board on the floor of the porch, he took out the cell phone he dreaded more with each use and punched in his old rodeo pal's number. The kid could be a plant, a way for the rustlers to get information without arousing suspicion. Which would make perfect sense . . . if his old rodeo pal was one of them.

"The Legend," A.J.'s voice greeted, using the same nickname as the men who had threatened Sammy Jo. "What's up?"

Luke glanced toward the top of the cabin. "Your cousin. He's roofing."

"Yeah, he told me about that. He's doing a good job, I hope?"

"Not bad. I was just surprised when I found out you were related," Luke continued. "You never mentioned a cousin."

"What's to mention? We all have cousins. I'm sure almost everyone in this state is cousin to somebody," his friend joked.

"Never knew you two were related to Winona Lane, either," Luke said, trying to keep any trace of hostility out of his voice.

"Oh, that's just me," his friend corrected. "Winona's *my* aunt, not Devin's. He's my cousin from my mother's side."

"Guess that would explain the different last names," Luke said, wondering if A.J. had a bruise along *his* right cheekbone. "Hey, when are you and the other guys meeting up next at the café?"

"Tomorrow afternoon," A.J. answered, his voice as calm and easygoing as ever. "Want to come?"

"Yeah," Luke ground out. "I think I will."

"Good." A.J. laughed. "I told the others 'The Legend' was back in town, but they said they wouldn't believe me until they'd seen you with their own eyes."

"It will be good to see all of you, too," Luke assured him.

And he'd find out once and for all if the rustlers were his old rodeo pals or if they knew who else it could be.

AFTER WORK, SAMMY Jo rehearsed what she'd say in her head as she made her way over to the Collinses'. But every variation of the lines she came up with was sure to take the smile off Luke's face—not something she relished seeing. Especially since they hadn't seen each other alone since they'd kissed.

Maybe if she worked with Luke's horse some more, it would help. Phantom needed all the training he could get. Besides, Luke was still busy working on the cabins. He hadn't even known she'd come by earlier with the trailer.

Sammy Jo and Bree worked with Phantom for almost an hour. Coaxing him to drop his front knees down into the bow position was easy. Convincing the horse not to roll over and scratch his back, as was the natural tendency, was a lot harder.

"Sammy Jo! Bree!" Luke called, running toward them as fast as his cane would allow with Delaney by his side. "I think the rustlers are back."

Sammy Jo's gaze shot toward their property line. Had the men driven through her gate again? Used her land as a way to enter or exit?

Beside her, Bree let out a gasp. "Did you call the sheriff?"

"Not yet," Delaney said, her voice breathless. "We wanted to check with you first, but we've searched everywhere and can't find him."

"Who?" Bree demanded, her face now as distressed as theirs.

With a jolt, Sammy Jo understood what was going on and her stomach clenched. "The rehab horse."

Luke's brows shot up in surprise. "You know where he is?"

Sammy Jo nodded.

"Oh, thank God," Delaney exclaimed. "We thought he'd been stolen and poor Luke had no idea how he was going to break the news to you."

He'd been concerned how to tell *her*? Sammy Jo looked straight at Luke, her rehearsed lines forgotten, and said simply, "I had to take him back to camp."

Luke held her gaze a moment, then gave her a nod as if no further explanation was necessary.

"You should have left a note on the dry-erase board or something," Delaney insisted. "When Luke went into the barn and saw the empty stall—"

"It's fine," Luke said, cutting her off. "At least we know the horse is safe."

"Luke, I'm so sorry," Sammy Jo said, stepping toward him. "I—"

"Oh, my, look at the time," Bree interrupted. "Delaney, shouldn't we go feed the horses their dinner?"

Del cast Sammy Jo a quick smile. "Yes, we should."

"Need help?" Luke asked.

Bree took Delaney's arm and pulled her away. "Nope. We've got it. We'll see you two later."

The Adam's apple in Luke's throat bobbed up and down, and the anxious expression he'd worn when he and Del first arrived returned to his face.

Slowly, his head turned . . . and Sammy Jo stared at him, not daring to breathe or say anything until Luke made the first move. And for a moment, all they did was look at each other.

Then Luke reached out, took her hand, and grinned. "Want to go on a trail ride?"

LUKE LED PHANTOM toward the barn to gather his tack.

"But how will you get on?" Sammy Jo insisted, following behind. "Phantom doesn't always bow. What if he tries to roll? We haven't trained him with the saddle on yet. What if he rolls over on your leg?"

"He won't roll," Luke assured her.

"How do you know?"

"Because he won't even think about it."

"What do you mean?"

He placed the saddle over the horse's back and tightened the girth. "I'm not going to have him bow."

"Then how are you going to get on?"

He met her gaze and grinned. "I'll mount up in the staging area."

"Use the raised decks? But you said they were for—"

"Greenhorns and gimps, I know," Luke said, leading Phantom out the barn door.

Sammy Jo retrieved her own horse, who she'd ridden over and placed in one of their outside paddocks, then rejoined him.

"What changed your mind?" she asked, watching him hobble up the platform and slide onto Phantom's back from above.

He gave her a direct look. "You."

"Me?" Her sweet face looked more flustered than ever.

"You are the one who convinced me to ride," he explained. "And you were right. Once I get my leg over the saddle and give it time for the muscle to relax, the pain isn't so bad."

She hesitated. "About those kisses . . ."

"Yes?" he prompted, his gaze drifting toward her mouth.

She rode Tango up beside him. "Well . . . after you saved me—"

"I had to save you," Luke said, his pulse racing from her close proximity. "What would your father have said, if I didn't? We don't need to give him another excuse to be mad at the Collinses or he might not approve our final inspection."

"Oh, is *that* why you rescued me?" she teased, her smile infectious. "What about the kiss? Was that to appease my father, too? Because I don't think he'd be happy about that."

"Counteracts saving you, doesn't it?"

"Yes, it does," she agreed.

Luke held her gaze. "But it doesn't really matter what he thinks, only what you think, right?"

"I suppose."

"So what do *you* think?" he pressed.

Sammy Jo's face lit up with a big smile. "Between you riding in like the infamous Legend of Fox Creek and then kissing me . . . well, I'm thinking you're trying to win my heart."

Luke grinned. "Oh, you do, do you?"

She was pretending to be as self-assured and flirtatious as always, but he saw the uncertainty in her eyes as her expression turned earnest and she asked, "*Are* you trying to win my heart?"

In answer, Luke leaned toward her and cupped her chin with his hand. "Whatever it takes, sweetheart."

Her eyes widened. "Does that mean—"

He brushed his mouth over hers, then affirmed, "I'll do whatever it takes."

Chapter Eleven

HE CALLED ME *"sweetheart"*! Sammy Jo had been so scared at first because Luke didn't indicate anything had changed between them. But after that brief kiss in the staging area, they rode out across the fields and stopped under a tree with low-hanging limbs near the riverbed. The green leaves formed a natural umbrella canopy, and under the false pretense of needing a moment of shade, Luke leaned toward her and kissed her again.

There was no doubt in her mind now. Luke *wanted* to kiss her. Again and again . . . which meant . . . he must be falling for her!

"Careful there, cowboy," she teased. "Don't lean so far forward that you fall off your horse."

"If I do, I'll just have to stay out here all night," Luke said, his tone playful. "And you could stay with me."

"Except we're not supposed to date," she reminded him.

"For how long?"

She smiled. "My father didn't specify, but I think he meant forever."

Luke drew toward her again. "But he didn't specify."

"No, he didn't," she said, her voice breathless as Luke gave her another light kiss.

"He didn't say anything against *this*?" Luke coaxed.

She shook her head.

"Then we won't date," he said, his voice husky. "We'll just kiss."

Sammy Jo laughed. "I never imagined in a million years you'd ever talk to me this way."

He placed a light kiss on the end of her nose. "What way?"

She smiled. "Like the sweet-talkin' cowboy I've always dreamed about."

"Does your dream cowboy have long hair and a limp?"

"He does now," she said, and then added, "but both of those things can change. Your hair can be cut and your limp fixed with the surgery."

"What's wrong with the hair?"

She tucked the locks falling over his forehead back under his hat. "I have trouble seeing your eyes and can't tell if you're looking at me."

"Trust me." He let out a soft chuckle. "I'm always looking at you. Even if I pretend I'm not."

Sammy Jo closed her eyes as Luke's mouth drew toward hers again. He was warm and soft and her head swam dizzily as he deepened the kiss. His arm tightened around her, drawing her even closer, until she feared *she* might be the one to fall out of the saddle. Especially when her horse shifted beneath her.

She broke away from Luke and caught her balance. "Whoa, Tango. Easy, boy."

The horse tensed and pricked his ears forward. A moment later, Luke's horse did the same, and a loud engine roared to life somewhere in the neighboring field.

"Is that coming from the Owenses'?" she asked. "I thought they're supposed to be away for the rest of the summer."

Luke frowned. "They are."

He rode out from beneath the tree and she followed. The sound grew louder the closer they rode toward the property line.

"Sounds like a tractor," she told him.

Luke shook his head and pointed. "Bulldozer."

"What?" She gasped as she focused in on the bright orange machine pushing against the wall of the Owens barn. A moment later there was a resounding high-pitched crash as the entire building collapsed. Several figures who stood on the sidelines clapped. She squinted, trying to get a better look at them. "Who are those people?"

"I don't know the man with the yellow hard hat," Luke said as they rode forward. Then he cast her a look of warning. "But the couple with him is Winona Lane . . . and your father."

"My father? What would he be doing over there?"

Sure enough, when the group turned, she saw it was him. And her father saw her too . . . with Luke. She knew the moment he recognized them from the way his dark brows drew together and his cheerful expression dropped into a deep scowl.

Luke tipped his hat in greeting toward the town posse, introduced himself, and inquired, "What's going on here?"

The man in the hard hat identified himself as Marc Hughes and said, "Tearing the whole place down to make room for a new housing development, Fox Creek Estates."

"What about the Owenses?" Luke demanded, the shock of the announcement evident in his voice.

"They sold me the property last week," Mr. Hughes informed them.

Luke narrowed his gaze. "Looking for any more land for your project?"

The guy grinned. "Not at the moment, no. But after I get done with this piece, I'll make you an offer for your ranch if you're interested in selling."

"We're not interested," Luke said, his tone bitter. "We'll never sell Collins Country Cabins."

"Never say 'never,' " Sammy Jo's father interjected.

"Dad!" she exclaimed. "What's your part in all this?"

"Mr. Hughes wanted to consult with me about zoning before filing building permits," her father said. "And he wanted to talk to Winona about a loan from the bank."

The woman smiled and Sammy Jo asked, "Shouldn't that be done *at the bank*?"

"Yes, of course," Winona assured her. "Mr. Hughes has to submit a formal proposal for approval. These are just preliminary talks."

A truck drove up the driveway and parked beside them. The same truck Sammy Jo had seen in the Collinses' field the night she was threatened. Harley Bennett stepped out.

"Nice bruise on your right cheek," Luke drawled.

Sammy Jo glanced at Luke and saw him glaring at Harley, his jaw drawn tight. Harley glared back at him, and when Sammy Jo glanced at the placement of the bruise on Harley's face, she realized he'd been the man Luke had tackled to the ground and punched. He'd been the one who had held the gun to her chest.

"I see you got your truck back," she said, her voice pinched with the anger welling up within her.

"Yeah," Harley said, glancing around at the rest of them. "The sheriff found it along the side of the road and returned it to me just this morning."

"Lucky you," she said, pursing her lips. "No doubt she's ready for some more action."

Harley slapped his hand on the hood of the pickup. "She sure is. Hey, Uncle Marc, what do you think of my three-quarter-ton gal?"

Mr. Hughes gave a nod of approval and Sammy Jo glanced from him back to Harley. *"Uncle?"*

LATER THAT NIGHT, Sammy Jo slammed the pan of pork chops down on the picnic table behind their house. "Don't you see?" she exclaimed. "Harley Bennett is working for his uncle and trying to sabotage Collins Country

Cabins so they'll either be forced to sell or lose their land to the bank."

"The only thing I saw," her father said, stabbing a piece of the savory meat with his fork and shoving it onto his plate, "was you with that . . . that *Collins* boy."

"Luke," Sammy Jo corrected. "His name is *Luke*."

"You promised me you wouldn't date him if I gave the Collinses the permits," he said, seizing a baked potato off one of the other plates she'd brought outside on the tray.

"We haven't been on a single date," she said, her cheeks growing warm. "We were exercising the horses."

"Before you left the Owens property this afternoon, I heard him call you 'sweetheart' three times."

Sammy Jo smiled. "He did, didn't he?"

"That's *not* funny," her father said, glaring at her. "You gave me your word."

"Like you gave your word to Mom when you stood at the altar the day you married and vowed to love her *till death do us part*?"

"Don't bring your mother into this."

"Why not? Do you think I like seeing you with that Winona woman any more than you like seeing me with Luke?"

"I didn't think you had a problem with her."

Sammy Jo raised her chin. "And I didn't think you had a problem with Luke, just his father."

"I *don't* have a problem with Luke. *Unless* . . ." he said, scrunching up his face and issuing her a warning look, "I hear him call you 'sweetheart' one more time."

LUKE DODGED FOUR heavyset middle-aged guests meandering down the path, circled the group of giggling girls from Travel Light Adventures, and wove around a couple wayward toddlers. Bursting through the front door of his family's house, he almost tripped his ma with his cane.

"What the blazes is wrong with you?" his father demanded.

"Dad, one of the rustlers is Harley Bennett. I'm sure of it."

His father nodded. "I suspected as much."

"But do you have proof?" Bree asked. "You know the sheriff won't do anything without concrete evidence."

"He had a bruise in the same spot I punched the one holding Sammy Jo," he replied. "His truck was at the scene even if he claims he wasn't."

"Not enough," Delaney said, shaking her head. "But I installed the security cameras up on the roofs of the house, the horse barn, and hay barn, and the top stands in the arena."

"What about the cabins?" Luke asked.

"There's one facing the whole row closest to the house and the camera from the horse barn shows the cabins on the other side. After dinner I can take you into the office and show you the views on the computer screen."

"Ryan helped her install them," Bree said, smiling as she said her fiancé's name. "They made sure the new cameras are hidden in places the rustlers can't see them."

"I hope so," Ma fretted. "We don't want them to set any more fires."

"Or steal any more cattle," Luke's dad added. "We

can't advertise weekend roundups if we don't have any cows."

"These rustlers need to be caught," Bree agreed. "I had a call today from Mr. Hamilton, the father of the bride paying for the big August wedding. It seems someone tipped him off and told him we've been having some trouble. I spent over two hours assuring him that no one in his wedding party would be in danger."

Ma sunk into a chair at the dining room table and used her hand to fan herself. "Oh, my. If we lose that contract—"

Bree groaned. "Yeah, I know. This whole mess makes me wonder if I should postpone my own engagement party until *after* our guest's August wedding is complete."

"Don't you dare!" Grandma warned her. "We could all use some happy celebrations around here. You can't let those rustlers ruin your plans."

"You're right, Grandma," Bree said, raising her chin. "I just wish we knew what they want."

"We do," Luke informed them. "A Mr. Marc Hughes bought the Owens ranch next door and had a bulldozer knock their house, barns, and everything else flat."

"It's true," his father said, backing him up. "I went over as soon as I heard the noise and talked with the fella myself."

"He's also Harley Bennett's uncle," Luke added, "and plans to build a housing development. *Next door.* Where there's no river, no grove of trees, nothing compared to what we have here. I'd bet anything he wants Harley and his friends to drive us out so he can buy our land cheap and build even more houses."

"But the Owenses have been our neighbors for years!" Ma exclaimed. "I know Mrs. Owens mental health is in question, but I never thought they'd ever sell."

"They might need money to cover her medical expenses," Delaney said, wiping her young daughter's hands at the sink.

Meghan ran toward Luke and tugged on his pant leg. "Onkle Uke, you want to play hide 'n' go seek?"

Luke remembered it was his turn that night to keep watch, and the fact he now knew at least one of the men he was seeking to expose filled him with new resolve.

"Yes, Meggie," he said. "I *do*." Then he glanced over at his sister. "Don't you worry, Bree. Next time the rustlers return, we'll be ready for them."

SAMMY JO PULLED off her sheets hoping the lively tune "Dancing with My Cowboy," which she'd set as her cell phone alarm, wouldn't wake her father.

She glanced at the time—1:45 a.m. She only had fifteen minutes before she needed to meet Luke for the second watch at the Collinses'. Even though everyone had split into teams and rotated shifts, four hours of sleep every other night was taking its toll and giving each of them dark circles beneath their eyes.

Turning on a small, dim light on her dresser, she dabbed a touch of cream-colored foundation beneath her lower lids to brighten her complexion. Not that Luke was likely to see it in the dark. But who knew? What if they went into the house for breakfast in the morning? She'd still want to look her best.

Luke might not see her too well until dawn, but he'd be able to smell her. Smiling, she sprayed a few short squirts of apple blossom scented perfume on her wrists and collarbone.

Her handsome cowboy might also want to kiss her. In fact, she was counting on it. Grabbing the tube of strawberry lip gloss, she opened the cap and proceeded to apply it to her mouth so that her lips would be silky soft.

Next she searched her closet for clothes. Ditching the pajamas, she pulled on a pair of dark jeans and a black T-shirt with the intention of blending into the dark night. And even though she hoped Luke would wrap his arms around her to keep her warm, Montana nights could be cool, so she also took a thin, lightweight black jacket off the hook and draped it over her arm.

Slipping into her boots, she went over to her bedroom window, raised the screen, and was about to climb out when she heard her father call her name.

Oh, no. She hesitated, wondering if she should reply or just hurry out over the windowsill and escape while she still could without having to answer a bunch of questions.

Her father had said he would *like* her to stay in at night but it hadn't been a direct order, and besides, at twenty-seven years old, she could do as she pleased without her father's permission. It's just sometimes . . . he disagreed with that line of thought. To him, she was still his little girl. Which was another reason, besides being lonely, that she wished she wasn't an only child. His expectations wouldn't be nearly so high if she had a couple extra brothers or sisters like Bree, Luke, and Delaney.

"Sammy Jo."

He didn't want her to spend time with Luke; that's why he was calling her at this hour of the night. But then, why didn't he come into her bedroom and face her outright?

"Sammy Jo!"

He called her name louder this time, with more force, and she stiffened with alarm. Something about his voice didn't sound right.

"Dad?" She went out into the hallway and glanced into his bedroom but his bed was empty.

"Here."

She spun around toward the bathroom . . . and saw him kneeling on the floor in front of the toilet. "Are you sick?"

Turning on the light, she caught sight of his pale face as he nodded.

"What do you want me to do? Get you some towels? An antacid? A can of ginger ale?"

He grimaced and bent over, pressing his hand against his stomach. Then he looked up at her with a pleading expression and asked, "Take me to the emergency room?"

Chapter Twelve

LUKE DISMISSED DELANEY and Zach Tanner and took their position in the shadows outside the hay barn. With the cows locked up tight inside and the added security cameras, he didn't see how the rustlers could possibly steal any more of their cows without getting caught. But he did look forward to spending some private time with Sammy Jo.

His gaze kept drifting toward the property line and he wondered what was taking her so long. Had she overslept? He should have gone to her house to escort her across the field. He didn't like the idea of her coming over alone in the middle of the night. What if the rustlers caught up with her again?

His gut wrenched tight as his mind tormented him with images of the possible things they could do to her. He couldn't let them touch her. Not *his* gal. For if they hurt her, they hurt him. And he'd hunt them down and give them a new legend they wouldn't soon forget.

A soft shuffle sounded behind him and he blew out a sigh of relief and spun around, planning to remind her of the danger these men posed.

Except it wasn't Sammy Jo. A masked figure with a strong arm punched him in the face, knocking him backward. Luke tried to recover his balance to return the blow, but his bad knee buckled under the unexpected shift in weight. He landed on the ground and the impact set his leg on fire with a pain far worse than any he'd experienced with the rehab horse.

For a moment he couldn't see, the pain was so intense. And when his vision cleared it was only to witness a fist coming at him a second time.

"Andy Macpherson has a message for ya," his attacker wearing the black ski mask taunted. "Stay away from Sammy Jo or you'll lose a lot more than cattle."

Another dark figure appeared from out of the trees and Luke groaned, realizing he was in trouble. But when the one who spoke raised his fist to punch him a third time, the newcomer intervened by grabbing his attacker's arm.

Luke squinted through the darkness and realized the guy who saved him was the new kid they'd hired to work on the cabins. Devin punched his opponent and pulled off the guy's mask.

"Harley Bennett," Luke growled, rolling over. He reached for his cane, which had fallen from his hand and landed several feet away.

Harley gave Devin a violent shove against the barn wall and ran off the same way he'd come.

Devin bounced off the wall and rubbed the back of his head. "Do you want me to go after him?"

Luke shook his head. "Nah. It won't matter now—we know who he is."

The sound of running feet made them both look toward the new men approaching. Luke hoisted himself up with his cane, and calculated the odds of two against four.

You need to get your knee fixed. The words repeated themselves in his mind, urging him to call the doctor for an appointment. He didn't look forward to his upcoming operation, but the surgery couldn't be as bad as getting his body smashed by a band of half-wit rustlers like Harley Bennett.

Then a voice called out, "Luke?"

It was Ryan. Which meant the other three figures must be his brothers—Dean, Josh, and Zach.

"Glad to see ya," Luke assured them, "but what are you all doing out here? I thought we were doing shifts?"

"Not tonight," Ryan said, laying a hand on his shoulder. "Bree got a frantic call from Sammy Jo a half hour ago saying she couldn't make it."

"Couldn't make it?" Luke repeated. "Why not?"

Ryan shrugged. "She didn't say, but Bree thought something suspicious might be going on and didn't want you out here alone."

"Why didn't Sammy Jo call me?" Luke demanded.

"She did," Josh answered, "but you're in the dead cell zone."

"Who's this?" Dean asked, gesturing toward Devin.

"New hire to help me with the cabins," Luke explained. "He helped chase off Harley Bennett, too."

"What are you doing out here?" Zach asked the kid. "Did Bree call you, too?"

Devin shook his head. "No. I was camping out in one of the unfinished cabins so I could get an early start on the roof tomorrow—I mean, *this morning*—before it gets too hot. But I couldn't sleep with everyone walking around all over the place."

Luke gave him a nod. "Glad you're a light sleeper. And, Devin—thanks."

The kid shrugged. "No problem."

A scream from the direction of the house turned their attention.

"Sounded like Delaney," Luke said, alarm coursing up his spine anew.

The Tanner brothers ran toward the Collinses' house, and when Luke caught up with them, the rest of his family was already assembled outside on the front porch.

"What happened?" Luke demanded.

"I went to the kitchen for a glass of water, and one of the rustlers ran right past me and out the door!" Delaney said, her voice choked with emotion.

"Somehow they *knew* we'd all be outside looking for you," Bree told him. "Even Ma, Dad, and Grandma were outside the house when it happened."

"Luke, your . . . your face is bleeding," Ma said, her voice rising higher with each word. "Did they hurt you?"

He ignored the pain still throbbing in his knee and

gave his mother a half grin so she wouldn't worry. "No, but they tried."

"I think this time they used Luke as a distraction instead of a fire," Ryan warned.

Luke's father frowned. "But they didn't steal any cows."

Bree scowled. "No, but they stole a fistful of cash from the office."

"And my bingo money from the cookie jar," Grandma added.

Luke's ma broke down in tears. *"And my purse!"*

SAMMY JO STOOD by her father in the hospital room awaiting his prognosis. He'd complained his stomach ached, and when he'd arrived in the emergency room, he'd actually emptied the contents of his stomach in a bucket the nurses shoved under his chin. He looked better since that episode, but her father still appeared pale and weak.

"I'd say he has a case of mushroom intolerance," the doctor announced, coming through the door to join them.

Her father shook his head. "I didn't eat any mushrooms."

Sammy Jo frowned. "Dad, what did you have for dinner?"

"Winona brought over some homemade beef stew."

"She must have put some mushrooms in with the other ingredients," the doctor surmised.

Sammy Jo's dad shook his head. "No. *Impossible*. It

must be something else. Winona *knows* I have bad reactions to mushrooms."

"Andy," the doctor said in a calm, gentle voice. "There were mushrooms in the bucket you got sick in."

After the doctor went back out, Sammy Jo got a text on her cell phone from Bree.

Rustlers returned. One came after Luke. Knew he'd be alone. How would they know that?

Sammy Jo glanced at her father and back at Bree's text. *Winona!* The old, crabby banker woman must have given her father the stew on purpose . . . knowing that she would have to take him to the doctor . . . and wouldn't be able to go over to the Collinses' to protect her man!

Sammy Jo's fingers furiously typed the keypad. *Is he okay?*

Bruised ego. Bruised jaw. Knee not so good.

Oh, no! Sammy Jo's chest tightened. *Not his knee!*

LUKE JOLTED AWAKE, sprang off his bed, and assumed a guarded position off to the side of his interior window. He'd barely slept, but he couldn't have imagined the scuffling sound.

Nope. He didn't. There it was again. Something was climbing *up* the same drainpipe he slid down when using one of his escape routes. And it wasn't an animal. Had Harley Bennett come back? Did he think to finish him off for good this time?

Luke stepped forward to peer out the window, but jumped back when he realized the climber was almost up to the ledge. A second later, a gloved hand raised the window screen and grabbed hold of the inside sill.

Not wasting a second, Luke lunged forward on his good leg, grabbed the intruder, and hauled him through the window and pinned him on the floor.

"Luke!"

He froze and glanced at the long locks of curly dark hair. "Sammy Jo? What do you think you're doing?"

She rolled over and sat up. "I heard you were hurt and I had to see you."

"Yeah, but you could have used the front door."

"I didn't want to wake anyone up. I know it's been a rough night. I haven't even slept yet and it's almost dawn."

"If you had fallen," Luke said, glancing out his second-story window, "you could have been hurt."

Sammy Jo waved her hand as if to brush off his concern. "We used to climb that drainpipe all the time when we were kids."

"But you're not—" He glanced down at her chest and then his gaze dropped lower to her nicely curved hips. "You're not . . . a kid anymore."

"I haven't changed *that* much. Besides, you're the one I'm concerned about," she said, reaching up and tracing each one of the bruises on his face with her fingers. "It's all my fault. I never should have left you alone."

"Why did you?"

"My father was sick and needed me to drive him to the hospital."

"Tonight, of all nights?" Luke asked. "He must have been faking."

"No, he wasn't. The doctor said he had a reaction to the mushrooms Winona Lane put in his stew. She knew he can't eat mushrooms and she had access to the key to the gate the rustlers drove through. I think she's one of them."

"That's the woman who's always pestering my ma at the bank," Luke said, taking Sammy Jo in his arms. "And you said she and your dad are dating, right?"

Sammy Jo nodded.

"Your father has had a lifetime feud with my parents and even went so far as to delay filing our permits. And he, too, had access to the key to the gate."

Sammy Jo sucked in her breath. "My father is innocent. He wouldn't intentionally make himself sick."

"Are you sure?"

"Positive."

Luke tightened his arms around her. "Then why did Harley give me a punch from your father and warn me to stay away from you?"

"Harley made that up!" Sammy Jo exclaimed in a sharp whisper. "He made that up because *he* wants me to stay away from you. When he saw us together at the Owens ranch, he must have got jealous because *he* wants to date me."

"I'm not going to let him near you," Luke promised.

Sammy Jo kissed the top of his chin. "And how are you going to do that?"

Luke bent his head and kissed her warm, inviting mouth. "I'm going to keep you here in my arms 24/7."

"And never let me go?" Sammy Jo teased.

Luke grinned. "Not ever."

Sammy Jo leaned back and smiled up at him. "Why, Luke Collins, if my ears didn't deceive me, that *almost* sounds like a marriage proposal!"

Marry Sammy Jo? They hadn't even officially dated, but as he leaned in to kiss her again, the thought took root. Who knew? Maybe someday . . . he *would* ask her.

DESPITE THE SWEET-TALK and a multitude of kisses that sent her head spinning, Sammy Jo convinced Luke he really did have to let her go home so she could check on her father. The sun's rays peeping over the horizon brightened the fields and, when she arrived at her door, illuminated the face of the woman walking toward her.

Sammy Jo tensed. "Winona, what are you doing here?"

"One of my friends who is a nurse at the hospital called to tell me she saw Andy in the emergency room and I was so upset I had to come over right away to see if he was all right."

"He will be now, no thanks to you," Sammy Jo said, narrowing her gaze. "You put mushrooms in his stew!"

"No, I didn't," Winona protested, her eyes wide. "I know how sensitive he is to those things. Please let me in to see him?"

Sammy Jo shook her head. "No, I think it's best you leave."

"Haven't *you* ever made a mistake?" Winona pleaded.

Yeah. The biggest mistake she'd made was leaving Luke alone. She should have called someone over at the

Collinses' to come take her father to the emergency room. Luke's family might be feuding with her father, but she could trust they'd help out in an emergency and never do anything to put him in danger.

"I have to explain," Winona cried. "I have to tell him it wasn't my fault. I didn't know there were mushrooms in the stew."

Sammy Jo frowned. "Weren't you the one who made it?"

Winona shook her head. "No, it was Loretta Collins. She brought over some stew to thank me for helping her access her safe deposit box."

Luke's ma made the stew? Sammy Jo eyed the woman in front of her with suspicion. "Go home, Mrs. Lane. If my father wants to speak to you, he'll call you later after he wakes."

Once the woman saw Sammy Jo was not going to let her inside, she turned and left, a deep scowl etched upon her face.

"Who was that?" Sammy Jo's father called as she passed his bedroom on the way to her own.

"Winona."

"Here? Now? What did she want?"

"She wanted to see you," Sammy Jo informed him. "But I said no. She also claims Loretta Collins made the stew."

Her father raised his head off the pillow. "She's lying."

"I think so, too," Sammy Jo admitted. "But how do you know for sure?"

He motioned her to step into the room and sit on the

edge of his bed. "Our junior year of high school, Loretta and I both ended up in the local doctor's office the same day. It was the first time we really got to know each other." He paused and a faint smile touched his lips. "Apparently we'd eaten the pizza in the school cafeteria and hadn't realized there had been mushrooms hidden beneath the cheese and other toppings."

"She's allergic to mushrooms, too?"

Her father nodded. "Worse than me. If her skin comes into contact with them, she breaks out in a rash and can't breathe. Believe me when I tell you Loretta would *never* put mushrooms in any dish. Even for a friend."

"I doubt Winona is her friend," Sammy Jo said, raising her chin. "Especially if Winona is working with the rustlers to tear Collins Country Cabins apart."

Chapter Thirteen

AFTER SLEEPING IN to recuperate from the excitement the night before, Luke and his family gathered around the kitchen table for breakfast, even though it was nearing noon.

"The PI we hired has tracked Susan and Wade Randall from state to state and says they're headed back to Montana," Bree reported. "The money they embezzled from us must be running out because they tried to rob a bank in Wyoming, but they got scared off before they could go through with it."

"Why would they head back to Montana?" Luke's father asked. "What do they have here that's worth the risk of getting caught?"

"Help?" Luke suggested. "When Mrs. Owens confessed to working with Susan and Wade last month, she threatened there might be others. How much money did the rustlers take when they slipped into the house last night?"

Bree frowned. "Not much. When I went in the office to recalculate what was in the cash box, I realized there was only thirty-five dollars missing."

"Those thieves stole twelve dollars from my cookie jar," Grandma complained. "Now how am I going to play bingo this week?"

"Twelve dollars isn't that much," Delaney assured her, and quoted back one of the elder woman's own sayings, "and '*you can't lose what you don't have,*' right, Grandma?"

"Right, sweet pea," Grandma grumbled. "But I didn't plan to lose. I was hoping to win a bundle of money this week and use it to save our ranch."

Luke turned toward his mother. "How much money was in your purse?"

"None."

"Then what was the point?" Luke's father barked, shaking his fist. "Why would the rustlers risk being caught for a measly forty-seven dollars? Why didn't they steal the computers or TVs or the new horse tack Delaney just bought?"

"Or the cows or horses?" Delaney added.

Luke set his jaw. They didn't come over just to throw a few punches his way either. "They've been playing us this whole time," he said, pushing away his unfinished plate of eggs and toast. "First they set a fire to distract us while they steal our cows, but they only take six. Why not more? Then they surprise us by coming from the opposite direction and steal a few more. Next they send Harley to distract me and pull all of you outside so they can sneak into our house to steal forty-seven dollars? There's got to be something bigger they're after. Something worth a whole lot more."

"Like what? Ma's 'valuables'?" Bree joked.

Ma sucked in her breath. "Oh, no!"

Luke grinned. "Don't worry, Ma, your valuables are locked up tight in your safe deposit box at the bank. They can't touch them."

"They could if they had the key." A look of horror crossed her face. "I usually keep the key in my purse."

Bree gasped. "That's why they stole your purse?"

Ma nodded. "Except I took the key out after my last episode with the bank's assistant manager, Mrs. Lane, and put it in the zipped pocket of my jacket for safekeeping so I'd have the key on me at all times."

"Why? What happened with Mrs. Lane?" Delaney asked, looking confused.

"I don't trust that nosy woman," Ma explained. "She has the master key to open the security boxes, but she doesn't have the key that opens my private lockbox *inside* the security box and I think that drives her nuts. She'd love more than anything to know what kind of valuables I have."

Luke glanced at a new text message from Sammy Jo on his cell phone. "Winona Lane could be working with the rustlers. Andy Macpherson told Sammy Jo that Winona's been short on money since her husband passed away last year."

"Our ranch managers also heard you say you had 'valuables' tucked into your safe deposit box," Luke's father reminded Ma. "And who knows how many people they might have told."

"What if they are all working together? Against us?" Ma asked, the color draining from her face.

Luke's father grunted. "Wouldn't surprise me. They may want your 'valuables' thinking it will cause us financial loss, but we all know what they really want. *Our ranch.*"

"No," Luke said, shaking his head. "They want the money they'll get by *selling* our ranch to that land developer next door. Del, did you review the surveillance tape?"

"Yeah, but all it caught was Harley hitting you from behind."

"We'll start with him," Luke decided. "If the sheriff brings Harley Bennett in on charges of assault, maybe we can find out who he's working with."

SAMMY JO HELPED each of the nine-year-old girls from the horse camp decorate their row of stalls at the Fox Creek Fairgrounds. The annual town fair would bring in hundreds of people this week, including three prominent judges who would award ribbons to the group with the best presentation.

Their main competition appeared to be the girls from the 4-H club across the aisle, but her girls' posters educating the public on horse safety was more colorful than theirs.

"I think we have a fair shot," Sammy Jo said to the expectant group of faces surrounding her.

"Will you sleep here with us?" one of the girls asked.

"No, I'm needed somewhere else, but Jesse will," Sammy Jo said, smiling at the camp owner.

"Lucky me." Jesse groaned. "I brought a sleeping bag, but it'll be nothing like my bed at home."

"Which is why you and the girls need to stay," Sammy Jo teased. "The stalls at the fairgrounds aren't anything like our horses' beds at home either. Strange noises, strange smells."

Jesse nodded. "I told the girls we'll have to give them lots of attention throughout the night so they aren't too panicked during their performance in the arena tomorrow."

"I wish you all lots of luck," Sammy Jo said, giving Jesse and the girls a big smile.

"You, too," Jesse replied, and motioned behind her. "Here comes your sweet-talkin' cowboy."

Sammy Jo turned toward the tall, good-looking man coming down the aisle. "Luke! What are you doing here?"

"I talked to Ryan and his brothers," he said, his tone filled with excitement. "They said all cattle shipments are on hold till after the fair because of the amount of traffic coming in."

Sammy Jo caught her breath. "You think your cows could still be here in Fox Creek?"

"Maybe," Luke said, and tipped his hat in greeting toward Jesse and the throng of girls still decorating the stalls with rolls of blue and white streamers. "I checked the holding pens at the auction house while the sheriff brought Harley in for questioning."

"And?" she prompted.

"They were empty. But then," he continued, his eyes taking on a sudden gleam, "I met with A.J. and my old rodeo pals at the café and they said they've heard rumors some of our stolen cattle might be hidden in with some of the others here at the fairgrounds."

Sammy Jo glanced all around her. "Here?"

"What do they look like?" Jesse asked, raising her brows.

"Black Angus," Luke told her. "A dozen of them branded with a 'C' on their rear flank."

"What kind of 'C'?" one of Sammy Jo's girls asked. "A big 'C' or a little 'c'?"

Luke glanced at the child and grinned. "Don't they both look pretty much the same?"

"No," said another. "She means is it like this?" The girl curled her hand to form the letter. "Or smaller?"

"The size of your hand," Luke clarified.

"Sometimes," said a different girl, "if you fill it in, a 'C' can look like an 'O.'"

Sammy Jo's gaze darted toward Luke. "We saw some cows here with an 'O' this morning. I assumed they were what was left of the Owens stock after they sold their property."

Luke took her hand and pulled her away from the others. "Show me."

Sammy Jo led him toward the cattle barn, but as they searched through the herd, none of them were marked with a brand in the shape of an "O."

Except one. Sammy Jo gasped. "Look!"

They drew toward the roped-off area with the beef

cow and Sammy Jo touched the white freeze brand marking with her finger. "That little girl was right," she said, showing Luke her white thumb. "The rustlers filled the open side of the 'C' in with chalk!"

"I'll call the sheriff," Luke said, pulling out his phone. "The rustlers must have moved the others to a different location and we only have a few days to find them."

"We will," Sammy Jo said, reaching up to kiss him. "In the meantime, we'll load this one into a trailer and bring him home."

LUKE AWOKE TO an explosion and for a second he thought he was still in the army. He rolled out of bed, and lay low to the ground. His pulse raced and his breath came in short gasps. Then he realized he was on the hardwood floor of his own Fox Creek bedroom. Raising himself up to glance out his window into the sunlit field, he saw the ensuing puff of smoke rising from a circle of blackened earth and wondered if the rustlers had come back.

The night before they'd had a small victory. After he and Sammy Jo returned with the cow, everyone had been reenergized and had wanted to help keep watch. The rustlers came, but with the help of the Tanner brothers, and Sammy Jo, the Collinses had managed to scare the intruders off before they could steal anything. Even better, they were able to do it without rousing suspicion from their guests.

A few of the teen girls from Travel Light Adventures had come outside onto the front porch of their cabin and Ryan had yelled, "Stay in, we're chasing a bear."

None of the guests had ventured outside after that.

Luke hurried as best he could down the stairs, although his bum knee and use of his cane made the trek more difficult. A quick glance at the clock told him he'd slept in again. It was 9:45 in the morning, not the time of day he'd expect the rustlers to launch an attack. Especially with so many guests wandering around. Another explosion pierced the air as Luke made his way outside, and this time he could feel the vibrations in the ground beneath his feet.

Delaney ran out the door behind him. "Meghan? Where is she? I went to the bathroom and when I came out she was gone."

"She's right there," Luke said, pointing behind her. He scooped his little niece up with one arm and placed her on his shoulders.

"Is that who I think it is?" Del asked, pointing to the figure by the blast site and coming to an abrupt stop.

"*Grandma!*" Luke yelled. "What are you doing?"

Her white hair was tucked beneath the gray hard hat that his grandfather had worn during his days working as a miner in the nearby caves. The chin strap framed her soft round cheeks, and the light from the round headlamp shot straight toward his chest. She waved and gave them a big smile. "I'm testing a few sticks of my homemade dynamite."

Luke exchanged an exasperated glance with his sister, then turned back to the old woman and complained, "C'mon, really, Grandma?"

"It's too dangerous!" Delaney said, her eyes wide with alarm.

"Nonsense," Grandma argued. "Marshmallows aren't the only things I make well. Your granddaddy and I have been making our own homemade dynamite for near half a century. Comes in handy when I need to blow a stubborn root out of the garden."

"What if Meghan had wandered out here?" Delaney asked.

Grandma furrowed her wiry brows. "I can see plain as day she's right with you."

"You're going to scare the guests," Bree said, running out to join them. "We can't have them pack up and leave again."

"Better we lose a few guests than any more of our cows and hard-earned bingo money," Grandma told them. "We need to protect ourselves against those rustlers, and next time they come back throw a few of these sticks under their truck."

"She's serious!" Delaney exclaimed.

Luke grinned. "Grandma, I'm not sure that's legal."

"Nothing like old-fashioned firepower," Grandma said, waving one of the unlit sticks in her hand. "Luke, you used to *beg* me to give you some of these when you were younger."

His sisters glared at him and he ruefully admitted, "It's true."

"Handsome as he is, it doesn't look like the sheriff is doing much to help us," Grandma continued. "I figure we need to take matters into our own hands and deal with these rustlers once and for all."

Luke handed Meghan off to Delaney and walked forward to take the remaining sticks out of his grandma's hands. "Let me take care of these," he told her. "And let me worry about the rustlers."

"You have a plan?" his grandma asked, her expression hopeful.

"I do now," Luke said, and realized he had to take action before his eighty-year-old grandma landed them all in a heap of trouble.

The first item on Luke's to-do list was to pick up the phone and call for a doctor's appointment. His hand shook when he made the call, but after eight months of waiting, it only took two seconds to schedule the needed appointment for an updated exam and evaluation on his injured knee.

Somehow it made the second item on his to-do list even easier, and when he walked into the Macpherson living room to confront Sammy Jo's father, he didn't even break a sweat.

"Mr. Macpherson," he said, looking the startled man in the eye. "I want to date your daughter."

Andy threw down the newspaper he'd been reading and sprung out of his recliner onto his feet. *"No."*

"I'm not asking your permission," Luke warned. "I'm not sure exactly what the feud you have with my parents is about, but it has nothing to do with me and Sammy Jo."

"Rodeo is her life. She may have given it up for a season," Andy said, narrowing his gaze. "But I know she'll be right back out there again next year. You know how tight-knit the rodeo community is and you just aren't a part of that world anymore. Do you really think Sammy Jo would be happy dating a guy like you?"

"She says she wants to marry me," Luke said, standing firm.

Andy scowled. "She can do better than marry a cripple whose guest ranch is on the verge of going bankrupt. She only *thinks* she wants to marry you because she's known you longer than anyone and she's comfortable with you. But she doesn't love you. She just wants to marry to get her grandma's inheritance and figures . . . you'll do."

Luke did a double take and old fears from the past rose up to laugh at him and tell him he'd been *played*. Unwilling to believe it, he eyed Sammy Jo's father with suspicion. "Inheritance? What inheritance?"

Andy hesitated. "Her money won't save your ranch if that's what you're thinking."

That's *not* what he was thinking at all. His chest squeezed tight and for a moment he couldn't breathe. Had Sammy Jo tricked him? Had she only been *pretending* to care about him after all? She *had* brought up the subject of marriage pretty quick.

"I'd never marry for money," Luke assured her father.

Andy gave him a rueful grin. "Sammy Jo *would*. She'd give anything to be fully independent and get her own place instead of living with me. But she can't touch the money her grandmother left her till the day she marries."

"You're wrong," Luke said, his throat tight. "Money has nothing to do with our relationship."

"Are you sure?" Andy challenged. "Did she ever want

to date you before you came back to town? Did she ever show *any* sign that she was interested in you before? Or did she treat you like a . . . *younger brother*?"

Luke's gut twisted around as he chewed on her father's bitter words. He didn't want to believe him—he *wouldn't* believe him—until he talked to Sammy Jo himself. Still it was hard to quiet the questions raging within his head. One side of his brain said the guy was a liar, just trying to keep him and Sammy Jo apart. A logical move by a desperate father. But a small cold voice rose up from the other side and whispered, *What if it's true?*

Andy must have guessed from his expression he'd touched a nerve for the man gave him a broad smile. "Like I said, Sammy Jo doesn't love you. She's using you, just like you used her to get the permits your family needed to build the cabins. Isn't that the deal you made her?"

"Feelings *change*," Luke insisted.

"Yeah," Andy Macpherson scoffed. "Money does that to people."

Chapter Fourteen

SAMMY JO STOOD beside Bree in the center of Collins Country Cabins' brand-new gazebo looking up at the tall, peaked, wood-shingled ceiling.

"Can't you just see it?" Bree crooned. "This will make a wonderful stage for my engagement party."

"You'll want teal streamers, of course," Sammy Jo said, writing the item down on Bree's shopping list.

"Oh, yes," Bree agreed. "Teal and white, wrapped around each of these side pillars. The wedding invitations, bridesmaids' dresses, and the men's corsages will all be teal." She let out a happy sigh. "Ryan and I agreed we'd wait to marry early next summer, but now that I've been making plans, I wish it were sooner."

"Let's concentrate on your *engagement* party right now," Sammy Jo said, trying to get her friend to focus. "And you still have to get through that big one-hundred-guest wedding party coming in next week."

"We're ready for them," Bree said, spinning around with her arms flung wide. "Everyone has pitched in to help Devin, Luke, and my dad finish the cabins over the last few days. Even Ryan and his brothers, though it's time to harvest hay at their own ranch."

"Maybe now that the cabins are done, Luke will have more time to spend with *me*," Sammy Jo said with a smile.

"Maybe you're right," Bree teased. "Looks like he's coming for you now."

Sammy Jo turned her head, and sure enough, Luke had his gaze focused solely on her as he made his way forward. She gave him a big smile, but as he drew closer, she saw his clenched jaw and knew something wasn't right. *Not more trouble with the rustlers, I hope.*

"Bree, can I borrow your friend a minute?" Luke asked, his tone too tight for teasing.

"Only if I can have her back when you're done with her," Bree said, hands on her hips. "My engagement party is this weekend and I need my future maid of honor's help with the food list."

"I'll be back in a few minutes," Sammy Jo promised, and followed Luke over to the river where they could be alone. Maybe steal a few kisses?

The clear water trickled softly over the stones and she breathed in the clean earthen scent of the moist riverbank while waiting for Luke to greet her properly. But he didn't kiss her.

Instead, he demanded, "Do you have to marry before you can touch your inheritance from your grandmother?"

Sammy Jo froze. "Who told you that? *My father?*"

Luke nodded. "Is it true?"

"Yes. But . . . that's not why I'd marry."

"No?" He looked skeptical.

"For me it's all or nothing," she assured him. "I'll only marry for love."

"Your father has a different opinion."

"I bet he does," Sammy Jo said, and raised her chin. "But you didn't believe him, right?"

Luke didn't answer.

She gasped, a hole forming in her chest. "You *didn't*!"

"No," he said at last. "If I did, I wouldn't be here. But why didn't you tell me about the conditions for your inheritance?"

"Maybe because you never asked," she said, arching a brow.

"And flirting with me and kissing me has nothing to do with money?" he pressed.

" *'Money can't buy me love,'* " she quoted from the famous Beatles song.

"Money can't buy your father either," Luke said, his tone bitter. "Although I tried."

"You tried to bribe my father?" She stared at him, trying to figure out what was going on. "When?"

"About a half hour ago when he had the building inspector fail our cabin's final inspection for occupancy."

"Oh, no," she moaned. "Why would he *do* that?"

"Probably because I told him I wanted to ask you out on a date."

Her heart kicked up a beat and she smiled. "You did?"

Luke's expression relaxed. "Yeah. He didn't take it very well."

She smiled wider. "I bet he didn't." Then the gravity of the situation settled in her mind. If the Collinses didn't pass their final inspection, they wouldn't be allowed to use the guest cabins, which they *needed* in one week's time for the incoming wedding party or they'd be ruined. She pressed her lips together, then asked, "What can I do to help?"

Luke shook his head, then gave her a subtle half grin. "Persuade your father to change his mind?"

Sammy Jo stepped forward and took both his hands in hers. "Didn't we have this conversation before?"

"Yeah," Luke said, and his grin faded. "I guess we're back where we started."

"Not quite." Sammy Jo wrapped her arms around his waist. "Last time I couldn't do this." She reached up and touched his mouth with her lips. "Or this." She ran her fingers through the back of his long, honey-brown locks. "Or . . ."

"No way," Luke said, but although his tone remained hard, that warm, familiar gleam she loved returned to his eyes. "You are *not* cutting my hair."

SAMMY JO'S PROMISE to talk to her father didn't do much to alleviate Luke's fear that he'd ruined his family's chances of getting the final inspection on the cabins approved.

Of course his father didn't offer much support.

"Why on earth did you have to confront him now of all times!" Luke's dad shouted, waving his hands in the air. "Everyone around here worked their backsides off trying to get those cabins finished in time and then you go and blow it. You and Sammy Jo haven't dated for twenty-seven years. Couldn't you wait a little longer? At least until our inspection passed?"

Luke's guilty conscience dove down deep and left a sickening ache in the pit of his stomach. "You're right."

"Of all the half-brained, foolish things to do! What were you thinking? That he'd let you—" His father paused in the middle of his tirade and stared at him. "What did you say?"

Luke swallowed his pride and repeated the words he never thought he'd ever say to him. "You're right. I was wrong. And what I did was stupid."

His dad stared at him a moment as if thrown off track and not sure how to respond. "Well," he said after a moment, his voice gruff. "At least we got that cleared up."

After his father stormed off, Luke walked over to the cabins, the fresh scent of the wood shingles they'd used to side the exterior walls filling the air. And the scene with the building inspector replayed itself over again in his mind.

The county official had made a show of pulling out his measuring tape and glancing at the building plans. Then he grinned, his face smug, as he announced, "Sorry, but these cabins haven't been built to code."

Luke knew as soon as the inspector spoke that the accusation was false. He and his family had triple-checked the measurements to make sure they met all code requirements.

"Why don't you try it again?" Luke suggested, trying to keep his temper under control as he nodded toward the man's measuring tape. "Maybe you read the numbers wrong."

"Nope. I didn't," the inspector said, stashing the tape in his pocket. "Looks like you'll have to tear the whole cabin down and start over."

It was at that moment that Luke realized Andy had given them the permits to build the cabins, but *never* intended to let them pass inspection so that his family could use them.

All their efforts had been for nothing.

His ma came toward him, hand in hand with Meghan. "Luke, don't let your father upset you. He means well, but his manner isn't always . . ."

"Appropriate?" Luke prompted.

She sighed. "He's a wonderful man with a big heart locked up inside. I just wish you'd get to see it more often. I try not to get in the middle of these disputes. But that doesn't mean I don't care." His ma put her arm around his shoulders and said, "Sometimes I think you must wonder why I married him, but your father's a good man. Not only does he work hard to put food on the table but he protects us . . . or tries to, the best he can."

"Ma, you haven't always agreed with Dad's opinions, have you." It wasn't a question, but a statement.

She smiled. "No. Not always. I don't always approve

of the way he treats you three kids. I didn't approve of his feud with Andy Macpherson when it first started, and I still don't."

"Dad said the feud had something to do with an old love triangle?"

Ma nodded her head and sighed. "Andy and I dated for a while in high school. Then I met your dad, who was Andy's best friend at the time. One day they were walking me home, when a car ran off the road and hit a power pole right in front of us. Sparks came showering down and lit the neighboring field on fire. As you can imagine, since I'd barely escaped the fire that killed my parents when I was younger, I panicked.

"And while Andy tried to put out the flames, your dad did his best to comfort me and make me feel safe. I never went out with Andy again, and he got angry. He accused your dad of taking advantage of my emotions. All I know is that I fell in love with your dad that day and I've loved him every day since.

"But he and I started dating—your father never should have punched Andy in the face for bringing me flowers and trying to win me back, and neither one of them should have held a grudge against the other over something so silly for so long. After all, we're *neighbors!*"

Ma let out another sigh. "I expected them to forgive one another when Andy married and then had Sammy Jo, but . . . I guess they'd gotten so used to hating each other that they forgot how to be friends." She shook her head. "The point is . . . if anyone's to blame for this mess we're in, it's *them*, not you."

Luke leaned in and gave her a quick kiss on the cheek. "Thanks, Ma."

"Onkle Uke," Meghan called, tugging on the bottom of his pants. "Can you play with me now?"

Luke glanced down at his niece and grinned. "Yes, I sure can. In fact, I have a present for you."

"For me?"

Meghan giggled with delight as he fetched his old marshmallow shooter and a small bag of homemade marshmallows out of the first cabin and proceeded to show her how to use them. She had trouble at first, then as Luke knelt beside her and guided her hands, Meghan was able to shoot a marshmallow at Ryan and Cody as they walked past.

"Hey, what's that?" Cody asked, his interest piqued.

"Meghan, why don't you show him?" Luke said, nodding toward Ryan's seven-year-old boy.

Luke watched his niece stick the extra marshmallows in Ma's jacket pocket. Then Meghan took the marshmallow still in her small hands, placed it in the plastic tube, and showed Cody how the shooter worked as if she'd turned pro.

"Teaching her young," Ryan commented with amusement.

"Every kid should have one," Luke said, and his mind returned to the failed cabin inspection. *Just like every kid should be able to grow up in a place like this and not have to worry about where they'll be in another year or two.*

If they had to sell, Luke knew he'd be okay. He'd never needed much to survive. He could buy a new tent to sleep in. And Bree would be fine. She'd be gone soon anyway after she married Ryan. But what about Ma? Dad? Luke's grandma, who had lived here three-quarters of her life? What about Del and little Meggie who had nowhere else to go and no way to support themselves?

When he'd promised his family he'd build the cabins, what he really meant was that they could count on him. That he would pull his share to make the ranch succeed.

"Hey, watch out for the flying marshmallows," Ryan joked, pulling him back out of range. "Now look what you did. I'll have to get Cody one of those things. Just as soon as you agree to stand up with me when I marry your sister."

Luke leaned to the side to dodge another wayward marshmallow. "Be in your wedding party?"

"We'll pair you up with Sammy Jo," Ryan promised.

Luke frowned. "But if she's maid of honor, then that would make me—"

"My best man," Ryan affirmed.

"I'd be honored," Luke said, "but shouldn't you give that role to one of your brothers?"

Ryan gave him a look like he was crazy. "And risk dividing the Tanner household by choosing one over the other two? No way. I told them they'd all be groomsmen."

Luke grinned and slapped Ryan on the back. "Well, okay, then."

The tension in his body eased, and as Luke watched the kids play, he thought of Ryan and Bree's wedding, and Sammy Jo, and realized no matter what happened, there were still many things for them all to look forward to in the future.

Like his grandma liked to say, *"If ya don't like what's behind you, don't look back. If ya don't see something in front of you worth looking at, keep going till you do."*

He'd find a way to save Collins Country Cabins from financial ruin, even if they lost the use of their cabins, and the big incoming wedding contract.

Somehow, *he*, like his father, would make sure his family remained safe.

"Luke! Ryan!" Delaney shouted, running toward them and waving her hands. "Come quick. Bree and I watched the video surveillance tape from the other night and we've got something to show you!"

SAMMY JO FACED her father by the tack shed, unwilling to give him an inch of ground in their argument over the Collinses.

"I do not want you going over there and getting yourself hurt," her father said, raising his voice.

"I am not going to get hurt," she insisted, giving her horse an affectionate pat.

"Someone had a gun on you. What if he'd pulled the trigger? Or what if someone knocked into him and the gun went off by accident? What then?"

"Then we wouldn't be having this conversation," Sammy Jo said, narrowing her gaze. "How did you hear about that?"

Her father's expression hardened. "Doesn't matter. What does matter is that you were in danger."

Tango snorted, echoing her own reaction. "You know

who threatened me?" she demanded. "It was your friend Harley Bennett, the guy you tried to fix me up with for a date. Is that the kind of man you want me to marry?"

"No," her father said, his tone sharp. "I was wrong about him."

"Then maybe," Sammy Jo said, pressing her advantage, "you could also be wrong about Luke."

"He's not the man for you either," her father stormed.

"Because he's a Collins?"

"Yes. *No*. He's . . . he's . . . far too assertive."

"Yes," Sammy Jo said, and smiled, thinking of the way Luke had transformed back into his former self both inside and out over the last few weeks. "And I'm glad he is. Luke is the one who saved me from the rustlers that night."

"He wouldn't have had to if you weren't there," her father pointed out.

"I've been helping the Collinses keep an eye on their ranch to keep the rustlers from stealing any more cows."

"Don't you have enough to worry about with your job at the horse camp?"

"I love the Collinses and will do whatever I can to help them."

Her father scowled. "You *think* you're in love with Luke."

"I know I am. And you had no right to tell him about my inheritance."

"Of course I did. The guy is only pretending interest in you. Do you think I bought that little act he did when he came over for dinner, pulling you onto his lap and calling you 'sweetheart'?"

Sammy Jo flushed. "He may have gone a little overboard."

"He'd do whatever it takes to get his hands on those building permits."

"He'd never hurt me."

"Then why does he allow you to come over into a hostile environment?"

"Now I think *you're* the one who's going overboard. I'd hardly call Collins Country Cabins hostile territory. They're dealing with some nightly theft, but no one's come to any harm."

"Except *you*."

"Dad, I'm fine. Really."

"Well, I'm *not* fine with this at all. I'm concerned for your safety."

Sammy Jo rolled her eyes. "Look—"

"Let me finish," her father said, holding up his hand. "I'll make you another deal. You stay away from the Collinses and avoid all contact with them, and I'll make sure their cabins pass their final inspection."

"Using your job to manipulate people is wrong," Sammy Jo spat. "Especially when you use it to try to manipulate *me*. Is this why Mom left? Did you try to manipulate her, too?"

Her father's eyes widened. "Don't you dare try to twist this conversation around. You may hate me right now, but I have to do what I think is best. Now do we have a deal or not?"

"Stay away from the Collinses?" Sammy Jo asked, glaring at him. "For how long?"

"Six months."

She gasped. "Never in a million years would I agree to something so outrageous as that!"

His expression darkened. "If you do not agree, then you'll have to go live with your mother in Wyoming."

He'd kick her out? Her eyes stung and with an inward groan she tried to hold back the tears she knew would follow. Tears would be a sign of weakness and her father would think he could overtake the conversation and win.

"I make enough money to rent my own place," she retorted. It was true. Although there weren't any rentals in Fox Creek, which meant she'd have to find a place miles away from the town—and people—she loved. Not to mention, she'd need to find a stall for her horse, which would cost almost as much as her rent, and pay for utilities, insurance, food, medical, and other costs.

Her spirits plummeted. She'd taken the job at Happy Trails Horse Camp because she loved it, not because it brought in a whole lot of income. If she moved out, she'd need to find a better-paying job. And the thought of leaving the girls she worked with filled her with dread.

"You can't afford to move out," her father taunted, as if reading her thoughts.

She raised her chin, determined to remain strong. "I can live with the Collinses. I'm sure they'd love to have me and if I'm right there it will be even easier for me to help keep watch at night."

"Everyone knows the Collinses are on the brink of bankruptcy and possible foreclosure. If they don't have the cabins available to host the incoming wedding party, they won't have enough money to keep their place. Then you'll all be out of a home. Do you want to be responsible for that? Knowing that if you'd just agree to stay away for a few months you could save them?"

"I *do* hate you!" she shouted. "How could you do this to me?"

"Because *I* love you, whether you believe it or not. And I'll do everything within my power to protect you."

A hot tear fell down over Sammy Jo's left cheek. She swiped it away but more followed until, unable to keep up with them, she gave up. "If I *do* agree to your '*deal*' what happens after six months? I can resume my relationship with the Collinses with no further interference from you?"

He nodded. "Yes."

"And I can date Luke?"

He hesitated, then said, "Yes. If he still wants you."

Of course Luke would still want me. Why wouldn't he? And they could still talk on the phone, and text, even though Luke had an aversion to cell phones and text messages. But he could learn. And they could Skype, see each other through their laptops. Military families were often forced to separate for months at a time, sometimes even years. Surely she and Luke could handle being apart for six months. She'd have to miss Ryan and Bree's engagement party but she could still be in the wedding early next summer.

"If you love the Collinses as much as you say you do," her father taunted, "you'll sacrifice your own desires and do what's best for them."

At the moment she thought her father was a monster, but considering her choices, she knew he was right. Without the final inspection approval on the cabins, the Collinses' ranch would fail. If the wedding party pulled out, there's no way they'd be able to fill the empty cabins in time to recoup the money they needed. Bree had told her how desperate they were. The guest ranch was barely surviving week to week.

Her stomach twisted tight at the thought of losing six months with Luke. But if the Collinses lost the ranch and he moved on . . . maybe even back to Florida . . . well, it was possible she could lose him either way.

Just agree and then sneak over at night to see him. The thought had merit. After all, why should she keep her word to a man who would put her in a position like this in the first place?

"Okay," she said through gritted teeth. "I'll accept your deal. But you better have your inspector friend run out to reverse his decision and give the Collinses approval for occupancy *this afternoon*. And you better not say another word against Luke or any of the Collinses in my presence *ever* again. Especially when Luke and I start dating at the end of January, six months from *today*."

Her father held her gaze and gave her a nod. "And if you break your promise to me and I find out that you've seen any of the Collinses behind my back, I want you to remember who still holds the ownership papers on Tango."

Sammy Jo's heart lurched violently in her chest and she shook her head, unwilling to grasp what he was implying. He couldn't possibly mean to take away her baby. Not the one who'd comforted her most year after year when she felt no one else was around. *No way.*

"After you turned eighteen, we talked about transferring the horse into your name but we never got around to it. Tango still belongs to me, and if you defy me and break this deal, I *will* sell him."

Sammy Jo looped her arms protectively around her beloved barrel racer's neck and gasped. "You *wouldn't!*"

LUKE STARED AT his cell phone, his hate for text messages growing stronger with each incoming text. The thing was pure evil. In fact, a demon must have gained possession of Sammy Jo's phone because she would *never* type in the words scrawled across his screen.

She couldn't see him anymore? Not for six months? What kind of nonsense was that? There had rarely been a day in the past or since his return home two months before that they hadn't seen each other.

Maybe her father wrote it.

Yeah, that was it. Her father must have picked up her phone and decided to kick him while he was down, as if the blow of failing the cabin inspection hadn't been enough.

Then that afternoon the building inspector showed up out of the blue and tore down the failed inspection notice. Without even remeasuring, the man put up a new sign that granted them approval for occupancy . . . and it was even signed.

Luke's family had been as dumbfounded as he, but while they celebrated, he looked across the property line to the Macphersons' house, a sick ache tormenting his gut. No doubt Andrew Macpherson had a hand in this somehow, and after rereading the texts he had a pretty good idea *why*.

He could see what must have happened as clearly as if he'd been present, and his chest tightened, pinching his heart, as his mind reeled again and again around one dreaded question.

Sammy Jo, what have you done?

Later that night, Luke drove the gator over the fields to the Macphersons' backyard and tossed a couple pebbles against Sammy Jo's bedroom window to draw her attention. Usually she left her window open, but tonight it was cooler than it had been in a long time. He bent down to pick up a few more stones when the glass pane lifted and Sammy Jo stuck her head out.

"What are you doing here?" she asked, her soft whisper full of alarm. "I told you I can't see you."

"Or what?" Luke asked, careful to keep his voice low. "Your father will send the inspector back out to revoke our cabin approval again?"

"No," she told him, and she glanced behind her as if to make sure they were alone. "My father threatened to sell my horse."

"Of all the low, dirty, rotten things—" Luke broke off before he said something that would sink him down to her father's level. "I'm not going to let him take your horse and I'm not going to let him keep me from seeing you either."

Sammy Jo dropped her elbows down on the window ledge and cupped her cheeks with her hands. "I've tried to reason with him. But he won't listen. I guess I'm not as persuasive as I thought because this is one fight I don't think I can win."

He leaned forward and brushed his mouth across hers with a quick kiss. "Yes, you can."

"How?"

Luke handed over the video disc in his hands. "Our surveillance tape caught your father on our property the other night. He's with the rustlers. Your father has been the one trying to sabotage our ranch all along."

"No." Sammy Jo shook her head. "You must be mistaken. My father might have manipulated your permits, but he would never do something like that. He'd never steal anyone's cows, or light their hay on fire, or steal money, or . . ."

"Have me beat up?" Luke asked.

Sammy Jo shook her head again. "He wouldn't."

Luke took her hands in his and gave them a slight squeeze. "There's no doubt it's him in the video. He was speaking to Harley and a couple of the others before we chased them away."

"Did you hear what they said?" she asked.

"No."

"Well, then, maybe . . . maybe my father was trying to stop them."

"Doubt it. In fact, the way your father bent down in a huddle with the others, it looked like he was the quarterback in charge."

Sammy Jo held his gaze and remained silent a moment. Then she drew in a deep breath and asked, "So what do we do? Threaten my father with the tape and see if he'll sign over the papers for my horse?"

"No. I need to take the video to the sheriff."

Her eyes widened. "But if found guilty, my father could be *arrested*!"

Luke nodded. "That's true."

"You *can't*!" she exclaimed, her whisper harsh. "Not without talking to him first. His ways may be unfair and he may have let this feud with your family get him in over his head, but he's not a bad man, Luke."

"We'll let the authorities make that decision," he said, softening his tone.

Sammy Jo pulled her hands away from his. "No. Don't do this. You can't. No matter how mad I am at him right now, he's *still* my father."

"And he's still guilty of trespassing on our land," Luke argued, "and consorting with cattle rustlers."

"I can't lose him," Sammy Jo warned.

"And I can't let my family lose our ranch," Luke said, trying to get her to understand. "If we don't take action now, who knows if the rustlers will come back tonight? We need to stop this, once and for all."

Sammy Jo frowned. "If you love me—"

"Don't even try to play that card," Luke said with a shake of his head.

"You'll leave my father out of this," she finished.

Luke winced, but the faces of his own family flashed through his mind—Ma, Dad, Grandma, Bree, Delaney, and . . . little Meggie with her marshmallow shooter. His jaw tightened as he took in Sammy Jo's pleading expression, but the only answer he could give her was, "I can't."

"Then it looks like we just joined the family feud," Sammy Jo shot back. And the look of pain on her face as she slammed the window shut was almost his undoing.

Chapter Fifteen

SAMMY JO STARED at her cell phone, but all she saw was a blank screen. Bree used to tease her that if she ever had a day without any text messages it would be like facing her worst nightmare. And it was.

She thought about texting her friends to find out what was going on, but for the first time ever, she didn't know what to say. And it was obvious none of them wanted to talk to her.

What had Luke told them? Were Bree and Delaney siding with their brother? Would they ever speak to her again?

Sammy Jo rolled off her bed to a sitting position and dialed Jesse's cell number.

"Hey, girl, what's up?" Jesse asked.

Sammy Jo summoned a smile and taking a deep breath she said, "I just wanted to check in on the girls and see how everything was going at the fairgrounds."

"We won the poster competition! The girls were very excited, but disappointed you weren't there."

"Yeah, me, too." She tried to keep her voice vibrant and pumped, but her tone dropped off on the last word. It seemed like she was missing out on everything at the moment.

"They can tell you all about it next time they see you," Jesse promised. "Oooh, I've got to go. We've got to get the horses back into the arena for another showing in twenty minutes."

Sammy Jo ended the call, wishing they could have talked longer. She could go over there and join in the fun, but she was afraid she wouldn't be able to keep up the happy charade for very long and didn't want the girls to see her upset.

Instead, she dialed the number of the only other person who could possibly understand how she was feeling. Her mother.

"*Mom,*" she cried after telling her mother what happened with Luke and her father. "You were *right*—I can't make Luke love me."

"I'm so sorry, baby," her mother said, the commiserating ache in her voice palpable.

Sammy Jo sniffed. "But I was so sure Luke had fallen for me. I *wanted* him to love me."

"Did he ever tell you he loved you?"

An onslaught of tears flowed freely down her cheeks, leaving her face a sloppy mess. "Noooo," she wailed, and knew she sounded like little Meghan or the overly emotional teenage Walford twins, but she couldn't help it.

"And I can't force him to feel something he . . . just . . . *doesn't*."

"I couldn't make your father love me, either, baby," her mother said softly. "I waited and waited, thinking he might change over time. I thought if I kept house, cooked all his favorite meals, stayed with him long enough . . . that one day he'd forget about his old crush on Loretta and his eyes would light up when he saw *me* enter the room."

"Dad doesn't know what love is," Sammy Jo said, wiping her nose with a nearby tissue. "He never should have let you go."

"But I had to let *him* go," her mother said, the ache still in her voice.

"And you think that's what I have to do with Luke?" Sammy Jo choked on another sob, unable to fathom life without Luke.

Maybe she'd overreacted when he said he couldn't leave her father out of the prosecution of the rustlers. Maybe he did love her but just couldn't go against his own family any more than she could. But he'd never *once* told her he loved her. Not once. And here she was hoping for a marriage proposal? When they'd never even *dated*? She let out a hysterical laugh that came out as a half sob, half shriek.

"Are you okay, baby?" her mother asked with concern.

"Yeah, I will be," Sammy Jo promised, and let out a deep sigh. "How did we ever become so delusional?"

"I don't know."

She heard a sniff from the other end of the line. "Mom, are you crying now, too?"

"I've gotta go. But I'll call you soon. Maybe you can come visit."

"Yeah, maybe."

But leaving Fox Creek was the last thing she wanted to do right now. All she wanted was Luke. She hung up, her heart wrenching from the memory of the look on Luke's face when he'd turned away from her window.

Her biggest fear wasn't a blank screen on her cell phone. Or losing Luke for six months. No, her biggest fear, her worst nightmare, was the possibility she'd lost him *forever*.

LUKE WALKED OUT the door of the main house, and made his way down the path past the row of cabins on his left. The teen Travel Light Adventure girls hung out on the front porches, their joyful giggles grating on his nerves. Despite their claims of enduring great hikes and camping experiences, it appeared their most thrilling "adventure" was flirting with Devin, who the Collinses had hired on full-time as a ranch hand now that the cabins were done.

Devin tipped his hat in greeting as he passed by the girls, which made them giggle all the more . . . and the nearby Walford twins clench their fists.

Luke veered away from them, wishing his camp on the other side of the property was still intact, a place he could go to be alone. He chose the next best place, the barn. But before he could enter, Ryan's son, Cody, cut him off as he chased Meghan around with the marshmallow shooter until she laughed so hard she fell down.

Seemed like everyone was happy today. Drawing in a ragged breath, he tried to recall one of his own happier times. Pushing images of Sammy Jo's smiling face aside, his mind latched on to a memory from his younger days, involving their infamous marshmallow wars.

He didn't wish harm to come to his family and certainly didn't want their cattle and other belongings stolen, but he had to admit that hiding out and keeping watch for the rustlers this past month had brought back a certain kind of sharp, focused intensity to his life. The kind he used to have with his childhood friends, or while conquering bulls in the rodeos, and then with his buddies in the military.

He liked being part of a team and liked leading one even more. But he was afraid his leadership had cost him something he valued even more than his love of covert "missions." Protecting his family, his new team, may have cost him the love of his life.

Luke wondered what Sammy Jo was doing at that moment. Would she ever forgive him for turning in her father?

He walked into the barn and led his horse out into one of the grassy paddocks. Running his hand down the sleek coat of Phantom's neck, he said, "You don't have to change for me. It was silly for them to ever think they could teach you to bow."

Upon saying the last word, the horse twitched his ears and dropped his front legs down to the ground, then lowered the front of his body as if to roll. But he didn't. Phantom looked at him with big, brown, expectant eyes, as if waiting for his next command.

Luke didn't want to disappoint. He slid onto the horse bareback and gave him a pat and the accompanying order, "Up."

Holding on to a section of Phantom's mane, he shifted his weight to maintain his balance as the gelding rose up to his full height on all four legs. Funny, this time, getting on had hardly even hurt. He gave the horse another encouraging pat and grinned.

She taught you to bow.

And she'd taught him how to live again. *Really* live.

When he'd found out his best friends he'd left behind in the military got killed, he'd been so upset he'd been reckless. He'd driven his motorcycle too fast on the wet pavement that night, not knowing if he wanted to live or die.

Afterward he drifted, still not knowing what he wanted to do. When his father's accident called him home and Grandma offered to split the ranch between them all if he stayed, it seemed like a good idea.

But it wasn't until Sammy Jo started following him around with that big flirtatious smile on her lips, and challenged him to get up on the horse, and kissed him, that he realized . . . he wanted to live.

"Bet Phantom's glad you're back," his father said, coming up and leaning over the fence. "How's the leg?"

"Not bad," Luke admitted. "It's been getting lots of exercise lately."

As Luke led Phantom into a walk around the paddock, his father said, "You did right, turning in that tape to the sheriff. I know how hard that must have been for you, considering . . . Sammy Jo."

Luke didn't say a word, but tapped his foot against Phantom's side to take him into a slow jog.

"I'm sorry I yelled at you over the results of the final inspection," his father continued. "It wasn't your fault. You weren't the one who was wrong. *I* was."

He was apologizing? Luke frowned and rode his horse closer. His father had never apologized to him before, but his face looked contrite, his tone sincere.

"I never should have let this feud thing come between you and Sammy Jo either," his father continued. "You need to go after her, Luke. Make things right between you."

Luke set his jaw, wishing it were that easy. "I let her down."

His father grinned. "Well, you can't please everyone all the time, can you?"

Luke held his father's gaze a moment and knew his ole man was referring to the fact he'd made it hard for Luke to please *him*.

"No, it seems I can't," Luke admitted.

"But that doesn't mean we should hold on to our grudges forever, does it?" his father asked, then looked him in the eye. "Don't push away the ones you love like I did. You don't want those kinds of regrets."

Touched by his father's rare moment of candor, Luke thought of Sammy Jo and said, "You're right, I don't."

A shrill *ring!* echoed from the inside of Luke's shirt pocket. He took out his cell phone and looked at the caller ID, hoping it was Sammy Jo.

But it wasn't. His gaze jerked toward his father. "My

friend A.J. says he was using the latrine at the café and
overheard one of Harley's men say they've got our cows
in a new holding facility twelve miles outside of town off
Route 106. Because the sheriff brought several of Harley's
gang in for questioning today, they're planning to put
them on the train and ship them out by dawn."

"We've got to stop them," his father said, a growl returning to his voice.

Luke gave a nod. "You can call the sheriff, but I'm
going after what's ours."

He expected his father to argue, call him a hothead,
or too impulsive. But his father gave a nod, his face tense,
and replied, "I'm going with you."

SAMMY JO SAT in front of the living room TV watching
the video Luke had given her. It was a copy, which meant
that by now the Collinses must have handed in the original to the sheriff.

The lighting was dim but there was no mistaking her
father's image as he came up around the side of the rustlers' pickup. They didn't have the trailer with them this
time, so she imagined they'd planned to try to sneak into
the main house again and then make a fast getaway.

Her father motioned to Harley and the other rustlers,
clearly recognizable without their black ski masks, and
they all came toward him. Her father bent down and
pointed in different directions as he spoke to the other
men in the huddle. Then all except her father pulled on
the masks and ran across the field toward the Collins

house. Obviously they still didn't know about the Collinses' newly installed security cameras.

In the next set of frames Sammy Jo watched her father jump into the driver's seat of Harley's truck, start the engine, and drive off toward his own property. The rustlers approached a side window of the Collins house by the garden but appeared to trip over a low-lying wire. No doubt Luke's grandma had been responsible for that.

Then other figures appeared—the Tanner brothers from one side, and the Collinses from another. Sammy Jo hadn't been there that night, as it was supposed to be her and Luke's night off. She'd heard the rumble of a truck drive through her property, but had no idea it had been her own father driving it out to the road.

The video ended, but she had heard that the Tanners and Collinses had managed to chase the rustlers off.

What if she *had* been there that night . . . and had come face-to-face with her father? What would she have said to him? What was she to say to him now? Had he also been there the night she was threatened? Is that why he knew about it? But then why hadn't he confronted her about it sooner?

He couldn't have been there. No matter how he had gotten mixed up with these rustlers, he would never allow them to point a gun at her. She had to believe that. In fact, by driving the rustlers' truck away, her father had left the guys without a ride. Had he intended for them to get caught? Or did he plan to drive around and pick them up from the road?

She needed answers.

Going from the living room into her father's adjoining office, she opened the appointment book on his desk. She flipped through the pages and saw a date circled in red pen, the same date the video had been taken. Obviously he'd planned to meet them there. But why? She couldn't believe her father had been engaged in criminal activity.

She riffled through the stacks of papers on his shelves, trying to find information showing why he might have been at the Collinses' that night. One document in particular caught her eye. An invoice with the name of a Canadian slaughterhouse in the heading. Apparently her father ... was selling them two dozen Black Angus cows. The invoice was addressed to him. Except he didn't own any cows ...

Her stomach lurched and for a moment she thought she would be sick. Dread shimmied up her spine. Her chest tightened. Her head spun with images of her father smiling at her over their home-cooked dinners, cheering her on at all of her rodeos, and happy times in the past when her mom was still around. Did her mother know what kind of man he was? Did *she*? Sammy Jo took a couple deep breaths to steady her nerves and realized that if her father could do such things to the Collinses, then she didn't know him at all.

A click from the front door brought her back into the living room, with the paper in her hands and her heart breaking. Her father stepped into the house, his face familiar, and yet she viewed him as a stranger.

He took one look at her, then glanced at the video on the TV that had automatically looped around and started playing a second time.

"How c-could you?" Sammy Jo demanded, her voice low and her body trembling.

Her father's eyes widened, then he turned around, shut the door, and came toward her.

Instinctively she backed away. "Did you have Luke beat up? Were you there the night Harley held me at gunpoint?"

"No!" her father shouted, his face aghast. "It's not what you think."

"Oh, no?" Sammy Jo raised her chin. "Dinner was an hour ago. Where were you?"

He closed his eyes for a moment, and when he reopened them, they were filled with tears. "The sheriff called me in for questioning."

"What did you tell him?"

"That I have nothing to do with the Collins theft. I told him I was there that night trying to *protect* the Collinses. I knew Harley and the others were going to try to break into the house again to search for Loretta's key. I tried to stop them, but they wouldn't listen to me."

"What about this?" she said, holding up the invoice from the slaughterhouse. Her gaze bore into his as she waited for his answer.

His throat worked as he swallowed and a bead of sweat rolled off his left brow. "They're trying to set me up. Use me as their scapegoat if things go bad."

"Who's 'they'?" she asked, keeping her distance.

"The new developer who bought the Owenses' place, Harley and his gang, Winona. They knew of my longtime feud with the Collinses and asked me to help put the Collinses out of business. I figured a little mischief wouldn't hurt, and I thought if the Collinses sold their property and moved, I wouldn't have to look at them anymore. And you wouldn't keep running over there every day chasing after Luke."

"How could you do this?" Sammy Jo cried. "I believed in you. I told Luke you were innocent. I *trusted* you."

"I didn't know what they planned to do at first," he said, rubbing both his hands over his face. "After they stole the first set of cows, I told them I didn't want any part of their scheme. But they threatened if I didn't keep my silence they'd take that paper to the authorities, along with a couple incriminating emails where I stated I'd do anything to see the Collinses leave the area."

"You let them drive through our property, didn't you?" she accused.

He nodded. "The first time, yes. After that, Winona stole my key and had an extra made without my knowledge. It was when she put mushrooms in my stew that I knew I was in trouble. They're going to make all of this look like it was my idea. And you're going to leave me just like your ma."

"Secrets . . . destroy . . . lives," she said, emphasizing each word. "You should have told Ma you were still in love with Loretta before you ever married her. Instead of holding a grudge against Jed, you should have told the sheriff what that town posse planned as soon as they approached you. And above all else, you should have told *me* what was going on."

"You know about . . . Loretta?" her father asked, his voice hesitant.

"Of course I know. Ma told me. She and I do *not* keep secrets."

Her father sank into a nearby chair. "I'm so sorry. I never meant for any of this to happen. I never wanted your ma to leave. Not really. I never meant to hurt the Collinses. Or you. I thought what I did would protect you, but I must have been . . . out of my mind."

Delusional.

Sammy Jo's heart seemed to skip a beat and the back of her throat ached as she took a step forward. "We all make mistakes, Dad, but when that happens we should do '*whatever it takes,*' " she said, her spirit lifting as she borrowed Luke's line, "to make things right again."

His shoulders slumped. "How?"

"Tell the sheriff what you just told me," she said, moving closer.

Her father shook his head. "I don't have proof I'm not any more guilty than they are."

"Then return what was stolen so there's no case against you," she pleaded. "Redeem yourself. Get those cows back before it's too late."

"I can't. I don't know where they are."

"Rumor has it, they're at the fairgrounds. Or at least, they were." She frowned. "Where would they move them?"

Her father sat up straight. "Winona once asked to meet me at a place not far from there. I didn't go."

"Why don't you check it out?"

"There's no guarantee that's where they're holding the cows."

She gave him a weak smile. "At this point, what do you have to lose?"

He hesitated. "I can't load up two dozen cows by myself."

Coming to stand beside him, she placed her hand on his shoulder. "No one said you had to do it alone."

LUKE HAD WANTED to leave immediately, but he got hung up making a few well-placed calls. Afterward he was waylaid by his sisters, who insisted they wanted to come.

"The sheriff and his men will meet us there," Luke assured them. "You'll only get in the way and be told to stand back."

"Don't you dare think you're doing this without me," Bree said, using her dominant I'm-older-than-you tone.

"Or me," Delaney agreed, whose concern was for the poor animals. "We have to save our cows before they're shipped off and slaughtered!"

The phone rang and Luke turned toward the kitchen wondering if it was someone calling him back, but a moment later his ma emerged, grabbed her jacket off a nearby chair, and headed toward the door.

"Where are *you* going?" Luke's father demanded.

"To the bank," she said, casting them a nervous glance. "The teller thinks someone broke into the vault and tried to bust open my safe deposit box."

"Our ranch managers?" Bree asked, and bit her lip. "Remember the PI said they tried to rob that other bank not too long ago. Do you think Susan and Wade Randall might be back in town?"

Ma narrowed her gaze. "I'd bet it was that Winona woman!"

"Maybe you should wait until I can go with you," Luke's dad suggested.

"No," Ma said, her voice firm. "I have to go now. I begged the teller to wait there so I could check the contents of my box and she agreed. Besides, she said the sheriff and his deputies are still there. I'll be perfectly safe."

The sheriff was at the bank? Realizing the authorities had their hands full and might be late arriving at the holding facility, Luke said to the others, "We're wasting time. We need to move out."

They hooked the cattle trailer to the back of the old red ranch truck and Luke, his father, and his sisters all squeezed into the extended cab. His father drove. The heavy fair traffic held them up fifteen minutes more so that it was nearly sundown by the time they got past town and down Route 106.

Twelve miles out, Luke pointed to a large structure coming up on their left. "That's it."

The white rectangular building with the gray barn-style roof sat on an upward stretch of land, with nothing around it except open fields. A faded sign read Fox Creek Square Dance Hall.

"I don't see any cows," Bree said, and frowned. "Are you sure you have the right address?"

"Maybe they're inside," Luke said, but wondered if his rodeo friend had played him by sending him to the wrong location. He still didn't know if he could trust him. For all he knew, A.J. could be leading them into a trap.

"I don't see the sheriff either," Delaney said, her face tense.

"Or any other vehicles," their father said, pulling in the driveway. "Your mother and I used to come dance here when we were younger. As far as I know, it's still used for square dancing today."

"It may look like a square dance hall," Bree said, wrinkling her nose, "but it sure doesn't smell like one."

Luke nodded. "They're here."

His father pulled the vehicle around the corner of the dance hall and slammed on the brakes. Another truck and trailer, vacant, was already there, blocking their path.

Delaney pointed. "Doesn't that belong to—"

Luke jumped out of the truck with the assistance of his cane, and on the count of three, his father helped him fling open the large double doors at the back of the building.

Yep. Just as he expected. Their cows were inside. But they were with both Andy and Sammy Jo Macpherson. *Not* what he expected.

He froze, taking in their identical wide-eyed expressions and the flush of guilt that crept into their faces when they realized they'd been caught.

"You and your father are working together?" Luke demanded, staring at Sammy Jo and wondering where he'd gone wrong. How had he not seen this? The enormity of their betrayal struck hard, pummeled him from the inside, and left him grasping for possible explanations, although he truly saw only one. "*You* helped him steal our cows?"

"No!" Sammy Jo exclaimed, a horrified look crossing her face. "We're helping you to get them *back*!"

"Of course you are," Bree said, running to her friend's side to help her lead one of the cows out the door. "Luke, how *could* you think she'd ever betray us?"

The wounded look Sammy Jo shot him seemed to ask the same thing. And with a pang of remorse deep in his gut, Luke shifted his gaze to her father. "What about him?"

Andy Macpherson slipped a rope around another Black Angus head and said, "I may be a lot of things, but I ain't no cattle rustler."

Luke's dad stood in front of their neighbor, rifle ready, in case the man should try anything, but after a moment of staring each other down, Jed Collins moved out of the way.

The rumble of other approaching vehicles came from outside, and while the two fathers hurried after the girls, Luke pressed himself against the wall and crept forward along the perimeter, careful to remain out of sight. He glanced through a window and saw two more trucks, five men. Harley was one of them.

Where was the sheriff? Why wasn't *he* here? And where was his *own* backup?

As if in answer, a third truck sped into the driveway, the Triple T Tanner trademark marked on its side. Ryan and his three brothers jumped out, pistols drawn. The rustlers drew their own guns and aimed them at the young women.

Although Luke's pulse flew into a dangerously fast rhythm, and his gut clenched tighter than a harness on a bull, he was confident his team could overtake the rustlers. But first, they needed a diversion to get Sammy Jo, Bree, and Delaney out of harm's way.

There wasn't a moment to lose. Withdrawing the stick of homemade dynamite he'd confiscated out of his duffel, he lit the end with a lighter from his pocket. Then taking two steps toward the door, he pulled back his arm and threw it between the rustlers' trucks.

The blast took everyone outside by surprise, and as the rustlers flung themselves back, the Tanners moved forward to try to knock the guns from their hands.

Luke hurried to assist, straining his eyes to see through the smoke, and froze when a shot rang out, piercing the air. Off to his right he heard Delaney scream.

A few more shots rang out. Luke lunged toward a man in a brown jacket who aimed a fist at his father and twisted his arm behind his back. The man broke free and moved to retaliate, but Luke bent low and used his cane to hit the guy's legs out from under him. As soon as the other man fell to the ground, Ryan grabbed him and roped his hands.

Luke shoved another man aside, enabling Bree and Delaney to run around the corner of the building. He looked around and called for Sammy Jo, but the cows had run back inside the dance hall and their mooing cries made it almost impossible to hear.

An uneasy feeling shot through his chest. Where was she? Why couldn't he see her?

Two more vehicles pulled around the building, containing his friend A.J. and his other rodeo buddies, the second wave of recruits he'd been waiting for. Luke acknowledged his appreciation with a quick nod as they came toward the remaining rustlers from the opposite side.

"We're outnumbered," one of the rustlers shouted, and each of them scattered in a different direction.

Luke tried to catch one who ran past him, but with his limp, he couldn't keep up.

An engine roared to life and one of the trucks tore away from them, leaving a spiraling cloud of dust in its wake. Luke glanced toward the remaining rustlers and saw his rodeo pals had one cornered. Ryan and his older brother, Dean, were tying up another, while Luke's dad helped Josh and Zach Tanner subdue one more.

"One of them got away," Ryan said, helping his brothers haul the four they'd captured into the back of their truck.

"Harley," Luke said, gritting his teeth.

Bree and Delaney came running out and Luke glanced behind them and frowned. "Where's Sammy Jo?"

"I think he took her," came Andy Macpherson's strained voice from behind.

What? Luke cast a sharp glance toward the road, his entire body tense. If Harley hurt Sammy Jo in any way . . .

"Luke."

He spun toward her father and found the man on the ground, his face pale, and his shirt bright red. As Luke dropped down beside him, the unmistakable smell of blood wafted up his nose. "He's been shot," Luke called out, and his own father ran up beside them.

"I didn't want her to come," Andy said, gasping for breath. "But Sammy Jo's just so infuriatingly *persistent*."

"She *is*," Luke agreed, wishing for once that she *wasn't*.

"Hold on, Andy," Luke's dad told him. "We're gonna get you out of here."

Sammy Jo's father nodded, then reached up his hand and latched on to Luke's forearm, his grip hard as steel. "Please," Andy said, and looked up at him, his eyes pleading. "Don't let him hurt my daughter."

"I won't," Luke promised.

As if her father even had to ask. The thought of Harley driving off with *his* woman stirred up all kind of crazy inside him.

Chapter Sixteen

SAMMY JO WAITED until she heard the truck door open and shut, and the booted footsteps of the driver fade away, before she pulled off the tarp she'd hidden under in the rear truck bed.

When Harley ran toward the vehicle at the square dance hall, she'd been determined not to let him get away. And he'd been in such a hurry to escape, he hadn't seen her climb over the tailgate.

She scanned the street, dark and nearly empty due to the fact most of the town businesses had closed for the night. Even the lights in the sheriff's station had been turned off, which was unfortunate, since it sat right next to the very bank the rustler had entered.

How did he get in? Winona?

Sammy Jo climbed out of the truck and crept closer to the large front window. Keeping herself hidden, she peered around the edge, and there, inside and held at gunpoint, was Loretta Collins. Sucking in her breath, she pulled out her cell phone and called 911. Then after she reported the incident, she tried calling her father, knowing he'd be worried sick when he discovered her missing, but he didn't answer.

Her third call went to Luke and he picked up on the first ring. "Sammy Jo?"

"It's me. I hid in the back of Harley's truck and followed him to the bank."

"You're all right?" He sounded desperate, relieved, and heartsick all at the same time.

"Yes, I'm fine," she whispered, keeping her voice low. "But, Luke—*they have your ma!*"

She didn't elaborate on the danger his mother was in. Hopefully the sheriff would arrive in time to rescue Mrs. Collins before she came to any real harm.

Sammy Jo held her position by the window and watched Winona pull Mrs. Collins into the bank vault in the back. Harley followed, but stood in the vault entrance, his gun aimed at something behind the tellers' counter.

What if Winona and Harley took whatever they wanted out of the bank and got away? Was she supposed to just sit here like a stray dog and watch?

No doubt Winona had shut off all the bank's security cameras to make sure there would be no evidence except Mrs. Collins's testimony. Sammy Jo glanced at the video camera button on her cell phone, and her legs bounced up and down, ready to move.

Except her ears still rang from the way Luke had

ended their call—warning her to stay put. She wavered back and forth a few more moments considering her options. Then when Harley turned his head, she darted through the unlocked door of the bank and dove behind a manager's desk in the corner.

The door had closed behind her quickly without making much noise. But one person had seen her. The young woman sitting on the floor behind the tellers' counter. From their current positions they had an open angled view of one another.

Another witness.

Rope bound the woman's hands and her mouth had been gagged with a white cloth. The teller's brows lifted, emphasizing the helplessness reflected in her eyes, and Sammy Jo put a finger to her lips, her heart pounding, hoping the woman would keep quiet and not give her away. If she did, Sammy Jo feared she might find herself in the very same position. Then she wouldn't be able to help anybody.

Harley stepped from the vault entry and Winona rushed out carrying a foot-long rectangular box that looked to be made of steel. Mrs. Collins followed, wringing her hands as Winona set it on the tellers' counter.

"Open it," Winona ordered, her eyes on Luke's ma.

Mrs. Collins shook her head. "No. There's nothing inside of interest to you."

Harley waved the gun he pointed as if to remind her it was there and Sammy Jo silently willed Luke's ma to listen to them.

"Loretta, rumor has it your wealthy parents died in a fire when you were younger and you were their sole heir.

So I got to wondering what could be so important that you would have to check the contents of this fireproof, double-combination locked box every two weeks? Two little birds told me they left you some 'valuables'? The family jewels perhaps?"

Mrs. Collins shook her head. "Like I said, what's inside is only valuable to me."

"We'll see about that," Winona taunted. "Now that we've managed to extract the numbers for the combination locks out of you, where's the key?"

Harley shoved the gun under Mrs. Collins's chin. "We don't need you to tell us, ma'am. We can shoot you here and now and crack the box open some other time."

Mrs. Collins broke down in tears and reached for her jacket pocket, but Winona stopped her by grabbing her wrist. "Hands in the air, Loretta."

Sammy Jo's heart went out to Mrs. Collins as she raised her arms. The poor woman looked absolutely terrified. And she had a right to be. There was nothing as hair-raising as having someone pull a gun on you.

She watched Winona reach into Mrs. Collins's jacket pocket, scrunch up her face in disgust, then withdraw a handful of white sticky goo.

"What's this?" Winona demanded. "Are you deliberately toying with me?"

Sammy Jo noticed Mrs. Collins seemed as surprised as everyone else.

"My—my granddaughter put some marshmallows into my pocket to save for later," Luke's ma told them. "And . . . they must have melted in the heat."

Harley glanced out the front windows toward his truck. "Winona, forget it. We need to take what we can and get out of here."

Winona shook her head, and gave him a sharp look. "Just another minute," she said, inserting the key into Mrs. Collins's steel box. "I *have* to see what's inside!"

Harley gave her a wary glance, but didn't say another word.

A loud *snap!* drew everyone's attention and even Sammy Jo leaned forward to see what Mrs. Collins had locked away for so long.

Winona opened the lid, withdrew a fabric drawstring bag and, pulling it open, dumped the contents onto the counter. "Photos?" she exclaimed. "There's nothing here but a bunch of *photos*? And . . . a broken chicken bone?"

"A *wishbone*," Mrs. Collins corrected, lunging forward to take the two pieces from the assistant manager's hands.

Winona let her keep them. "But Susan and Wade Randall said you had valuables. *Real* valuables!"

"The photos of my family are irreplaceable," Mrs. Collins said, her voice rising into an anguished squeak. "And—and Jed gave me the wishbone when he proposed. He'd told me to make a wish. I told him I loved him and wished to be with him forever."

"*How sweet,*" Winona drawled.

Touched by the tale, Sammy Jo's heart ached for Luke, and when she checked the screen on her cell phone, she saw he'd sent her a message. Luke—the man who hated texting—had sent her a text! She read, *Stay safe. Be there soon.*

She smiled, then with a start she realized the light from her phone had reflected against the wall and revealed her position.

"You want to come out of there?" Harley asked, his gun now aimed in her direction.

There was no point in resisting. She had no weapon. Except the record button on her cell phone, her tongue, and what Luke liked to call her "*special powers of persuasion.*"

Determined to get a complete confession out of Harley and Winona to help the Collinses and to clear her father's name, she shoved her fear down to the soles of her boots . . . and stood up.

RELIEVED TO SEE four squad cars lined up on either side of the bank when his father pulled the truck to a stop along Main Street, Luke hopped out of the passenger's side and held the door open for Sammy Jo's father. Andy refused to go to the hospital, insisting the bullet had only grazed his shoulder and that he needed to help get his daughter back.

Especially since the 911 dispatch informed them the sheriff and his deputies had been sent on a wild-goose chase all afternoon investigating a rash of phony 911 calls. Looked like the officers had finally made it to the right place.

Luke headed toward the sheriff, who stood outside the bank beside the front window. "What's going on? Where's Sammy Jo? My ma?"

One of the deputies moved to prevent Luke from coming any closer, but the sheriff, who knew Luke's past exploits well, motioned for the officer to let him through. "They're inside," the sheriff informed him. "But we can't get a clear shot. Sammy Jo's standing in the way."

Luke's jaw tightened as he peered through the window and assessed the situation for himself. He didn't see his mother at all, only Winona Lane and Harley Bennett, who had one hand wrapped around Sammy Jo's shoulder, and his other holding the gun he pointed at her.

Somehow she'd been caught. Again. Most likely while trying to "help." Because that's what she did. Except this time the authorities wouldn't let him in to save her. He'd need to find a way to revamp his internal game plan.

From behind, Luke heard Andy Macpherson argue with the same deputy who had let him through. "But my daughter's in there!"

"With my wife!" Jed Collins's voice added.

Glancing over his shoulder, Luke saw the Tanners pull up to the curb behind them. The four rustlers they'd tied up were still in the back of their truck, ready for delivery to the sheriff's station next door.

But the additional vehicle had drawn the attention of a few late-night onlookers coming out of the café across the street. They needed to do something quick before more people arrived and Harley took Sammy Jo hostage as a means to escape.

Luke let out a low, frustrated growl similar to his father's. Maybe he should have brought another stick of his grandma's dynamite along with him to create another diversion, but he'd used the only one he had back at the dance hall. Now he'd have to rely on his tactical skills . . . like he had in the past.

Leaning in beside the sheriff, he peered through the window again and reported, "Harley's let go of her and stepped aside. If I can get Sammy Jo to drop, can you get your guys inside to take control?"

The sheriff nodded after listening to the rest of Luke's plan and radioed his men standing on the other side of the building to prepare for Luke's signal.

"On the count of three," Luke whispered, and held up his hand, signaling with one finger, two fingers, three.

Luke glanced through the window again and yelled at the top of his lungs, "Sammy Jo, *snake!*"

He didn't know if she'd remember the code word. At the time, she hadn't even been on his team. He held his breath, waiting for her reaction, and hoped he hadn't inadvertently placed her in greater danger. His heart drummed an extra beat against his chest, but then he watched her drop to the floor.

Both Harley and Winona stared at her, startled for a moment, then as the sheriff and his men burst through the door, they redirected their weapons. Rapid gunfire rang out as the officers tried to shoot the guns from Harley's and Winona's hands. Winona dropped hers, while Harley held on and aimed at one of the officers coming toward him.

Luke wasn't going to wait another moment. Crouching low, he pushed through the door behind the officers, grabbed hold of Sammy Jo's feet, and dragged her out backward. Then, scooping her into his arms, he pulled her around the side of the building, and collapsed on the ground with the woman he loved in his lap.

"Are you all right?" he asked, his voice breathless and his heart pounding like a machine gun.

She nodded, then frowned. "Luke, where's your cane?"

He shook his head and shrugged. "No idea. All that matters is that I've got you."

Holding her tight against his chest, he brushed his hands over her hair again and again, until his erratic breathing slowed.

Several sirens filled the air as other emergency vehicles arrived at the scene. Then just seconds later there was a flurry of shouts and people running around them as several groups of people exited the front of the building. A few of the deputies led Harley and Winona away in handcuffs, and the sheriff emerged with another woman and Ma. His mother ran into his father's arms, and then after she gave him a hug, she gave Andy Macpherson a hug, too.

"We've got your ma!" Luke's father called over to him. "They locked her and the teller up in the bank vault."

Andy took a step toward Luke, his eyes on his daughter, but two paramedics grabbed his arms and pulled him back to look at his wound.

Luke pulled *his* attention back to Sammy Jo, and lifted her chin so he could look at her face. Her dark brows were uplifted, her beautiful eyes filled with tears, and her lower lip trembled.

"You're not ever going to do something like that again, are you?" he whispered.

Her head gave a violent shake. "No. But, Luke, it was Winona in charge this whole time, not my father. I've got proof," she said, holding up her cell phone. "Winona hired the rustlers. She made a deal with the builder who bought the Owenses' property. She's orchestrated everything. And she's been working with Susan and Wade Randall, your embezzling ranch managers!"

"Shhh," Luke whispered, shutting her up with a kiss. "There'll be plenty of time for talk later."

"But they—"

"Later," he repeated, and this time when he kissed her lips she didn't argue.

SAMMY JO BROUGHT the tray holding the homemade chicken noodle vegetable soup and thick, crusty, Italian bread slathered with butter into her father's room and set it on the end table beside his bed.

"How are you feeling?" she asked, checking the bandage covering his left shoulder.

"The pain's lessened," he said, his mood much improved since their ordeal at the bank two days before. "I think I'll be back to work at the planning department in no time."

"The builder who wanted to turn the Owens property into a housing development unexpectedly put the land up for sale today," Sammy Jo informed him. "After I got that confession out of Winona and Harley on my cell phone, everyone connected with them has been either 'going on vacation' or 'moving to another state.'"

"Goes to show how many people Susan and Wade Randall were spoon-feeding profits when they posed as ranch managers and embezzled the Collins money," her father muttered.

"Winona had set up a special bank fund for the Randalls to slip the Collinses' money into," Sammy Jo informed him. "In return, they were giving her a cut of the money. She blames the Collinses for scaring the Randalls off and taking away her incoming share."

"As if it was rightfully hers," her father scoffed.

Sammy Jo nodded. "Winona thought if she could force Collins Country Cabins into foreclosure, she could recoup her loss by selling their land to the builder next door. With Harley and his friends' help, of course."

Her father shook his head. "I never should have trusted her. And when I suspected she was up to no good, I should have warned the Collinses before she stole away more of their money."

"They're hurting financially, but the good news is, everything is set for when the big wedding party comes in next week. The money they receive from that should help them survive."

"Unless someone else is on the Randalls' payroll." Her father sat up in the bed and frowned. "Does anyone know where Susan and Wade might be now?"

"Bree says the private investigator they hired has tracked them across several Midwestern states, and it's possible they might be headed back to Montana. But they are still on the move and he just can't seem to get ahead of them."

Her father hesitated, then asked, "Did the Collinses say anything about me?"

Sammy Jo pursed her lips. "They aren't pressing charges, if that's what you mean. In fact," she said, arching her brow, "Jed has invited us over for dinner as soon as you're up for it."

Her father's expression softened. "He did?"

"Yes," she said, and smirked. "I told him you'd be happy to bring dessert—humble pie."

Her dad chuckled. "I'd better bring two. I owe Loretta an apology as well."

A triple knock sounded on the bedroom door and Sammy Jo met her father's gaze. "Are you expecting company?"

"Maybe," he said, and when he turned toward the door his eyes gleamed and his face took on an expectant expression.

The door opened and Sammy Jo gasped. *"Mom?"*

"Hi, baby," she said, wrapping her in a giant hug. "How are you?"

Sammy Jo looked at her mother's happy, smiling face, and back to her dad, then said, "Great. I think everything is great."

After all, if there was a chance it might work out for her mom and dad after all this time, after everything that had happened, then she had to believe there was hope for her and Luke, too.

In fact, she'd tell Luke she wasn't giving up on him this very night . . . just as soon as they came face-to-face at Ryan and Bree's engagement party.

LUKE TAPPED HIS cane against the edge of his seat as he waited for the doctor to come back with the results of his newest X-rays. He didn't think he'd be able to get in so soon, but someone else had canceled and the receptionist had been eager to have him fill the open slot.

The door opened and Luke froze, unable to breathe. Then the doc said, "Good news. I don't think you need to have the surgery."

"What?" Luke stared at the images the doctor brought up on the computerized screen on the wall in front of him. "How is that possible?"

"Well, it's been a while since your accident and it's given your torn ACL ligament time to heal. With the recent physical activity, your muscles have strengthened around the old wound, giving it better support. So I have a few recommendations for you."

"Yes?" Luke asked, giving the doctor his full attention. He'd do whatever the doctor suggested. Anything, if it meant avoiding the surgery.

"First, keep riding . . ."

Luke came home from his appointment feeling like he'd just won the lottery. *No surgery. No being put out with that risky nitrous gas or sleep cocktail or whatever medicine they used these days.*

Even more importantly, the doctor had said that if he agreed to physical therapy twice a week and kept up with the riding, he should make a full recovery. It would take time, but he *could* look forward to a day when he would no longer need the assistance of a cane. A day when he would be *whole*.

He glanced at the cows back in their pen, munching on the hay Delaney had tossed in for their evening feed, and shifted his gaze to the influx of guests bringing suitcases to their assigned cabins.

Bree had found out one of the newcomers was a country singer and hired him to perform at the engagement party. Luke's sisters had spent most of the day decorating the backyard gazebo in teal and white streamers and Sammy Jo had hung a banner that read Congratulations, Bree and Ryan.

He couldn't wait to see Sammy Jo tonight. She'd been over almost every day, as usual, and they'd talked about what happened at the bank, but they hadn't spent much time alone.

Besides helping Bree get ready for the engagement party, she'd stopped in at the horse camp to see her kids and tended to her father's shoulder wound. Luke hoped now that the feud had been called off, her father would *finally* allow her to date.

At least that was the plan.

The Walford twins ran up beside him as he headed down the path toward the horse barn.

"Mr. Luke, guess what?" Nora exclaimed, shuffling the load of towels in her arms.

"Bree isn't going to make you do any more laundry?" Luke teased.

"No!" both girls squealed in unison. *"We're going to the engagement party with Devin!"*

"Both of you?"

"Yes!" the girls cried, their excitement almost contagious.

"Those awful girls from Travel Light Adventures were chasing him and poor Devin had nowhere to run and hide," Nora explained. "And so we—"

"We used our key to open one of the empty cabins," Nora cut in, talking over her sister. "And he was so grateful that he agreed to be our date!"

Luke arched his brow and asked, "You don't mind sharing 'Dreamy Devin' with each other?"

"Not tonight," Nora assured him.

"We're just so happy to all be together," Nadine agreed, giving her twin a high five.

Luke thought of Sammy Jo and his own sisters and how they'd all grown up together. The happiest moments *were* the ones they'd shared. *"The more the merrier,"* Grandma always said. His thoughts returned to the engagement party and he began to formulate a new plan, one that would make it extra special . . . for all of them.

Nora looked over his shoulder and gasped. "There's Devin now."

As the twins dropped off their load of clean towels in the cabin beside them, and ran to catch up with the new ranch hand, Luke chuckled.

If only everyone could be that happy.

LATER THAT EVENING, Luke searched through the faces of dozens of guests, waiting for Sammy Jo to show.

The Walford twins, dressed in matching sparkly, blue, off-the-shoulder dresses, giggled as they passed by on either side of Devin, their arms looped through his.

He spotted his niece, Meghan, and beside her, Delaney with Zach Tanner, and it looked like they might actually be *flirting*.

Then his gaze slid over to his sister Bree, stunning in her brown cowboy boots and fashionable red dress, one of her own designs. Ryan held her hand, keeping close, his eyes never straying too far from hers. Except to glance at his son, Cody, who greeted everyone and seemed to think tonight's party was all about him.

A second later Luke spotted A.J. Malloy. "Hey, thanks for coming. Tonight and . . . that night at the dance hall."

A.J. shot him a quick, easy grin. "Couldn't let you get all the credit. The town will be talkin' about that one for years to come. This time we'll *all* be legends."

Luke laughed at the reference, then admitted, "I didn't know whose side you would take when you found out your aunt was involved."

A.J. shrugged. "She's only an aunt by marriage. And even if she wasn't, she got what she deserved. But hey, you better not stand here talkin' to me all night. Look over there. Isn't that your woman?"

"Indeed it is," Luke said and, tipping his hat, took his leave.

"Luke Collins," Sammy Jo said, weaving her way through the throng of people as she made her way toward him. "I have something to say to you."

"Well, I guess that's good because I have something to say to you, too," he said, his tone matter-of-fact.

She looked beautiful wearing a sleek, purple gauzy thing that emphasized her figure in all the right places.

And her long dark curls had been pulled away from her face in a soft twist at the back of her head. While he preferred her hair down most times, the style *did* expose her neck—which Luke was mighty tempted to lean down and kiss. Especially as she stopped short and stared up at him.

"D-did you get a haircut?" she stammered, her eyes wide.

He took off his hat to reveal the short chop he'd received at the barber. "They took a little off the top."

"More like four inches!" she exclaimed.

"You like?" he teased.

"I—I do, but—" She narrowed her gaze. "But what I wanted to tell you was that my mother came to visit and—"

"Your mother is here? Now?" Luke's spirits plummeted. Something wasn't right. Sammy Jo had that stubborn scowl on her face, the one that said she'd already made up her mind about something and she'd fight anyone who dared to try to change it. His jaw tightened. "Are you going to live with your mother?"

"I hope so," Sammy Jo told him, her tone wistful.

Obviously she hadn't forgiven him. He drew in a deep breath, his pulse racing, and said, "I'm *sorry* I accused your dad of being a rustler and trying to sabotage our ranch."

Sammy Jo shrugged off his apology as if it didn't make much difference. "Anyone would have suspected him, given the evidence."

"You can't go," he said, swallowing hard. "I can't let you go to Wyoming."

"Wyoming?" she repeated. She gave him a puzzled look and then laughed. "When I said I hoped to live with my mother, I meant *here*. I'm hoping she decides to stay."

Luke released his breath and relaxed. "Well, that's okay, then. *We're* okay, right?"

"That's what I wanted to tell you," Sammy Jo said, and gave him a teasing smile. "I'm the one who's not letting *you* go. I won't push you, but when you're ready to finally fall in love, I want you to know . . . I'll still be here."

"No, actually," he said, glancing around and then taking her hand and moving her closer to the front of the gazebo. "You need to be right *here*."

"What? Luke, what are you doing? You just made me bump into those nice innocent people and now everyone's looking at us."

"My beloved sweetheart, Sammy Jo," he said, drawing her into his arms. "*I love you. I adore you. With all my heart.*" He grinned when her eyes widened and it became clear she recognized the sweet-talkin' verse. "And I've decided I just don't want to date you. I want to marry you."

The music suddenly shut off, more faces crowded around, and Luke didn't think he'd ever seen Sammy Jo look so nervous.

"You want to marry *me*?" she asked, as if half-afraid this was all a hoax.

He watched his future bride glance over at his sister Bree, who smiled and pulled the cord unfurling the second banner. One that let Sammy Jo know this wasn't just Ryan and Bree's engagement party. It was *theirs*.

"You said you'd only marry for love and so I'm here

today announcing to all these fine people, *on bended knee*," he added, dropping down onto his good leg, "that I love you and I want you to be my wife. The only question is . . . do *you* love me?"

"Yes." Tears sprung into her eyes and for a moment it didn't look like Sammy Jo could speak. Then with a brilliant smile and more force, she repeated, *"Yes!"*

As she helped him back up onto his feet, a loud cheer rose into the air, followed by a tumultuous roar of thunderous claps from the people in the crowd around them. But Luke didn't pay them much attention. The minute his new fiancée flung herself into his arms, he lowered his mouth to hers and kissed her.

"Now that you've agreed to this deal, you know I'm not going to let you back out, right?" he teased.

"I wouldn't want to," Sammy Jo said as she wrapped her hands behind his neck. *"Never in a million years* would I ever want to."

"And you'll promise to love me all that time?" he pressed.

She nodded. "Of course!"

"And kiss me every day? Morning, noon, and night?"

"Luke Collins," she said, giving him one of those big, flirtatious smiles he loved. "I never knew you could be so persistent."

He grinned, then moved in for another kiss, one she'd remember forever, and promised, "Whatever it takes, sweetheart. Whatever it takes."

Keep reading to discover the very first book
in fan-favorite Darlene Panzera's new series . . .

MONTANA HEARTS:
HER WEEKEND WRANGLER

Bree Collins has finally come home to Fox Creek,
Montana to manage her family's guest ranch. She
knows she can handle any challenges that come her way,
but when the infuriating Ryan Tanner reappears in her
life, Bree suddenly has doubts about her ability to stay
professional-and away from the handsome cowboy.

Ryan Tanner is in a bind. He needs to train a young foal
for the upcoming show but its mother would rather
bite his hand off. Just his luck the cute cowgirl from his
past arrives back in town. Bree just so happens to have
a reputation for taming animals of this nature. Ryan is
willing to make a deal with her, but he has no intention
of being swayed by her sweet smile or the tenderness
she shows his young son.

Yet when fate brings them together, falling for one
another becomes the easiest thing in the world. Ryan
might just want to wrangle this cowgirl's heart . . . but
will Bree give him the chance?

Available Now from Avon Impulse

An Excerpt from

MONTANA HEARTS: HER WEEKEND WRANGLER

"'BEST WISHES FOR A *speedy recovery, you redneck rascal!*'" Bree Collins snorted, slapped the greeting card back onto the display rack, and picked up another. " *'Sending up heartfelt prayers that you'll get well soon.'* " She shook her head and tried one more. " *'Dearest Father . . .'* "

Definitely not *that* one.

What was with these cards anyway? They were inscribed with messages that were either too personal, too distant, or completely inappropriate. Maybe she should get her "dear ole dad" a gift instead.

Glancing around the Fox Creek General Store, decorated country-western style for the tourists, Bree spied a rickety old wooden bookcase. A book would be better than a game of marbles, a stuffed jack-a-lope, or a "Welcome to Montana" mug. Her father could read while his injuries healed.

Except she had no idea what kind of stories he liked. She and her father had never been close. And he'd never had much time to read while running the family's twenty-four-cabin guest ranch. But now? He'd have to find *something* to do while he recovered or he'd drive her mother and grandma crazy. Maybe he'd like a volume of crossword puzzles?

She walked over and tugged on *Puzzles and Games*, a newer book wedged tightly between the thick, dusty jackets of *The Secret History of Yellowstone Country* and *Ranching Ain't What It Used to Be*. And the entire bookcase leaned toward her.

Catching the frame of the shelves with her hands, she spun around, and used her body weight to shove the burdensome book beast back into position. But every time she stepped away, the case threatened to fall. Somehow the bottom had become unbalanced. She glanced at the clerk behind the counter and opened her mouth to call for help. Then Ryan Tanner walked toward her and she involuntarily jumped in place.

They'd grown up together, riding the same school bus and sharing the same classes day after day right up through the twelfth grade. But after high school she'd relocated to New York to attend college. Then she put her business degree and love of fashion together to snatch the assistant managerial position at the Manhattan branch of Silvain's, a national fashion retail conglomerate that specialized in hip clothing and accessories. Over the years she'd run into Ryan only briefly during her occasional visits home.

And she had no desire to see him now.

Ryan was the kind of guy a girl dreamed about but could never have. At least, not exclusively. He was a charmer who took the opportunity to flirt with every female he met. And he'd tried to charm *her* the night of their high school senior prom, the night her horse died, in an attempt to delay her from getting home too soon . . . and saying goodbye.

Of course, they were adults now, both almost twenty-seven, she with her glowing résumé and he with a seven-year-old son. She thought she'd forgiven him and let bygones be bygones.

She was wrong.

RYAN TANNER HAD finished paying for the floral bouquet tucked under his arm and was headed toward the exit when he noticed her. He'd heard Jed Collins had taken a nasty fall off his horse the day before, planting him in the hospital. But if Bree was back in Fox Creek, well, then, her father's condition must be serious. He stole a look at her beautiful face, took another few steps toward the door, then stopped.

It wasn't the need to offer condolences that made him turn back around. Everyone knew Bree and her two younger siblings, Luke and Delaney, didn't get on well with their dad. No, it was the doubt he saw flickering in her eyes that unsettled him. Bree was one of the most confident, capable, career-oriented women he'd ever met. What could have happened to make her change? Had Jed's condition taken a turn for the worse?

He thought he should at least give her a quick hello. For old times' sake. Not that they'd ever been best of friends or dated, although . . . he wished they had. Just once. Before worldly ambitions drove her away to the farthest reaches of the country to pursue her glamorous career.

Ryan tipped his straw Stetson in greeting as he approached. "Brianna Lee Collins, back from the big city?"

She hadn't seen him coming until he was just a few feet away. Startled, she practically jumped right out of her boots, and the bookcase behind her wobbled. Ryan bolted forward, ready to offer assistance, but then she leaned back, pushing it upright, and smiled. "Just visiting."

He nodded to the blue hard-shell suitcase by her feet. "You haven't been home yet?"

She shook her head. "I took a cab from the airport. Luke's coming by bus and Delaney flew in last night. She's picking us up so we can meet my ma and grandma at the hospital and go in to see my father together."

Bree's honey-brown hair was shorter, just past her shoulders instead of the waist length he remembered. And in the past she'd always worn beaded earrings, necklaces, bracelets, and rings, but today she wore no jewelry.

Even her plain, white sleeveless blouse and jeans were different from the sparkly clothes she used to wear. And yet, she was still just as beautiful. Maybe even more so.

She gave him a quizzical look, and with a jolt, he realized he was staring.

Bree nodded toward the flowers. "Hot date?"

He grinned. "Something like that."

Then he switched the cream-colored rose bouquet from one hand to the other and the crinkle from the cellophane wrapper filled the awkward silence. He knew he should go, but didn't want to. Not yet.

Ryan cleared his throat and asked, "How *is* your dad?"

"Ma says his condition is stable. Scans showed some brain-swelling, so the doctors put him into an induced coma for a few days. But they think—"

Her shoulder slid down a notch and . . . so did the bookcase. A couple of books from the highest shelf flew past her head and hit the hardwood floor with a *thump*.

Ryan stepped closer. "Need help?"

Bree's gaze shot to the top of the teetering case. "Nope." She gave him another smile. "I've got it."

She sure did. He could see now it was her body holding the bookcase up. The thing moved every time she did, which meant—Bree was trapped. But one would never know it from her expression or from her calm, upbeat tone.

Yep, instead of accepting his help, Bree Collins held up the heavy monstrosity and stood there smiling as if she didn't have a care in the world. He swallowed a laugh and grinned. He doubted Bree would ever admit she *needed* anyone. He'd heard from mutual friends she was a top dog in the corporate world and no doubt it was that *"I've got it"* attitude that led to her success. However, he wasn't the type to leave a damsel in distress. Whether she wanted his help or not.

Tossing the bouquet aside, he reached forward to place an arm on either side of her to steady the unit, and Bree yelled, "Close enough, Tanner!"

His face just a foot away from her own, he looked straight into her dark sapphire eyes. "What did you think I was going to do, kiss you?"

She lifted a brow. "Don't you kiss all the girls?"

He dipped his gaze toward her soft pink lips and he lowered his head even closer. "For your information, *darlin',*" he drawled, "I save my kisses only for the best."

That got her attention. She gasped, her mouth forming a perfect O.

"Now duck," he instructed.

"What?"

"I'll hold up the bookcase while you duck under my arm and get out of there."

She locked gazes with him for a fraction of a second, then brushed her head against him as she moved under his arm to escape her awkward position. Her hair was so silky soft it tickled and sent a jolt of awareness coursing through him. And as she stood up on the other side, her eyes widened as if she, too, had been uncomfortably aware of their close proximity.

He waited until she'd stepped back a safe distance,

then rocked the shelves until a marble rolled out from beneath the bottom of the unit.

She gasped. "No wonder I couldn't get it to stay up."

Ryan retrieved the flowers he'd intended to give his aunt, and to prove he was a true gentleman, and not the kiss-'em and leave-'em cowboy Bree implied, he handed the roses over to her with a mock bow. "If you needed help, all you had to do was ask."

To his satisfaction he didn't think he ever remembered Bree looking so flustered.

"I—" Her mouth formed that tantalizing O again. "I suppose I should thank you."

He waited, and when she didn't say anything he prompted her with a wink.

Just when he thought he'd seen it all, Bree blushed. "*Thank* you, Ryan."

He tipped his hat and grinned. "Nice to see you, Bree."

Then he took his departure, finally heading in the *right* direction—toward his son, who licked an ice cream cone and stood waiting for him by the door.

BREE'S FACE CONTINUED to flame as she stared at the father and son duo. Cody looked just like Ryan, same brown hair and brown eyes. She'd never met him, but her friend Sammy Jo kept her updated on all the local info and had sent her a picture when he was a baby. Now seven years old, he was a solid, sturdy, little boy. With that same heart-melting grin.

She raised the delicate bouquet of cream-colored roses to her nose and their beautiful fragrant scent took her back to her teens, a time when she'd been a starry-eyed, hopeful romantic with endless possibilities for the future spread out before her.

No man had made her feel that way in a long time, certainly not her two-timing ex-boyfriend she'd left behind in New York. He'd been a charmer, too . . . and had hurt her almost as much. Yes, she was *through* with romantic relationships. At least for a while. She needed to find a new job now that she'd been unexpectedly cut— one of the dangers of dating the boss. And handsome, knock-your-socks-off charmers like Ryan Tanner would be strictly off-limits.

Bree waited a good ten minutes to make sure he was gone before she left the store. She'd had every intention of asking for help with the bookcase—but she would *not* ask for help from a Tanner, especially *Ryan*. She'd had enough of his kind of "help."

Besides, she'd once heard him say to another, *"Bree Collins isn't worth my time."* If he didn't think she was worth his time, then she certainly wasn't going to trouble him or allow him to tarry any longer than necessary on her account.

She rubbed a hand down each of her arms, soothing her sore muscles. Then she realized she'd been so disturbed by Ryan and the wobbly bookcase that she'd forgotten to buy her father a gift. She glanced at the flowers in her hand. They would do.

Outside, she scanned the single street running

through the mite-sized Montana town for a sign of her siblings. She glanced at her watch, and a few minutes later her slender, blond sister pulled up to the curb in a red, paint-peeled pickup truck.

"Bree!" Delaney's face broke into a huge smile as she jumped out of the driver's side and ran around the front to give her a big hug. "It's been too long."

Bree smiled and, despite the too-tight squeeze, fiercely hugged her younger sister back. Then she choked out, "Del, I can't breathe."

"Sorry." Delaney loosened her grip and laughed. "Didn't mean to strangle you."

"It wouldn't be the first time," Bree teased, and laughed along with her. It *had* been too long. Almost an entire year. She glanced back at the truck. "Where's the baby?"

"No baby," Delaney said, opening the side door and helping her daughter out. "She's two and a half, a 'big girl' if you ask her."

Meghan, wearing a pretty strawberry print sundress, nodded and pointed to herself. She looked a lot like Delaney. Same fair hair, skin, and sprinkling of freckles across the nose.

"Look how you've grown." Bree dropped to her knees beside the little girl, wishing she'd bought a gift for her as well. "Meghan, do you remember me?"

Meghan shook her head, making her blond ponytails swing back and forth, and wrapped her arms tight around her mother's leg.

"How could she?" Delaney asked with an amused

grin. "She was only eighteen months old the last time she saw you."

"She saw me a week ago on Skype."

"Images through the computer aren't the same."

No, they weren't. Bree bit down on her lip. She should have purchased an airline ticket to see her niece sooner. Instead, she'd let her crazy busy work schedule get in the way.

"And Steve? Where's he? Couldn't your husband get off work?"

Her sister shook her head, the laughter fading from her eyes. "He didn't come."

"Why not?"

Delaney shrugged and Bree suspected there was something her sister wasn't telling her, but they would have time to talk later. Right now a bus approached and the rumble of the motor drowned out all other sound.

The bus let out a loud *swoosh* as the door opened to let off passengers. One of them was their brother, Luke, the middle child of the family, a year younger than Bree and two years older than Delaney. Luke spotted them, and slowly crossed the street, hobbling along with the help of what looked to be a hand-carved wooden cane.

"Did you know Luke was hurt?" Bree hissed in a sharp whisper.

Delaney gasped. "No. I—I didn't."

Not waiting for him to reach them, Bree asked, "What happened?"

"Motorcycle accident," he replied, taking the last few steps. "Right after I got out of the army."

"Last July? That was ten months ago," Delaney accused. "Why didn't you tell us you'd been hurt?"

"What, this?" Luke leaned on his good foot and lifted his injured leg. "This is just a scratch. I took more of a beating in Iraq." He gave them a look that said he really didn't want to talk about it and shrugged. "I figured no sense worrying anyone."

Bree poked a finger into his chest. "Ma's going to be mad that you didn't tell her. Grandma, too."

"Yeah, I know." Luke's jaw tightened. "But what's done is done."

Bree knew that feeling. To lighten the mood, she teased, "You can't use that short hiking stick as an excuse not to give us a proper greeting. Come here, you."

Luke didn't chortle with laughter like he did back in the days before they'd each left home, but he did give her a quick grin, even if it did seem forced. "How about a high five?"

Bree slapped the palm he raised like they'd always done and her heart eased.

Luke gave Delaney a high five next and then his gaze drifted to the little girl still clinging to her mother's knee. "Would you like a high five, too?"

Meghan hesitated, then a smile stole across her face, puckering her cheeks. "High five!"

"She talks?" Luke asked as they watched their niece reach a stubby hand in the air to meet his.

"Meghan's using short sentences and learning more words each day," Delaney informed them. "Giving high fives is one of her favorite games."

"Mine, too," Luke agreed. "It's one of the things I *can* still do."

Bree noticed he still wore his dog tags around his neck. And his honey-brown hair, a shade darker than her own, wasn't the short, military cut she remembered. Now it fell down over his forehead in an unruly shag that was sure to send Ma running for the scissors. He also appeared thinner than she'd last seen him. Grandma would take that as a challenge to fatten him up with homemade breads and meat pies.

They hadn't seen each other for almost a year, not since they all came home last June for her birthday. Afterward Luke got out of the service and went to Florida to live on a boat and do odd jobs. She'd flown back to New York, and Delaney and Meghan had relocated with Steve to California. They'd still kept in touch through phone calls and Skype. But when had they lost touch so much that they'd started keeping secrets from one another?

She glanced at Luke's cane again. Did he think she wouldn't care? Or wouldn't understand? Before she could question him further, Luke pointed to Delaney's barren ring finger and asked, "Where's Steve?"

Bree gasped. She'd been so caught up in their hug and seeing Meghan again, and Luke, that she hadn't noticed. Now her sister had her full attention.

Delaney hesitated, glanced back and forth between them, then in a quiet voice said, "We're divorced."

About the Author

DARLENE PANZERA WRITES sweet, fun-loving romance and is a member of the Romance Writers of America's Greater Seattle chapter. Her career launched when her novella "The Bet" was picked by Avon Books and *New York Times* bestselling author Debbie Macomber to be published within Debbie's own novel, *Family Affair*. Darlene says, "I love writing stories that help inspire people to laugh, value relationships, and pursue their dreams."

Born and raised in New Jersey, Darlene is now a resident of the Pacific Northwest, where she lives with her husband and three children. When not writing she enjoys spending time with her family, her horse, and loves camping, hiking, photography, and lazy days at the lake.

Join her on Facebook or at www.darlenepanzera.com.

Discover great authors, exclusive offers, and more at hc.com.

Give in to your Impulses . . .
Continue reading for excerpts from
our newest Avon Impulse books.
Available now wherever e-books are sold.

GUARDING SOPHIE
A Love and Football Novella
By Julie Brannagh

THE IDEA OF YOU
Ribbon Ridge Book Four
By Darcy Burke

ONE TEMPTING PROPOSAL
An Accidental Heirs Novel
By Christy Carlyle

NO GROOM AT THE INN
A Dukes Behaving Badly Novella
By Megan Frampton

An Excerpt from

GUARDING SOPHIE
A Love and Football Novella
by Julie Brannagh

Hearts beat and sparks fly when two
people find shelter in each other.

Seattle Sharks wide receiver Kyle Carlson needs
to escape and Noel, Washington is the perfect
place for him to do it and figure out his next
step. He likes the seclusion and predictability
of the small town . . . until the biggest surprise
of his life turns up in the local grocery store.

She swallowed hard. She looked down at her hand clasped securely in his. There was so much to say, but for once, she'd like to spend a couple of hours sitting on the couch with nothing more pressing to do than enjoy herself.

"I have to tell you this," he said. "I'm kinda into you. I have been since we were in school." He let out a long breath. "Are you okay if we take this slow?" He peered at her through a mop of dark, shoulder-length waves. His full lips twitched into a shy smile. "I don't want to screw it up," he confessed.

It was probably a huge line he'd used with women before, but hearing something so bashful coming from the normally confident, handsome, funny Kyle charmed her. Even if it wasn't original, it worked. She licked her suddenly dry lips. "I like you too."

"That's good to know," he said. He squeezed her hand.

"I wonder how things would have been different if I'd gone to the prom with you instead."

"You were a bit unavailable in those days."

"Yeah. It wasn't working, no matter how hard I tried to convince myself it was. Of course, then I met Peter, and that was even worse." Maybe she should change the subject. No one wanted to hear about the train wreck that was her love life. She still had a tiny flicker of hope in her heart that things could be different.

Somehow, law enforcement would keep her ex away from her, she'd meet a man she wanted to be with and who wanted to be with her in return, and her life would be happy. She didn't have to plan her entire future in the next ten minutes.

"I've had some sketchy relationships over the years too," he said. They stared at each other for a minute or so, and he grinned at her. "How about that movie? What would you like to watch?"

She'd rather spend the evening talking with him and continuing to catch up on the past ten years, but maybe he preferred the relative safety of a shared activity that would not require baring one's soul. They had plenty of time to explore each other's thoughts and dreams. Maybe sitting on the couch holding hands was the best medicine for both of them right now.

"That's a good question," she said. "Do we watch something we've seen before, or do we take a risk?"

"What's your favorite movie?" he said.

"*Pitch Perfect*," she said.

He clicked the TV on, hit the Amazon Instant Video icon, and located the downloadable movie. "I know I'm supposed to say something like I love the *Fast and Furious* franchise more than anything," he confided. "Don't tell anyone, but I own the *Pitch Perfect* DVD. It's in Bellevue."

"You're not a *Fast and Furious* fan?"

"Don't let it get out," he joked.

"That's aca-awesome, Kyle."

They watched the bar on the screen as the movie downloaded for a few seconds.

"I'll bet you sing along too," he said.

" 'Titanium' is one of my favorite songs," she assured him. "And I sing 'Since U Been Gone' in the car. At least I did when I *had* a car."

"We can sing it in my car." He moved closer to her on the couch as the download ended. "Want something to drink before I click Start on the movie?"

"No, thank you. I'm fine," she said.

"You are, aren't you?"

She laughed as he moved closer.

"I have one more thing to confess," he said as he reached out to cup her cheek in his hand. He slowly rubbed his thumb against her jaw. Her heart was going as if she'd chugged a four-shot latte, and the memories came rushing back. She remembered a thousand nights of football games, pizza, and hanging around on the beach with her friends. She remembered Kyle as a laughing teen with wavy, tumbled dark hair, sparkling dark eyes, and the confidence of someone who believed life held only good things for all of them. She thought that charmed life would go on forever.

They weren't high school students anymore. They'd both had their share of joy and pain as they'd ventured into the adult world. The stakes were higher now, especially since they'd confessed a mutual interest. The pain in her heart, if this did not work out, would be a momentary annoyance compared with the anguish she would feel if she exposed Kyle or his family to danger as the result of her unhinged, vengeful ex.

"What if he finds me?" she whispered. His couch wrapped them in a cocoon of overstuffed comfort.

"We'll deal with that later," he whispered back. "I've wanted to kiss you for years now, Sophie. I think you want to kiss me too."

An Excerpt from

THE IDEA OF YOU
Ribbon Ridge Book Four
by Darcy Burke

In the fourth sexy and emotional novel
in the Ribbon Ridge series, movie star
Alaina Pierce just wants peace and quiet after
a tabloid scandal that rocked Hollywood . . .
but a hot and steamy affair with a gorgeous
Archer brother is the perfect distraction.

Evan Archer rounded the larger of his parents' two garages and was immediately hit by the smell of smoke and the peal of an alarm. He instinctively pressed his hands to his ears and looked up at the apartment on the second floor of the garage. Smoke billowed from an open window. Despite the excruciating sound, he ran toward the door, threw it open, and vaulted up the stairs. The door at the top, which led to the apartment, was open. The acrid scent of smoke assaulted his lungs as the scream of the alarm violated his ears.

A woman stood beneath the alarm madly waving a towel.

Evan strode to the dining table situated in front of the windows and pulled a chair beneath the smoke detector. He said nothing to the strange woman, but nevertheless she moved out of his way. He stepped onto the chair and promptly pulled the battery from the alarm. Blessed silence reigned. He closed his eyes with relief.

"Thank you," she said, draping the towel over her shoulder. "I am so sorry about this. Who are you?"

He didn't look directly at her but recognized her immediately. "You're Alaina Pierce."

"I know who *I* am. Who are you?" There was a guarded, tentative look in her eyes. He universally sucked at decoding emotional expression, but that was one he knew. Probably because he'd seen it in the mirror so much when he'd been younger.

He jumped down off the wooden chair and returned it to the table. "I'm Evan Archer. Are you staying here?"

"Yes. Sean didn't tell you?"

"Nope." Evan hadn't seen his brother-in-law today, but that wasn't unusual. He and Evan's sister Tori lived in a condo in Ribbon Ridge proper, while Evan lived fifteen minutes outside the center of town with their parents in the house they'd all grown up in. "Should he have?"

"Maybe not. My being here is a secret."

Then it made perfect sense that he hadn't told Evan. He was terrible at keeping secrets. "I suck at secrets." And knowing when to keep his mouth shut.

"I see. Well, do you think you could keep me a secret?"

Maybe. If he didn't make the mistake of blurting it out without thinking. "I guess."

"Hey," she said with more volume than she'd used before. "Would you mind looking at me so I can see if you're telling the truth?"

He forced himself to look straight at her. She was beautiful. But not in the glamorous movie star way he'd expected. She wore very little makeup, not that she needed any at all. The color of her skin reminded him of rich buttermilk, and her hazel eyes carried a beguiling sparkle. They were very expressive and probably her defining feature. Along with that marquee smile he had yet to see.

"Do you have a superpower that allows you to detect lies?"

Her mouth inched up into an almost-smile. "Yes, I do. It's a side effect of being ridiculously famous."

"Good to know. I was only moderately famous, so that's a skill I don't possess." He was also fairly lousy at lying. How could he recognize it in someone else? He looked away from her, settling his gaze on the still-smoky kitchen. "I'll do my best not to expose your secret."

An Excerpt from

ONE TEMPTING PROPOSAL
An Accidental Heirs Novel
by Christy Carlyle

Becoming engaged? Simple.
Resisting temptation? Impossible.

Sebastian Fennick, the newest
Duke of Wrexford, prefers the
straightforwardness of mathematics
to romantic nonsense. When he meets
Lady Katherine Adderly at the first ball
of the season, he finds her as alluring as
she is disagreeable. His title may now
require him to marry, but Sebastian can't
think of anyone less fit to be his wife, even
if he can't get her out of his mind.

"I take it you have something you wish to say to me, Your Grace."

He still hadn't released her. She was warm and smelled heavenly, and the grip of her hand grounded him. Here and now. That's what mattered. Not the past. The past was a broken place of mistakes and regret.

The April evening had turned chilly and Seb finally let her go to remove his evening jacket and settle it over her bare shoulders.

She pulled the lapels together across her chest.

"Is it to be a long discussion, then?"

Seb reached up to lift the coat's collar to cover more of her exposed skin, but he found himself touching her instead, stroking the soft warm column of her neck and then resting his hand at the base of her throat, savoring the feel of her speeding pulse against his palm. His heartbeat echoed in his ears, as wild and rapid as Kat's, and the longer he touched her, the more the sounds merged, until he could almost believe their hearts had begun to beat as one.

He shook his head. That sort of romantic drivel led only to misery.

But he couldn't bring himself to stop touching her. And

he couldn't deny he wanted more. Leaning down, desperate to know if her flavor was as sweet as her scent, he pressed his mouth to her forehead.

"Your Grace?" she whispered, the heat of her breath searing the skin above his necktie.

He pulled back and lifted his hands from her, remembering who he was, who she was. He was a master at guarding his heart and avoiding intimate moments. She was the woman who'd thrown over multiple suitors during each of her seasons.

"We must speak to your father."

Even in the semidarkness, he could see her green eyes grow large. "You've changed your mind?"

Excitement hitched up her voice two octaves, and Seb wished he'd changed his mind, that he wouldn't have to disappoint her, or her sister and Ollie. If he hadn't wasted all his reckless choices in youth, he might allow himself a bit of freedom now. But controlling his emotions, regimenting his behavior, clinging to logic and order—that had seen him through the darkest days of his life. Control had been his salvation, and he was loathe to let it go.

"No. But Ollie tells me that he and Lady Harriet—"

"Plan to elope."

"You knew?"

"She just told me when you walked off with Mr. Treadwell, and I fear they're quite determined."

He jumped when she touched his arm, her exploring fingers jolting his senses, until each press, each stroke along his collar and then up to the edge of his jaw, made him ache for more. She caressed his cheek as he'd touched hers in the conservatory before sliding her hand down to his shoulder, gripping him as if to brace herself.

"Won't you reconsider my suggestion, Your Grace?"

When she lifted onto her toes and swayed toward him, a flash of reason told him to push her away, to guard against her feminine assault. But the thought had all the power of a wisp of smoke and dissolved just as quickly when he reached to steady her and found how well she fit in the crook of his arms.

He'd been a fool to drag her onto the balcony and touch her like a man without an ounce of self-control.

"If you're going to let me hold you this close, you should call me Sebastian."

"If we're to be engaged, you should call me Kitty."

He hadn't agreed to the engagement and still loathed the notion of a scheme. And yet . . . he couldn't deny the practicality of it. It would forestall Ollie's ridiculous plan to elope, satisfy the Claybornes and allow the young couple to marry, and, best of all, it would keep all the spirited misses eager to make his acquaintance—as his aunt had so disturbingly put it—at bay.

"I'm afraid you'll always be Kat to me. Never Kitty."

"Very well. Is that your only condition?"

His skin burned feverish. He loathed lies. Hated pretense. And yet he loathed nothing about holding Kat in his arms. With her velvet-clad curves pressed against him and her thighs brushing his own, he found himself tempted to agree to her subterfuge. Almost.

"I have two more."

"Go on."

"We end it as soon as we're able." If holding her melted his resolve this thoroughly, what sort of wreck would he be after weeks in her company? "You can jilt me if you like. However you wish to do it. And we tell my sister the truth of what we're doing and why. Pippa's far too clever not to see through a falsehood."

"Agreed, Your Grace."

He caught the flash of white as she smiled and moonlight glinted off the curve of her cheeks. Pleasing her stirred an echo of pleasure in him, and it disturbed him how much he wanted to see her smile again, wanted to bring her pleasure, and not just for a moment.

Lifting a hand to caress her cheek, Seb drew Kat in close, dipped his head, and took her mouth in a quick mingling of chilled flesh and warm breath.

An Excerpt from

NO GROOM AT THE INN
A Dukes Behaving Badly Novella
by *Megan Frampton*

In Megan Frampton's delightful
Dukes Behaving Badly holiday novella, a
young lady entertains a sudden proposal of
marriage—to a man she's only just met!

1844
A coaching inn
One lady, no chickens

"Poultry."

Sophronia gazed down into her glass of ale and repeated the word, even though she was only talking to herself. "Poultry."

It didn't sound any better the second time she said it, either.

The letter from her cousin had detailed all of the delights waiting for her when she arrived—taking care of her cousin's six children (his wife had died, perhaps of exhaustion), overseeing the various village celebrations including, her cousin informed her with no little enthusiasm, the annual Tribute to the Hay, which was apparently the highlight of the year, and taking care of the chickens.

All twenty-seven of them.

Not to mention she would be arriving just before Christmas, which meant gifts and merriment and conviviality. Those weren't bad things, of course, it was just that celebrating the season was likely the last thing she wanted to do.

Well, perhaps after taking care of the chickens.

The holidays used to be one of her favorite times of year—she and her father both loved playing holiday games, especially ones like Charades or Dictionary.

Even though he was the word expert in the family, eventually she had been able to fool him with her Dictionary definitions, and there was nothing so wonderful as seeing his dumbstruck expression when she revealed that, no, he had not guessed the correct definition.

He was always so proud of her for that, for being able to keep up with him and his linguistic interests.

And now nobody would care that she was inordinately clever at making up definitions for words she'd never heard of.

She gave herself a mental shake, since she'd promised not to become maudlin. Especially at this time of the year.

She glanced around the barroom she was sitting in, taking note of the other occupants. Like the inn itself, they were plain but tidy. As she was, as well, even if her clothing had started out, many years ago, as grander than theirs.

She unfolded the often-read letter, suppressing a sigh at her cousin's crabbed handwriting. Not that handwriting was indicative of a person's character—that would be their words—but the combination of her cousin's script and the way he assumed she would be delighted to perform all the tasks he was graciously setting before her—that was enough to make her dread the next phase of her life. Which would last until—well, that she didn't know.

Sophronia was grateful, she was, for being offered a place to live, and she didn't want to seem churlish. It was just that she had never imagined that the care and feeding of poultry—not to mention six children—would be her fate.

Which was why she had spent a few precious pennies on a last glass of ale at the coaching inn where she was waiting for the mail coach to arrive and take her to the far reaches of beyond. A last moment of being by herself, being Lady Sophronia, not Sophy the Chicken Lady.

The one without a feather to fly with.

Chuckling at her own wit, she picked her glass up and gave a toast to the as yet imaginary chickens, thinking about how she'd always imagined her life would turn out.

There were no members of the avian community at all in her rosy vision of the future.

Not that she was certain what her rosy vision of the future would include, but she was fairly certain it did not have fowl of any kind.

"All aboard to Chester," a voice boomed through the room. Immediately there were the bustling sounds of people getting up, gathering their things, saying their last goodbyes.

"Excuse me, miss," a gentleman said in her ear. She jumped, so lost in her own foolish (fowlish?) thoughts that she hadn't even noticed him approaching her.

She turned and looked at him, blinking at his splendor. He was tall, taller than her, even, which was a rarity among gentlemen. He was handsome in a dashing rosy-visioned way that made her question just what her imagination was thinking if it had never inserted him—or someone who looked like him—into her dreams.

He had unruly dark brown hair, longer than most gentlemen wore. The ends curled up as though even his hair was irrepressible. His eyes were blue, and even in the dark gloom, she could see they practically twinkled.

As though he and she shared a secret, a lovely, wonderful, delightful secret.